IMMACULATE
CONCEPTION

IMMACULATE CONCEPTION

A NOVEL

LING LING HUANG

DUTTON

DUTTON

An imprint of Penguin Random House LLC
1745 Broadway, New York, NY 10019
penguinrandomhouse.com

DUTTON and the D colophon are registered trademarks of
Penguin Random House LLC.

Book design by Katy Riegel

LIBRARY OF CONGRESS CATALOGING-IN-PUBLICATION DATA
Names: Huang, Ling Ling, 1989– author.
Title: Immaculate conception: a novel / Ling Ling Huang.
Description: First edition. | New York: Dutton, 2025.
Identifiers: LCCN 2024036915 (print) | LCCN 2024036916 (ebook) |
ISBN 9780593850435 (hardcover) | ISBN 9780593850442 (ebook)
Subjects: LCGFT: Gothic fiction. | Novels.
Classification: LCC PS3608.U22483 I46 2025 (print) |
LCC PS3608.U22483 (ebook) | DDC 813/.6—dc23/eng/20240823
LC record available at https://lccn.loc.gov/2024036915
LC ebook record available at https://lccn.loc.gov/2024036916

Printed in the United States of America
1st Printing

The authorized representative in the EU for product safety and compliance
is Penguin Random House Ireland, Morrison Chambers, 32 Nassau Street,
Dublin D02 YH68, Ireland, https://eu-contact.penguin.ie.

For the jealous

IMMACULATE
CONCEPTION

will have to leave the bathroom eventually. I've already been here too long reading the same alert over and over again. People are likely whispering already, wondering where I am. Five more minutes, and I'll go back to the gala. Submit myself to the hands gripping my elbow in concern, and the pitying eyes hungrily searching for signs of distress in mine. *I just saw . . . Are you OK?* As if the answer isn't written all over my face. A low wail escapes my throat and my chin wobbles dangerously. I turn the lock and step out of the stall before I can start to cry again. In the mirror, I prepare a smile, ratcheting it wider until I believe my own happiness. I will stay for the duration of the evening, not out of gratitude or courtesy, but out of obligation. The entire art world is here tonight to celebrate the new atrium named in my honor. Everyone except Mathilde, who is still missing. *Presumed dead.* My eyes keep snagging on those last two words. Among the many guests, there must be someone who knows where she is, and I need to find her before the presumption becomes truth.

EARLY STYLE

1

first saw Mathilde through the little oval window of her studio space. She looked so small beneath the trees that towered over her that it took a moment for me to find her, and to notice what was off about the scene: trees are not often indoors. She caught me looking, her lashes flicking upward in a gesture of annoyance, as if my very presence outside her door was a distraction. I smiled. She didn't.

We were both freshmen at the Berkshire College of Art and Design, and though everyone else in our class was always barging into one another's studios, pretending to look for this brush or that color while sizing each other up, no one dared to assume that kind of intimacy with Mathilde. Rumors swirled about her. She was Carolee Schneemann's assistant for a time. Maya Lin had included one of her early works in an anthology of young women who would change the future of art. Fabrice Hybert was allegedly her godfather. There were whispers that she was one of the Guerrilla Girls. She hadn't even applied to BCAD. When the first buffers—alleged art pieces—began sprouting up overnight, she received international attention for a series of protest performances against them. She was among the first to grasp the true purpose of those silvery sculptural lines that wove through cities, with screens on either side. They were barriers, insidiously designed to separate communities of different means. By creating eruvim, ritual halakhic enclosures, and basing them on inequality maps, she showed how the boundaries were the same, proving her hypothesis to be correct. This even though she, as an enclave kid, wasn't adversely affected. BCAD had practically begged her to enroll.

In classes, it quickly became clear that not only was she supremely gifted in any medium of her choice, but she also knew more about art than anyone, particularly in critical theory and history. In our first class with Professor Thomasina, we were asked to introduce ourselves and name our current favorite artist. It was meant to be a fun icebreaker, but I watched as we went around the room and students, with a sheen of sweat, grappled for the most impressive obscure artist they could think of—all of whom were known or cliché, even to me. As soon as a name was said, everyone snapped their heads up and down compulsively as if to say, *Yes, yes, I know that artist. I'm familiar with their work and, in fact, their entire oeuvre.* It was the first day of four years of classes, and everyone wanted to prove they had nothing to learn. Only Mathilde mentioned a name that invoked a surprised and momentary stillness.

"Remedios Varo?" She repeated the name again, hoping to elicit recognition. "*Vagabond? Creation of the Birds?*"

A slight shake of the head and some murmuring from other students. One boy surreptitiously typed on his phone under the desk.

"What do you like about his work?" Professor Thomasina asked.

"Her work," Mathilde said. "Right now, I'm inspired by the specificity with which she used tools to achieve exactly what she wanted. Sand, Masonite, decalcomania, soufflage . . . even quartz crystal sgraffito . . . nothing was off-limits. And instead of diluting her artistic language, this fluency of technique created it."

Professor Thomasina nodded slowly. "I remember her works now, yes. So original."

"Yes, exactly." Mathilde seemed happy to hear that someone else knew this artist she loved. But looking around, I thought that, like me, no one believed Professor Thomasina.

As one of the only non-enclave students, I had been worried about a lack of knowledge when I got to BCAD. During orientation week, I spent every night at the library, trying to catch up on all of the education I had missed. But it was impossible to grasp the entire history of our ancient field in that short amount of time, let alone familiarize myself with new artists and exhibits. Mathilde knew so much more than everyone, however, that it had an equalizing effect. Compared to her, we were all inexperienced. Instead of the panic my peers felt at her omniscience, I felt relief.

Outside of class, she was so introverted as to be unfriendly. The way she brushed past people, never noticing or acknowledging anyone, led us to believe she was hostile and competitive. Certainly she was as friendless as I was, although her loneliness was a choice. She seemed to recoil from human interaction, but that didn't stop me from being drawn to her. If I'd had a sister, I imagined she would look something like Mathilde. An intense gaze amplified her small, pointed features. She would have looked severe if not for the sweet fullness of her cheeks. When she passed me in the hallways, I had the urge to reach out and touch her. There was a surprising solidity to her slight figure, as if she created her own gravitational force. Anyone who got too close was in danger of falling into her orbit. Or maybe I was just so insecure that anyone with a strong sense of identity could destabilize me.

Although the BCAD campus sprawled across fifteen acres and had 1,703 students, there were fewer than twenty buildings, including dormitories. The student body was like a stack of unused canvases, grating against each other as we hoped to be the next masterpiece. It was impossible to exist without breathing in another artist's paint fumes or wading through their oversized ego. I always pinched myself as I admired the expansive green lawns dotted with clean brick buildings and gothic stone arches. It was the first time I was among other young artists, some of whom already had followings and pieces in prestigious galleries. They were all from enclaves, and many of them came from famous art families and were already minor celebrities. I found myself altering my history when I arrived. Little things, like saying I was from Miami instead of Gainesville. It was still miraculous to me that I had made it into BCAD, that I was walking in the footsteps of so many beloved artists. But no matter what I said, or how much I embellished, I couldn't shake the feeling that our lives had already been determined. I could see the way my classmates' careers would spin out over the next few years and decades. I could see the legacies they'd leave behind, eventually having their own golden art children—equally rich, talented, and connected. Comparatively, I was a nobody who came from nothing.

Without my scholarship, BCAD wouldn't have been an option. In my sophomore year of high school, the first buffers were erected in my neighborhood. We watched with eager anticipation as the sleek linear sculptures, reminiscent of silver snakes, were constructed. We felt lucky to be recipients of such beautiful public art pieces until my family was suddenly carved away from the rest of our community and every aspect of our daily life changed. Overnight, we were all assigned a designation. You were either an enclave kid or a fringe kid, and that title meant everything. As a fringe kid, I had to move schools, and my parents had to take such circuitous routes to work, they were eventually fired for persistent tardiness. Not only was upward mobility made impossible, but swimming in place wasn't even an option. It became too much of a hassle to see our old friends, and anyway, we didn't want to see them once the shame crept in. Presumably, these buffers were being erected all over the country, preventing contamination everywhere, but it was hard to even know if that was true. Normally, we would have found solidarity or solace online, but the new designations also dictated our online activity. Invisible buffers had been established on the internet so that websites were either enclave or fringe. Algorithms were no longer even vaguely related to our choices— they now corresponded to our IP addresses. I watched the possibilities of my life and self shrink to fit the algorithms, governed by these new limitations. The internet stopped being a place to connect to others or to exchange knowledge, and became a way to perform belonging in the world you had inherited.

Some people who were relegated to fringe status became obsessed with getting to the other side, something facial and gait recognition made impossible. But most, including my parents, began to indulge in a nasty snobbishness against anything cultural. If our lives were to be defined by inaccessibility, we could recontextualize that definition as a choice. A distaste for the interests of those who could afford to have interests. Art, which had never been truly democratic to begin with, was now an unattainable interest. My parents were first bewildered, then disturbed by my continued interest in it. They made it clear that they wouldn't spend a dime of their hard-earned money to support any of my artistic endeavors. I suppose it made them feel better to refuse, rather than to admit they didn't have anything to offer me.

Separated from any art store, I'd been forced to steal supplies. But there are so many colors you can make with just three. So many strokes to be taught from one brush. I made scarcity a good education. And even though I had so little, I had to hide it all for fear of my parents' ridicule, disappointment, and occasionally their wrath. As much as I disliked them, I also felt sorry for them. I couldn't have been the daughter they'd been conditioned to want.

When I got to BCAD, my mind couldn't help seeing a future in which all of my fellow students were stars and I alone a failure. I understood that if I wanted to ascend in this world, I would have to pull myself out of a warm, unrelenting sludge that perpetually sucked me down. I could feel the fringe on me, like a scent or shadow I couldn't shake, and I was worried everyone else could see it, too.

As a result, I preferred to work late at night when most of my classmates had gone home. It felt safer to keep my nascent projects from prying eyes. I would have a late dinner before heading to my studio space, that sanctuary of solitude, at eleven p.m.

One night, I noticed Mathilde's studio lights were still on. I looked in through the window quickly and saw that she wasn't there. I pressed myself against the door to better smell the delicious earthy aroma emitting from the large tree logs. I felt as if I were intruding on a deeply private moment, so at the squeak of an old window casement being closed in the building, I straightened and went down the hall to my own studio. I spent the next few hours drafting preliminary concepts for the upcoming Freshman Exhibit. For a while, I had been planning a work that would expose technology's limited ability for representation, but my new school affiliation changed the online spaces I could access, and technology was now an infinite resource rather than a constraint. I would have to change my initial idea, and I wasn't sure where to begin. I considered making a piece that would link so-called technological advances together. Something that drew a correlation between the invention of bullets and buffers, which I saw as an elongated bullet made static, forever blasting through cities, creating ruptures and boundaries. But I worried about the attention I would receive from creating an anti-buffer piece. Most of my classmates were antiestablishment, and would no doubt be suddenly interested in befriending me if they knew I had grown up fringe. I couldn't decide if that would make me feel more or less like an outsider. I was distracted by these thoughts, and a vague guilt pursued me the entire time, as if I'd seen or taken something I shouldn't have.

By three a.m., I was tired, unfocused, and unable to stay upright for more than a few minutes at a time. I packed up my things and went to the bathroom. I washed the dark charcoal off my hands with multiple pumps of soap and checked my face in the mirror for marks. I gasped—the stall door behind me was partially open, and a body was slumped on the toilet. Mathilde. I rushed in and grabbed her by the shoulders, righting her body. Her eyes flew open. She twisted away from me as if singed by my touch. I backed away, realizing how invasive I had been, even though I had acted out of concern.

"I'm sorry, I didn't mean to—"

"It's OK," she mumbled, waving a hand at me.

Drunk? I looked at her for a moment longer. No, not drunk. Sad. Her face was blotchy and swollen from crying. Her hands and arms were bleeding from different points. That explained her violent reaction to my touch. Pinpricks, maybe. Self-harm? But then I remembered the logs in her space. Splinters. "Do you need me to call someone?"

She shook her head without looking at me. "I just need to be alone."

"Mathilde, right? I'm Enka. We're in the same year, and my space is down the hall. Are you sure there's nothing I can do? Do you want me to stay with you? Or walk you home?"

She shook her head again, forcibly this time.

WHAT ELSE COULD I have done but leave?

I kept waking that night, startled by the appearance of her crumpled body. Each time I dreamed of her, I saw the expression on her face more clearly. The look in her eyes when they opened in surprise. How quickly that surprise became sadness. As if she were disappointed to find that she could still open them.

In the morning, I visited my studio as an excuse to pass hers. She was there, in the same clothes as the night before, looking lost as she stood among her logs. The blood had dried from the splinters, polka-dotting her arms. I stood in place until she noticed me. When she looked up, I watched my hand move up to her window, my palm filling up the entire space. I let it rest there for a moment, not sure what I was conveying but somehow certain it was significant. When I pulled back, I saw my handprint smudged on the glass and decided I liked it there.

From that day forward, I always pressed my hand to her window whenever I passed. It became a habit, and eventually, it didn't feel like I could go to my studio without the ritual. I would do it even if she wasn't there. She never gestured for me to come in or stepped out to speak to me. Mostly, she looked away. Maybe embarrassed for me.

A few weeks into this, I saw a handprint on the little window of my door. It was small and faint but unmistakable. My heart let out an erratic flutter.

This time, she came out of her room when she saw me.

I looked at her expectantly for a few seconds before she finally spoke.

"Why do you do it? The handprint thing." Her arms were crossed and wrapped around her body, as if she was cold.

"I'm not sure."

She looked past me, or through me, as she nodded fervently.

"I thought it might be a physicalization of our friendship . . . using a kind of substance and its accumulation as a show of time."

A sound of surprise escaped from my throat, startling us both. I quickly suppressed it.

"Everything is art to you, huh?"

She looked down, embarrassed, and wrapped her arms tighter around herself.

"I didn't mean . . . I mean, because it is to me."

She met my gaze tentatively.

Without realizing it, we had walked from her studio to mine.

"What are you working on? I saw through the window, but didn't understand . . ."

"I'll show you sometime," I said, panicking at the thought of showing my work to anyone, especially her. "Maybe tomorrow?"

"Why not now?" she asked softly, peeking through the glass.

I opened the door and trailed slowly behind her into my space.

"It's so . . . indoors."

I burst out laughing, her comment uncorking my nerves.

"Not everyone's working with a forest, Mathilde."

The ghost of a smile at the corner of her lips.

I explained my struggles with deciding which direction to go in for my piece and showed her some sketches. She chewed her lip furiously while listening to me.

"Have you always worked with technology as a medium?"

"Always. I think that expressing our technological moment while using it as the base material is contrapuntally interesting and has the most potential for subversion. I used to paint, too, but when I heard that the Dahl Corporation was giving full scholarships to students pursuing technology art, I jumped at the chance."

It wasn't a complete lie. But I hadn't told anyone how seriously I had pursued painting in the past, and I didn't plan on it. My love for oil began on a field trip to a museum in the sixth grade when I walked by a small painting on the way to the water fountain and stopped, startled by a feeling I can only describe as recognition. It was a painting of a wooden frame laid against a wall on a red surface. Inside the frame was a substance that was half wood, half transparent. I felt as if I'd caught it mid-transformation, and was witnessing something so vulnerable, exposed, and intimate. And I felt that it saw me in return: the shame, and the secrets adolescence was beginning to thrust at me. It reassured me that the lack of a coherent self, a self in the midst of change, could still be beautiful. I started crying before I reached the bathroom.

Once I experienced how artists could elicit such primal emotions, communicating with something beneath and beyond language, I became obsessed with the idea of doing the same. I signed up for art classes at school, not knowing that the teacher, Ms. Liu, would become the most significant person of my adolescence. She taught me the basics of sketching and painting, and generously introduced me to the work of countless artists by loaning me books and giving me ample individual attention. As the last school bell rang, I would run to her room, and she would let me paint while I waited for my parents to pick me up. I loved the tired feeling in my limbs; I found it gratifying to do something that exhausted my whole body. The endless colors I could make, that maybe the world hadn't seen before . . . the way paint clumped my arm hairs together or worked its way into the tooth of my denim. I was good at it, too. Even when I lost access to Ms. Liu and the high school with art classes, I was still the local prodigy in my small town, and that confidence led me to believe I would make it into the art school I deemed most prestigious.

The Berkshire College of Art and Design was known for being more progressive than other art schools, and it was the only one I was interested in because I needed to study with Professor Thomasina, the artist who had painted the piece that had provoked such an emotional response from me. I knew it was an object, but I couldn't help feeling like the painting understood me. That it captured something about my essence and reflected it back to me. That work of art was a balm in a family, school, and town that continually spiraled beyond my comprehension and control. I was certain Professor Thomasina would take one look at me and recognize who I was.

My visit to BCAD as a prospective student changed everything. When I saw the level of skill and creativity on campus, the space between me and my dreams widened. At BCAD, my so-called artistic genius would be mediocre at best. I was a good painter, but good doesn't compare with visionary. It felt hopeless to even try.

After this, I sank into a deep depression. Packed up the brushes that had become extra limbs and stuffed them into the storage closet along with the paints and gently stretched canvases. Still, I used a cheap online location scrambler to obsessively check the BCAD application website, wondering whether to apply. One day, the admissions site flashed with a banner announcing the newly created Dahl Fellowship for artists working with technology as their medium. I crawled out of my misery and forced myself to spend the rest of the year making a portfolio of art that intersected meaningfully with technology and culture. Either because the fellowship was so new that people didn't know about it, or because technology art had little appeal to my cohort, I was the only applicant. I was accepted, technology finally the savior it always promised to be.

MATHILDE'S PRESENCE IN my studio unnerved me. I couldn't tell what she was thinking as she assessed my sketches. Did she think they were stupid? "You're a sculptor?" I asked, as much out of curiosity as a need to distract her.

She nodded.

"How's your piece coming along?"

She flinched at the mention of her work. "It's not easy."

"Maybe I can help? Anything you can show me?"

She shook her head. "I would, but it doesn't make sense if it isn't the whole picture." She sighed and smiled at me. "Thanks for showing me your studies. I know it takes a certain amount of trust. In yourself and in the other person. And I never thanked you for the other night . . . the bathroom."

"Please. I didn't even do anything," I said.

She left the studio, closing the door before I could follow her. The next day, a piece of heavy cloth covered her window, obstructing any chance I had of reaching her.

For the Freshman Exhibit, I ended up staging my own version of a Noh play based on chūkan hyōjō, an ideal of ambiguous expression or neutral beauty in Noh theater. It was a term I had connected with as soon as I came across it. In this ambiguousness, I recognized an opportunity to interrogate the passive nature people assumed of me from my exterior. The mask, like technology, gave me a shadow self in which I could hide, or so I hoped, the fact of my being a fringe kid in a new enclave environment, which then liberated me to be myself. I made a rudimentary approximation of a Noh mask, a process that usually took up to a year. While most students stood next to pieces they had built or painted, I stood in my booth under a single light in a black robe. Popular karaoke tunes that were nostalgic and melancholy played from a small radio. I had elongated the sleeves of my robe with fabric scraps so that they dripped dramatically from my wrists and hid my hands. I wore the mask, which I had painted to look like the smiling emoji, and tilted my head, swaying from side to side and dancing when I felt like it. No matter what music was playing from the radio, my expression was one of happiness. It mirrored how stuck I felt in real life by the way people perceived me.

I got to the show early to set up and hoped to see Mathilde's finished work before everyone else. But she hadn't arrived yet, and her assigned space was empty. I stopped by Liesl's station instead, admiring her sculptures of extinct insects that reimagined how they might adapt to habitat loss. The chitinous pieces were secondary to the emotional resonances she hoped to evoke between them. Only a few of us knew that the primary material substance was Cheeto dust.

Criztina's interactive work consisted of only a table on which she performed body calligraphy. As hard as she tried, she was unable to dispel the idea that it was a free massage booth, and many were upset by the service they received. They had wanted more pressure, and could she at least even them out? Later, we laughed at online reviews we found on a rating service website, all of them complaining about the terrible massages they'd received at our school.

A small crowd had trickled in, and I joined them as they oohed and aahed at Mona's paintings, which were all identical except that they were dried in different sunlight. *Copenhagen* had a distinctly bluish tinge while *Tuscany* was mauve-tinted. Envy pricked my heart when I saw the large gathering around her simple paintings. It never occurred to me to be competitive or even jealous of men. For a long time, I'd worried that it was internalized misogyny before I realized that the only artists I respected enough to envy were women.

E-Noh-Ji was a success, but it didn't win the first-year prize. All evening, people had dashed past me toward an exhibit somewhere behind and to the left. When they passed me again, they did so at a much slower pace, with their eyes lowered. Other students left their pieces unattended to see what was going on, but I couldn't do the same because my piece required my presence. When the night began to wind down and guests finally stopped trickling in, I tore off my mask and all but ran to see what had been so captivating.

The back corner of the space was covered with metal. It had been converted into the cabin of a plane. It was hung with mobiles of loaned debris from 9/11. There were only two seats: one was taken by a painted wooden sculpture of Mathilde's dad, and the other was empty. Each visitor was asked to sit and hold his hand in what was a re-creation of his final moments.

Mathilde's dad was slightly turned toward the other seat. Beads of sweat were frozen around his temples and his glasses were askew. He looked worried, mouth slightly parted as if he were about to speak. His tie was crumpled around his neck and an old mobile phone sat in his lap. A speaker crackled, playing a faint recording of his last words. "I don't know if . . . will go through, but I . . . try. Mathilde, honey, I love you. You are the . . . and joy of my life. I . . . so lucky to have been . . . dad."

Even though our opening night was coming to an end, there was still a line for Mathilde's piece. When it was my turn, I sat down and took his wooden hand. I started to cry as I whispered a stream of apologies and comforts.

When I finally wrenched myself through to the next part of the exhibit, Mathilde was on the other side. I opened my mouth to congratulate her, but a sob escaped my throat instead. Wordlessly, I wrapped my arms around her body. I thought back to the day I had seen her in the stall, how sad she had looked. I saw how that day multiplied, stretched into weeks and months of Mathilde alone in her studio space with a block of wood, carving her father's likeness out of it. Getting as close as possible, while never actually being able to reanimate him.

There was a big party at a house where a few upperclassmen lived. Everyone had packed up their personal belongings and headed over, but Mathilde didn't seem to have any intention of leaving. I lingered, packing my things slowly until I worked up the nerve to approach her.

"I understand now, what you meant before. That it requires the whole picture."

She smiled thinly, her eyes glassy and unfocused. "Thank you."

Now that I was standing so close to her, it broke my heart to see how thin she had become, as if while working on her father, she had also taken the chisel to herself.

"Mathilde. I can't imagine how difficult this must have been for you to work on."

A look of terror crept over her face. "I can't leave him here."

I took my backpack off my shoulders and placed it on the ground.

"So we'll stay."

2

I started letting myself into her studio space while she was working. I would open the door quietly, shut it behind me, and sit on the floor, often staying for many hours. I thought that if I could observe the smallest of her daily actions, I could begin to understand the secret of her artistry. The first several times, she was surprised, and it took a few moments before she was comfortable continuing. Eventually, she barely noticed the interruption.

Mathilde had cleared the forest from her studio space, but it was still unlike any other. The rest of us accumulated paper and canvas, bits and bobs of material. Mini-fridges, crushed energy drink cans, and empty coffee cups. More pastels, paints, and even pets until the negative space of our rooms was completely eaten away by clutter.

Mathilde's room was empty except for a small desk with a single pencil and pad of paper. She stood in a corner, staring into space and swaying from side to side, whether consciously or unconsciously, I couldn't tell. She would end her sessions by walking quickly to the table and picking up her pencil. By my fifth or sixth unannounced and nearly unacknowledged visit, I began to feel how energy circled above her, culminating in images that struck her mind, visual lightning that traveled down her arm and onto paper.

When left alone in her room for the first time, I rushed over to see what divine dispatch she might have received, expecting the usual studies that would coalesce into an eventual work. On each paper, instead of a drawing or any kind of form, I saw the absence of form. Around that empty space, a torrent of words. Desires, urges, and other feelings. This was the first lesson Mathilde taught me: artists create works of art; geniuses curate an emotional response.

Mathilde worked in the afternoons, as soon as classes were finished. I continued my quiet studies with her during that time, and then worked on my own art at night. My own sessions were more inspired after watching her. When confronted with any artistic challenge or obstacle, I would often arrive at something interesting if I asked myself, *What would Mathilde do, or think, or say?*

I started bringing her dinner and offering to get her materials when I was at the art store. We began walking home together after our sessions. She introduced me to her favorite films, and I bought a record player for all the music she loaned me. It wasn't long before we spent all our waking hours together. And maybe our friendship was lopsided at first, or maybe there was something unnatural in the way I went about doing anything I could to get her to concede to my presence, but eventually, we had become real friends.

We were inseparable, waiting for one another before and after classes, sharing every meal, a bed, and sometimes even the same bathroom stall. We could tell with a glance what the other was feeling. I became especially adept at reading the outline of her body, her silhouette often betraying every emotion she had experienced that day. Our sudden intimacy was alarming yet thrilling. And I can't deny that I loved being seen with her. With our relationship, I had access to genius, which was a consolation when every crit session made me feel less and less like I belonged at BCAD. I had nothing to offer compared to my colleagues. No matter how much I searched for a self, my works were always deemed too reminiscent of already existing pieces. As a fringe kid, I was unavoidably ignorant of so many artists and pieces, and that ignorance was now on full display. It'd almost be preferable to plagiarize rather than unknowingly replicate a familiar idea, with less skill. Even when I did manage to make something somewhat original, it wasn't interesting. My classmates and professors were all enclavers . . . I didn't know their influences, and that lack of knowledge meant that I couldn't guess what they might want to see.

After particularly nasty crits in which I stood defenseless while my colleagues and professor intellectually tore my work to shreds, I would shower with the heat turned all the way up, hoping my skin would melt and reassemble, turning me into someone else.

Everyone wanted to be friends with Mathilde after seeing her work. Not only had she won the first-year prize, there were many gallerists circling, wanting to represent her. Still, Mathilde had chosen me over the many who had tried to get close to her.

Those who were jealous of our friendship retaliated with rumors as ugly as they were unimaginative. People made fun of how inseparable we were, whispering, "It's already been done by Teh-ching Hsieh and Linda Montano!" This reference made me inter-nally sneer. They'd needed a rope to bind them for that year. What Mathilde and I shared was deeper, a devouring that needed no vow.

Only once did the insidious murmurs worry me. It was said that between the two of us, Mathilde was the genius, but I was the beautiful one . . . because when two women are together, it's a social mandate that one is more beautiful. But I didn't feel beau-tiful, especially not next to Mathilde. In the early days of our friendship, I drew her often. It felt important to observe the phys-ical boundary that separated us when an electrical charge ran be-tween our minds. The wild tangle of black curls she spontaneously cut herself, usually out of frustration. The vulnerability of her round cheeks and childish freckles above a small and defiantly pointed chin. The insouciant jut of her lower lip, and the danger that lurked in the dark quivering pupils of her eyes. I traced every line, followed every curve. Is there anyone who knows a young woman's body better than her closest friends? By way of love or comparison or some combination of the two? Even the way I was beautiful seemed to lack imagination. Was I beautiful or just sym-metrical? Sometimes it made me feel good to think of myself as attractive, but mostly it paralyzed me. I was afraid there was something fateful in these whispers. That they would grow and solidify into something powerful enough to lock us into a para-digm we had no choice but to fulfill. One we wouldn't be able to escape.

Things began to change at the end of the year. Mathilde stopped going to classes, which didn't worry too many people. She had so little to learn from the professors, anyway. Then she stopped going to the cafeteria and the library. Stopped walking on the trails that wound around campus. Her working hours became less frequent. Most of the time when I slipped into her studio, I encountered an empty room, gathering dust because she spent her days in bed.

I had always heard that healing wasn't linear, but it was alarming to see how sharply Mathilde dropped off the edge of any quantifiable process. I started showing up outside of her room every morning, knocking gently before letting myself in, hoping to coax her into having breakfast with me. At night, I tucked her in and climbed in beside her. Sleep eluded her; she often woke after only a few minutes, crying out for her father or her mother, who had taken her own life shortly after her husband's death. When this happened, I whispered, "I breathe in, you breathe out." It became a sort of mantra, one I recited to help her fall asleep. She was so childlike in size, under the many layers of blankets I spread over her, that sometimes I felt as if she were my daughter. She was constantly fevered, and she became so thin, I could see the blue veins that coursed through her translucent body like streams. On the rare occasion that she was able to fall into a deep sleep, I ran my fingers up and down those tributaries, imagining where they emptied. I hoped that my presence could mitigate some of the loss of her family.

Maybe I even envied the grief that surrounded Mathilde. It was clarifying, burning away anything else that might distract her from art. A moat that kept her safe from the desires of others and her own. On the other hand, I was insatiable. All anyone had to do was look at me, and I was filled with a longing to be touched. I wanted to be serious, to be wholly dedicated to art and matters of the mind, but my body's hunger voided everything else, erupting with rashes and pimples when I didn't heed its call. I was especially drawn to art handlers, seemingly unable to resist the bit of taut forearm suspended between glove and sleeve. I tried dating more seriously exactly once, giving up precious time I could have spent with Mathilde for a few unsatisfying conversations and dinners. That brief relationship ended when he let slip that Mathilde's 9/11 piece seemed gimmicky to him. He looked at me apologetically as he said it, as if worried he'd said the wrong thing. He had. I regretted sharing myself with him, and went back to sleeping with multitudes of people, often just to shake off lust's pervasive talons.

On the nights when I'd left Mathilde alone, I would crawl out of some stranger's bed racked with guilt for not being with her. I'd bike to my room and take a quick steamy shower before morning classes, followed by a stop at the cafeteria to grab food to bring her. While she barely touched the fruit, whole wheat bread, and hummus, I took her computer and fielded emails. Every major gallery in New York, Miami, and Paris wanted to show her 9/11 piece. She had been put forth by an anonymous institution for the Biennale. Mathilde's inbox was an artist's dream come true. I sometimes pretended I was responding on my own behalf.

I opted to stay on campus during the summer, instead of going home. Mathilde was too vulnerable, and if I didn't take care of her, who would? I also couldn't imagine spending time with my parents and their willful disdain for everything I loved. After a day on their feet at ungratifying jobs, they would expect me to eat TV dinners and fossilize on the couch with them while conspiratorial anchors blasted at full volume. Much better to stay here with Mathilde and offer what I could in the restoration of her brilliance.

She slept most of the summer. I put old movies on and sketched at her bedside, fleshing out conceptual ideas I would work on once the semester started. Some days were better than others. The first time I made her laugh, a look of surprise came over her face before she abruptly stopped herself. Between the lines of her pained expression, I could read the guilt.

"You're allowed to be happy," I said. "Your parents would have wanted that."

"I know," she said, rubbing her face in an attempt to not cry.

In the moments when I felt like she was really present, I was rewarded with the most charismatic and intelligent person I had ever met. Even though she was far from 100 percent, the speed at which her mind made connections, and the way she bridged disparate tangents, was astounding. *Bill & Ted's Excellent Adventure* wasn't just a classic . . . By our third viewing together, she had convinced me of all the ways it was *the* classic, clearly an homage to Homer's *Odyssey*. She conversed in strands that suddenly cohered at the end of a thought the way an abstract painting could come together with visceral meaning. "Van Gogh and jazz are the same thing," she once said. When I looked at her blankly, she explained. "Van Gogh's gradual discovery of color in his paintings over a period of ten years gives us a way to understand how an individual can transcend oppression to find a loose and dazzling joy. Jazz does the same, but on a communal level. The jazz solo is a love letter to the maintenance and expression of self that still manages to remain in harmony with a greater community."

A moment of lucidity I remember especially well: for a week in July, the air-conditioning in the dorms stopped working. The heat felt solid, and moving through it was slow and strenuous. We stuffed our pillowcases and sheets in the small fridge, only taking them out when it was time to sleep. We sweated so much in her muggy room that I collected a small cup of our commingled fluids to use for watercoloring.

"It reminds me of home," I said to her. "It gets this swampy in Gainesville, and you can almost see the damp spreading through the walls. As a kid, I thought there was an invisible giant trapped there, painting a message from within. It terrified me."

The wet spots festered and bloomed into fantastic molds that I still unconsciously draw from time to time. Even now, I'm afraid that the damp somehow still clings to me, holding me in place or waiting to overtake the life I've tried so hard to build away from it.

"I thought you were from Miami," Mathilde said. *Shit.* The heat . . . I wasn't thinking clearly. But Mathilde's eyes were curious, not judgmental.

"I'm actually from Gainesville," I said. Once the door was open, more truths slipped through. "I guess it's embarrassing or something. Not as cool as Miami. And, you know, I'm fringe."

Mathilde put a hand over my paint-splotched sleeve.

"Don't be embarrassed about where you're from . . . It's part of who you are," Mathilde said.

"I guess I'm embarrassed about that, too."

"Why? You're an amazing artist and person. Certainly the best fucking thing to ever happen to me."

I had to bite the inside of my cheek to keep from grinning too wide. When I had visited BCAD the year before applying, this was the kind of friendship I had longed for. The students were all covered in grungy paint-splattered clothes, lost in philosophical conversation as they hurtled away from me with giant masterpieces tucked under their arms, leaving me in a cloud of fragrant linseed oil. Finally, I had found someone who didn't care about who I had been, only who I was becoming. Someone who dreamed the same dreams and spoke the same language.

While I was genuinely worried for her, looking after Mathilde was a necessary distraction from the paralyzing depression that came from being so terribly suited for the thing I most wanted to do. If she saw something in me, even if it was something I manufactured, I mattered. In some perverse way, by taking care of her, I was making myself indispensable to the institution, maybe even the art world at large.

MY PARENTS WERE given special buffer privileges to visit for a weekend, wanting to see me at least once during the summer. I was surprised, having fully expected they'd never set foot on campus again after dropping me off the first time. I was glad they wouldn't have a chance to interact with too many students or professors during this visit. They'd ruined my first few hours at BCAD, mocking everything they saw. I tried to reason with myself. It wasn't their fault . . . The buffer had physically cut them off from the art world. It was only natural for them to retaliate by closing their minds to what had been withheld. When they met Professor Thomasina at orientation, Dad asked her about a painting in her office, an abstract piece with muted grays, browns, and golds.

"That's one of my more well-known paintings. It's always a work in progress. Whenever I experience a specifically deep emotion, I transfer it onto the canvas with a material or color that feels appropriate in the moment."

Dad responded that it looked like a transfer he'd seen by a dog in a junkyard. I thought my face would never stop burning.

The only person they met this time was Mathilde. She was bedridden and thus charmless, so of course they only saw a tiresome obligation who needed constant care.

"Why is she so ill? Who are your other friends? There's still time to transfer." They were always angling for me to do something else, but this time they seemed to do so out of genuine concern. They were confused, as well, by the many changes they observed. The way I had begun to resemble Mathilde: how I dressed, my new interests, and especially my voice, which had become deeper and breathier.

"Don't lose yourself," my mom said.

But I couldn't wait to lose the person I'd been. What is college except the chance to try on many selves? My parents thought I was copying Mathilde, which hurt my feelings. It wasn't as one-sided as they perceived during their short visit. People are wrong about imitation, anyway. It isn't flattery but an attempt at closeness. Mathilde and I were exchanging parts of ourselves, our very identities a collaborative work.

As the start of our second year drew closer, Mathilde began to talk about withdrawing from BCAD—something that alarmed me.

"I don't know if I can do it, Enka," she murmured every day.

"Of course you can, Mathilde."

"I just feel . . . abandoned. I don't mean . . . You've been amazing. But sometimes I just want to never wake up. Because when I do, I remember that they aren't . . . I wonder what would happen if I just stopped moving. Would it be so bad?"

"You don't mean that, Mathilde." I stroked her sweaty temples and fed her ice cubes, one at a time.

"I just don't have it. Whatever it is that propels people forward.

I don't know if I'll ever have it again, don't even remember what it was like."

"You just have to go through the motions. The feelings will come after, I promise."

I tried not to take these conversations personally. But I couldn't help despairing at the thought that I wasn't enough for her. What would I do if she left? There had been little time to devote to other people—she was now my closest and only friend.

"I don't even have anything to show for the summer project," she said one day as I pleaded with her to reconsider.

"What about this? What are these?"

All summer, she had doodled in a little sketchbook by her bed.

Her eyes lit up, a rare occurrence. "This is the cactus lab. It was part of my family's old cactus farm. There wasn't much for us to do in the desert, so my dad made a cactus labyrinth for the local kids to play in. We spent so many days there."

We rarely talked about her childhood or her parents. I had learned to avoid those subjects early on in our friendship when I saw how her face would slacken when they were mentioned. I was surprised she brought them up now, but not surprised to hear that her upbringing had been artistic and unconventional.

"What if you built a model based on it? You could probably even submit these sketches for the summer assignment." The drawings were exquisite. Elaborate circular structures, spiky mandalas snaking off the pages.

She shook her head slowly and gently took the sketchbook from my hands. "This part of my life is just for me."

3

A hundred faces stare at me when I step out of the bath-room. Masks made of a mysterious pink substance, which leaks through the facial structures formed with enmeshed wire. I look toward the main wing, where everyone is mingling, and think about joining, but the Bosq pieces are so striking, they pin me in place. From where I stand, I have a clear view of every member of Mathilde's foundation board, likely the people in touch with her last. Klaus Wegner is wandering outside on the phone with a glass of wine glued to his lips. Otto Wiedenboch circles the fountain full of hybridized koi-piranha, no doubt look-ing for prey of his own. Polina is heading for the bar, Professor Abara is delicately patting his mouth with a napkin, and Monika is talking to one of the servers.

"There she is!" a loud droll voice exclaims.

I set my face in a careful smile before turning around to face Ira, finding him with my father-in-law. "The woman of the hour."

He crushes me in a hug, and the flowers on my dress release a heavenly scent that sours as it makes contact with the sweat and alcohol emanating from his skin. "You really shouldn't be touching any of the pieces," he says.

I drop my hand. Lost in thought, I hadn't realized I had been touching the gel of the nearest Bosq piece, squeezing it like a stress-relief ball. The fleshlike consistency is unexpectedly warm and comforting.

"They're so lifelike," I say.

"Well, they *are* life, Enka. The Plasticine is mixed with materials from the last surviving Ketumbe people."

"Right."

Materials. I try not to shudder. Bosq shares a small percentage of DNA with the Ketumbe people, but he was born and raised in an affluent Dallas enclave. He only recently discovered his heritage through Deszendant, and something about all of it makes me uncomfortable. But maybe the authenticity is what makes it so haunting. I only wish it evoked a stronger emotional response. Like most artists in the last few years, Bosq values concept over content. The pieces are visually unsettling, but they prioritize aesthetics and center Bosq. Aren't we supposed to be sad that our choices have caused the loss of the Ketumbe homeland, and, eventually, their existence? In recent interviews, Bosq almost sounds happy to have a sad history to co-opt for his own artistic gain. It reminds me of the climate art craze from a decade ago, before it became too problematic for being mostly performative, wasteful, and useless at enacting real change.

"Aren't you going to welcome me to the family?"

"Sorry?" Ira's question catches me off guard.

"The partnership. As the LORA's curator, I'll be working closely on the collaboration with Dahl Corp. All very exciting. I'm so interested to see how the pilot stage will go," Ira says.

"Welcome to the family," I say with as much enthusiasm as I can muster. "Excuse me." I make my way toward Polina. I don't have the patience to pretend I'm interested in anything Ira has to say tonight. At the bar, Polina takes one look at me and slides her glass over.

"You need it more than I do."

I reach for the drink, grateful for her directness.

When Mathilde and I were freshmen, Polina was already a senior. She was the bright star of the curatorial studies program, with an uncanny third eye for performance art that could easily be commodified and converted for online spaces. By the time we were sophomores, she was working at the Whitney.

"You've obviously heard?" Polina says.

"What do you know?" I'm unable to keep the desperate edge out of my voice.

She turns to me with a bitter look in her kohl-rimmed eyes. "Not much. They kicked me out."

"What . . . Who kicked you out?"

"The rest of the board," she said. "They wanted to . . . I didn't agree with their decisions. All I did was raise some questions, ask for more time and consideration, and the next thing I know, they've ousted me." She takes the glass from me and raises it toward Monika. I follow her gaze to my mother-in-law, who looks immaculate as usual in a dress dripping with diamonds, and hair that's aquatic in its continuous flow. She turns at that moment and catches me looking at her. Graces me with the famous smile she would never waste on me if we were alone.

"She led the charge," Polina says.

"Of course she did," I say, taking another sip. "So you don't know anything about where Mathilde might be?"

Her eyes widen. "Enka, it's so much worse than anyone knows. She hasn't just been missing for a few days. More like a year."

I bite my tongue in shock and watch a drop of blood disappear into the wine. "That's not . . . possible. We would have noticed . . . I or someone . . . would have known . . . Just last week, *The Lancet* was updated with new pictures."

"We kept it a secret for as long as we could. Kept pumping old content we scheduled beforehand. Another one of Monika's choices. I'm relieved someone either found out or leaked the information today. I was thinking of doing it myself."

"Does Monika know where she is?"

Polina shakes her head with visible disgust. "I doubt it. She's been so wrapped up in the details of this new partnership with Ira, she's probably forgotten all about Mathilde. When she first went missing, it was all about the logistics of covering our asses. I don't think she's even looked for her."

"But, so . . . when was the last time you saw her?"

"We went down to the Chinati Foundation and found that she'd taken off—"

"She ran away from the Chinati?"

"Yes. I had nothing to do with it, but they blamed me and used that as the official reason to call for my removal. That was the last time I saw her. In person, at least."

"What do you mean?"

"I received some texts from her after they'd already dismissed me from the board. I wasn't sure they were meant for me, or anyone. They seemed accidental."

"Do you still have them?"

She nods, producing her phone from a small clutch. "Are you sure you want to see?"

"Why wouldn't I?"

Polina lets out a shaky breath. "She wasn't well, Enka. We found a specialist. And we ran tests. We hoped that she would recover at the Chinati. You know, working was always cathartic for her. But this . . . we didn't know if there was any way back from this."

"I don't understand. Did something happen? Did she suffer a . . . mental break of some kind?"

"Here," she says, tapping on her phone. "See for yourself."

Two blurry desert landscapes that are nearly identical. Then, a ten-second video. The unsteady camerawork shows Mathilde's feet trudging in the sand before flipping to focus on her face. Her skin is leathery and covered with blisters, but she smiles hugely into the camera. Her lips are so cracked they look gouged. "Come on," she shrieks to someone behind her. A glimpse of something bundled in dirty white linen . . . a small dog? Whatever it is, it trails behind her, connected to her wrist by a length of rough rope. She starts to say something again but is cut off by the end of the video.

Who was she with? What had happened to her skin? Why was she sharing this with Polina, of all people? The glint in Mathilde's eye, the leprous skin, and the way all fat had been siphoned from her body . . . I feel a chill, as if my spine has been swapped out for an icicle. A wave of agitation sweeps over me, and my underarms stream with sweat. *Where are you, Mathilde? Can you really have left me all alone?* From the moment we became friends, she and I constructed ourselves in relation to one another. I've always had one eye fixed on her, each of her actions initiating an equal or opposite reaction. Everything I've achieved has been from trying to keep up with her, and I only know who I am in relation to her. What do I do if she's really gone? Will I also cease to exist?

4

A week before our second year began, I received a call from an unknown number.

"Hello?"

"Hi, this is Polina Ma. I'm a curator for the Whitney Museum. Is this Mathilde Wojnot-Cho's assistant?"

"Yes," I answered. It was the Whitney after all, and I was basically Mathilde's assistant.

They, like everyone, wanted to show Mathilde's 9/11 work, in an exhibit themed around loss. They also wanted to commission another piece to be shown with it. She sat up in bed when I told her the news. I watched as she processed this information for a few moments. "What could I possibly make to keep him company?" she whispered. Tears gathered in her eyes, threatening to spill.

I didn't know what to say. But it was the Whitney. I knew that I should give her some time to think it over, but I couldn't help myself. I begged her to consider it, promising it would be good for her to work on something new. Selfishly, I also knew she would have to stay in school to work on another piece. She would need the resources. She resisted, and every few days, I found myself on the phone with Polina, in the awkward position of having to make up reasons for Mathilde's lack of an answer. Part of me wanted to shake her. Being asked to show at the Whitney at such a young age . . . while she was still in school. It was something most of us couldn't fathom. To be asked was an honor. And yet there was no part of her that was gratified or excited about the interest. I was relieved when, three weeks later, she finally listened.

I was right—committing to a new work revived her. By the second month of the semester, she was often dressed and out of bed when I checked on her in the mornings. We started having meals together in the cafeteria instead of her room. And even though she hadn't been working on anything tangible, her mind had experienced a profound philosophical shift. She informed our professors that she was moving away from permanent works. She had been rewatching Yasujirō Ozu's films and was inspired by their quality of "mono no aware," the Japanese idiom for understanding the transitory nature of things. She wanted to explore transience as a tool for heightening artistic experience. She was also deeply moved by Susan Philipsz's sound installations, and the way she made presence out of absence. "Her use of sound is almost like color. It fills everything in, making us more aware of ourselves and the space around us. My youth has been defined by absence and impermanence, and if I'm to continue making art, I have to find ways of reconciling with them as the primary materials that have shaped me." The professors acquiesced, probably thinking it was just a phase, but understanding that Mathilde likely couldn't bear the idea of making anything that would outlive her parents.

She started working: weekend and night shifts at the local

Marriott hotel. I was surprised since I knew she had a full scholarship and a generous stipend from the school—my eyes had stung when I happened to see an opened check in her room. Her new job left her with very little time to commit to her Whitney piece, and that worried me. Polina called every few weeks with scheduling details, requests for the exhibit and the space, and each time, I had to find new ways of lying about Mathilde's progress. A month flew by, then two. She only had three left, not to mention the whole impermanent-works situation. I was baffled by the whole thing. Would she be making *anything* for the exhibit? How would the Whitney respond to great philosophical concepts that ultimately showed nothing?

Now that Mathilde was so occupied with her new job and the classes she had to make up from last year, I had more time to return to my work. I was proud of the head start I had given myself by staying and working through the summer. The ideas were all there; they just needed to be realized. For the Sophomore Exhibit, I was working on a piece about the loss of innocence. My studio space was piled high with things I had collected from junk shops and various online marketplaces: old Game Boys, Tamagotchis, and N64 cartridges. I glued these abandoned childhood items into small sculptural chains, making umbilical cords that dangled from the ceiling. My confidence in the piece vacillated wildly. Some days, I was sure it was a work of genius; other days, I was paralyzed with doubt. A month before the sophomore show, I finally let Mathilde see what I was working on. As I approached the door, I hesitated, regretting my decision to share it with her. What if she thought it was terrible?

She squeezed past me, entering my studio before I could protest or make excuses, and immediately snapped her head around to look at me.

"Are these umbilical cords? Or maybe I'm being too psychoanalytical . . . or anthropomorphic . . ."

"No, you're right—that's exactly what they are!" I was thrilled that she got it at all, and so quickly. "I wanted to . . . Well, it's an attempt to grapple with some of the binaries that I experience working with technology. Technology art and technology at large are rather male-dominated now, and I want to disturb that notion. As well as the idea that the biological and the digital are at odds with each other. We might all be hybrid creatures one day."

"I love it. The organic quality of the shapes, and the order you imposed on the materials with the natural progression of games mirroring our developmental growth. There's such a palpable sense of loss, too. Most people are afraid to use anything branded or evocative of a specific time, in an effort to create a timeless piece of work. They don't want to age the piece . . . and yet you've done exactly that. Aged it, used branding to portray the universal experience of time passing. It's so powerful."

Her praise fulfilled me in a way that nothing else had, and I savored the look on her face as she walked around, admiring the pieces from a closer vantage point, even touching some of them. A handheld *Tetris* game disassembled and strung around a Bop It.

"It reminds me a little of Judith Scott's works."

My face began to burn. Once again, I had unwittingly copied an artist I didn't know. But Mathilde's voice was gentle, without any of the lacerating quality of my peers in crit when they brought up the similarities in my works to other artists.

"She's a favorite of mine. A fiber artist who makes fabulous wild cocoons and other organic shapes with textiles. You take it in a completely different textural and contextual direction, of course. But there's something so emotional about both of your works."

"I'm not familiar with her," I confess.

Mathilde grins. "I'll show you later. She was an outsider artist for so long, before the establishment finally deemed her successful enough on their terms to be called a contemporary artist."

Mathilde must have seen the look on my face. "Enka, I didn't mean . . . That's just the terminology for someone without formal artistic training."

"Like me."

She stepped close and cupped my face with her palms. "No one is like you. You know that the fringe stuff doesn't mean anything to me, right? If anything, I envy you and other outsider artists. You work from experiences that are your own, and they have an emotional palpability that's often more universal than works by people who have grown up knowing what kind of art the market prefers. For the last few years, I've been engaged in this long process of unlearning what I know, all the history and the images that get in the way of my instincts. You're an inspiration to me."

A look of apprehension distorted her features. "Can I show you what I've been working on? For the Whitney?"

"Of course," I said, relieved that there was something to show me at all.

We walked across the street to the library. She opened a door to the left of the bathrooms and began walking down a set of stairs.

"I couldn't find a place dark enough until the library let me use this space. And then it took them a while to get situated. That's why I haven't shown you anything before." She flicked on a dim indirect light, and I saw twenty standing structures that made me gasp.

Mathilde hadn't been working at the hotel because she needed money but because she wanted to obtain Bibles without subsidizing religious institutions. She had stolen twenty Bibles from bedside tables and encased them in Perspex grids, with two silverfish in each one. They were now being stored in the dark basement of the library.

A month later, when they were finally moved to the Whitney, the pages had been eaten through by the insects, creating a beautiful latticework. The exhibit was profiled in *The New York Times* as "a powerful indictment of religion's random and often too-convenient interpretations of the Bible." Another article remarked that it "definitively crowned consumerism the new Christ, signaling religion's capitulation to capitalism." In an interview, Mathilde explained that after she lost her parents in quick succession, she struggled with her faith, eventually losing that, as well. The work served as a testament to that dual loss. When the exhibit was over, Mathilde gave the grids away. For years, people posted pictures from their books on a long-form open-access document. Phrases, patterns, and even poetry, parsed by the appetite of the silverfish.

5

A couple of weeks before the Sophomore Exhibit, our class was called into the gallery space. We walked by our tired works from the year before, excited to show how much we had grown in the span of twelve months. We assumed we were there to receive assigned spaces for the showcase, so students eyed the room, making mental notes on the ideal placement for their works should the need to barter arise. We were in for a rude awakening. Professor Thomasina waited for us to settle before she began to speak.

"A month ago, students at Caltech created a piece of generative software that made what they called 'weird art.'"

Students around me laughed. Wasn't all art weird?

"I assure you very little is funny about this new digital museum. With this software, anyone can type a few words into a box as a prompt, click 'generate,' and different works of art will appear."

"Anyone?" Gabriel asked from where he sat cross-legged on the floor.

"The creators have made the software open-source, so not only have they uploaded their artworks, but the general public can, as well. This digital museum has only been online for fourteen hours, and already, hundreds of thousands of people have uploaded and copyrighted their generated artworks. We expect this to continue and to proliferate at astonishing speeds."

I looked around at the other students, unsure of where this was going. Professor Thomasina had never looked so serious or grim. And she was speaking more formally than usual. Whatever this new technology was, she was clearly afraid of it. But I still didn't understand . . . How did this pertain to us?

"In light of this new development, we recommend that you search this digital museum for works that may be similar to yours. If you find something, assume that the copyright holder will pursue a cause of action against you. We can't afford to defend against these claims, so we recommend buying the rights to the preexisting work from them, destroying your work, or challenging them in court. We will not assist in any legal defense, so be prepared to spend a lot of time and up to tens of thousands of dollars. While their cases might be frivolous, the costs associated with them are serious. In order to reduce our risk as an institution, we reserve the right to remove your artwork from the exhibit if we find the potential for infringement."

She dismissed us shortly afterward, leaving us in a state of chaos. Some people were nervous. Others shrugged it off and tried to convince the rest of us that it wasn't a big deal. Who cared what some nerds did on the opposite coast? How would it affect us, the makers of tangible art?

In the privacy of my room, I searched the website Professor Thomasina sent in a subsequent email. Someone had typed in "gameboy" and "baby" and had generated something very similar to my umbilical cords. The work that had taken up most of my time for the last six months was now as obsolete as the materials it was composed of.

My adviser, Professor Wiedenboch, encouraged me not to participate, and in the end, I conceded. I was worried about the legal ramifications, but I also didn't think my pride could handle a public shaming. I had searched for things that could resemble my past works in the digital museum, only to find that everything was at risk. It seemed that I was only capable of making predictable derivative trash.

Mathilde didn't understand my decision. "What's so bad about derivation? Isn't everything derived? We just usually call it 'in conversation with . . .' Is it even possible to really copy someone? If someone tried their hardest to mimic another person, their unique life experiences and skills would still yield completely different results."

Easy for her to say. Mathilde was the only student whose works bore no similarity to anything in the Stochastic Archive. Our floundering professors pointed to her as proof that it was possible to create something new, but instead of giving us hope, it only bred resentment toward her. More than half of our class had pulled out of the Sophomore Exhibit. Seeing the critical acclaim for Mathilde's Whitney exhibit was difficult when my work was quickly losing any value it'd had. I had been worried the Whitney wouldn't respond well to an "impermanent work," but in fact, the entire art world was blown away with the idea. Non-object works and performance art weren't new, had always been a favorite of anti-capitalist artists who also wanted careers immune to market volatility . . . but the coincidence of Mathilde's impermanent works being born at the same precise moment as the Stochastic Archive created a defiant narrative that made her seem prescient. The fact that her art disappeared meant that it could attain a mythical status in the collective imagination. Her genius shone particularly bright against my dullness. I tried to console myself by pinning the blame on our chosen mediums. It was impossible to keep up with the way technology unfurled at the speed of light, forever out of reach, rendering my art constantly reactive whereas Mathilde was endlessly generative. I walked by a motivational poster one day that read "A rising tide lifts all boats." Whoever said that had clearly never been lost at sea, left alone and gasping for air among unrelenting waves.

I WENT HOME that summer to stifling heat and parental attention. I seethed under my dad's *I told you this art thing wouldn't last* grin. Now that I had been in an enclave for so long, the buffers were unbearable to me. From every window in the house, I had a view of them curling around the neighborhood, a silver vise choking me from growth. I stopped looking outside and watched mold trail across the blank walls while Mathilde was in Rome, having accepted the invitation to be one of America's representatives at the Venice Biennale. I missed her terribly. Each of my days passed exactly like the one before, and eventually, Mathilde's texts became the only reliable unit of time, each post or ping slicing through the humidity to reach me. She sent pictures of herself basking in perfect squares of buttery sunlight, her hands dripping with olive oil and fennel pollen gelato. Her lips were always the perfect bee-stung shade, colored by cheap delicious wine. While I ate and watched the same variations of food and TV every day, she traipsed to a different church, holy site, or palazzo. I didn't share much of my depressing daily life with her. On the rare occasions when she had time to talk and would ask what I was doing, what could I say? That I lost days to my phone, gorging on the lives of the classmates who weren't as affected by the Stochastic Archive? That I followed them as they did studio visits, went to exhibits during elaborate family vacations, and lived the charmed lives of artists? I'd begun to nurse my envy like a spoiled pet, and even though I knew it was unreasonable, I started to resent Mathilde for leaving me behind.

Students had begun dropping out of BCAD like flies, and I began to wonder if I should do the same. Every time I had an idea for a new work, I looked it up in the digital database, only to be confronted with my lack of originality again. A TV that played for the visitor a video of themselves from the moment they stepped into the building: commentary on the increasingly ubiquitous surveillance of everyone's lives. A labyrinth of iPads a visitor had to get through, only to end up at a mirror, the first and ultimate screen, the self, after all, being the thing we hope to discover or recognize in all screens. A ceremony in which people divorced their souls from their phones. All of my ideas had already been conceptually explored and shown online.

When Mathilde called, I detected a new lightness in her voice. Italian voices fizzed around her in our tenuous mobile connection, and I imagined her as one of many bubbles effervescing in a bottle of champagne. Until now, the world had left so little for Mathilde, and she had responded by narrowing the expectations she allowed herself to have. To see her opening up to the possibility of happiness was a great joy. The moss of resentment that slowly crept over my love for her evaporated when I remembered how frail and sad she had been during the first year of our friendship.

6

Two hands suddenly wrap around my waist, and I turn to find Mona. The martini she's clutching sloshes onto my arm, but she's sobbing too hard to notice.

"I always knew something tragic would happen to her. I painted her cards once, as part of my tar-art card exhibit? And her future was so bleak. Not to say I'm like a prophet, but she was such a genius. Of course there was a price for shining so brightly."

Mascara drips from her eyes, and I offer her a stitched camellia petal from my gown as a wipe.

"Thank you," she says. "Look at me. I'm a mess, and so selfish. I haven't even asked how *you're* doing."

She starts to sob again, and I feel helpless. I don't know how to comfort her when it's taking all my strength not to join in her despair.

She helps herself to another petal from my dress and presses it to her face.

"Do you remember that afternoon when Professor Thomasina told us the news?"

"Of course."

"Obviously it was a difficult time for everyone. I'm not saying I was the only person to be affected by it. But I do feel like it was worse for me, being one of the most promising painters at school. You were at least in the technology realm already, so maybe it was easier to accept? But the rest of us . . . to have conceptual ideas invalidate bodily labor in such a total way was hard to grasp."

After news of the Stochastic Archive broke, Mona stayed in her studio all night and day, quietly sitting in front of a blank canvas. If everyone hadn't been in a similar state of shock, someone might have realized something was wrong.

"I know that I wasn't as close to her as you were, but she changed my life. I, um, had a really weak night," Mona says. "Maybe a couple of weeks after the meeting, I was in my studio, and I don't know what came over me. It was like I was possessed with the sudden idea that I'd never found the perfect red. It made me so angry. And I dug a palette knife into my skin because I wondered if I would find the color I'd been searching for. You know how dull they are . . . it was almost impossible to break the skin, but I did. And I kept going and transferring it to the canvas. I hadn't meant to end my life, per se. But that's kind of what started to transpire. Anyway, Mathilde was passing my studio on her way back from a hotel shift, and she saw me and brought me to the hospital. I wouldn't be alive without her."

"Mona, I had no idea."

"She swore that she wouldn't tell anyone. But she didn't just save my life. The only reason I'm still a practicing artist today is because she convinced me to stay after the Stochastic Archive. She visited every day I was in the hospital. Whenever I thanked her, she would say that she only knew how to take care of me because of you. 'It's all Enka. I'm just doing what she would do.' I owe her everything, and now I'll never get to tell her how much she meant to me." Mona collapses into my arms, and I pat her arm tentatively.

I want to tell her not to talk about Mathilde like she's already gone, but I can't bring myself to say anything.

My vision blurs as I scan the crowd. More people seem to pour through the front doors every minute, and I start to feel sick. The same circle of people, pulled tighter each day. The fine art world is a nauseatingly claustrophobic world. New artists emerge and people devour their oeuvres in a frenzy, until they've been dissected so thoroughly, they don't exist anymore. I'm tired of the pettiness and the gossip, bored of the way everyone is unique and exacting and particular. People who have to invent sadnesses and rare illnesses, or bizarre processes, to feel special because as enclavers, every one of their basic necessities and desires has been met. I want to slip into some other stream of society. One of genuine— not manufactured—excitement.

Finally, I spot a pair of gigantic painted-canvas glasses perched above a nest of dirty blond hair. Despite the event being black-tie, Otto is wearing his uniform: long scarf, mesh shirt, and a kilt. A former punk musician turned avant-garde artist, he has mostly been entrenched in academia for the last few decades. He was a professor at BCAD, surviving one sexual assault allegation after another until, finally, he was persuaded to leave by joining Mathilde's foundation board. He always likes to say that he "discovered" Mathilde, and while that is wildly untrue and deeply offensive, I will get on my knees in gratitude if he can discover her now.

I make my way through the crowd, excusing myself from the people who cling to me, wanting to provide me with false comfort in exchange for whatever gossip I might offer them. I lose him for a moment, my view blocked by the long necks of a ballet company that has genetically crossed themselves with swans. Their movements are beautiful and graceful, albeit punctuated by the occasional squawk. They're getting ready to perform, accompanying the renowned pianist who plays with webbed fingers.

As a young artist, I had imagined this world—the higher echelons of the art industry—so differently. I certainly didn't picture this constant tide of flushed faces, drinking and talking and shoving hors d'oeuvres in their mouths. I had thought it would be wider and deeper. Cleaner. I had truly believed that if you worked hard enough, with enough creativity and dedication, it was possible to make your way to a greener pasture where everyone made pieces from a place of love and introspection. I had believed that good art prevails. Events like these remind me of money's total power to control and leech the substance out of everything. Sure, you can be a star in this world, as long as you keep your patrons interested and are willing to compromise everything to make them more money. Not too many women can succeed at one time . . . just enough to make the rest of us hungry, to believe it's possible. Part of the myth of Mathilde is that she and she alone is a genius. To the general public, she emerged fully formed. Almost no other artist gets as much autonomy as she does. As the beloved daughter of the art world, she is allowed, however begrudgingly, to do what she wants, because they know that her vision is so spectacular, they'll always be wowed and their coffers enriched. In this way, her autonomy creates more restrictions for those of us who haven't found our voices yet. Most of us never will without the time or the institutional and monetary support to experiment. It's quite possible, I realize, that many people here may be happy Mathilde is missing.

"OTTO," I SAY, reaching him just as one of his hands reaches for the model-artist Anya Jeslewski from behind. Or from the front. I can never tell. She went through a lengthy procedure a few years ago, replacing most of her spinal joints with ball joints. As a result, much of her body can swivel, making her something of a human Rubik's Cube.

"Enka! I just heard the news."

My stomach lurches. Has there been news about Mathilde?

"Oh? What news is that?" I ask.

Otto's eyes wander up to the heavens of the new LORA ceiling. "Monika just informed me that the second floor of this space will be kept empty, reserved for your works. I didn't even know you were still making art."

Disappointment swamps my body. I suppose the only silver lining of the news about Mathilde is that no one at the event has asked me what I'm working on. Until now.

"Oh, well, you know. It's been difficult with kids and everything else, but I'll get back to it soon."

"I remember how promising your work was before the Stochastic Archive, and I'm only sorry we weren't better equipped to help you all at the time. You know, it was a nasty shock for us, as well. So many of us had to pull our own works, even as established professors and working artists."

An image pops into my head of Otto, running around campus like a headless chicken. He had started a fire in the quad and was burning his sketchbooks one by one. Ripping the pages apart like he couldn't do it fast enough. It wasn't until we saw his panic that we began to understand how monumental the digital archive was for our industry. In many ways, we're still coming to terms with it."

I smile politely.

"Otto," I begin, unsure how to bring up Mathilde. "You must be so proud," I say instead, pointing at one of the nearby sculptures of what looks like a table runner with tribal scars arranged into an aesthetically pleasing design.

"Yes, Bosq continues to astonish me. He's really figured it out. Since his exhibit was picked for the LORA's opening, so many of my younger students have pitched new works that use their own Deszendant profiles. I wouldn't be surprised if it becomes its own genre soon—ancestry and heritage being one of the only things artificial intelligence can't riff on yet."

I want to tell him that mining our pasts for artistic works has always been a genre, just never one so literal. But correcting him won't persuade him to help me.

"Deszendant is one of Dahl Corp's services, isn't it?"

"It is," I say.

"Have you indulged?"

I shake my head.

"I haven't either. I have to admit, I'm a bit skeptical. I've heard things . . . probably untrue, but maybe you can confirm. The data collected from Deszendant genome scans . . . is it true that it's used for Project Naiad?"

"I wouldn't know. That's a question for my father-in-law. But, Otto. When was the last time you saw Mathilde?"

I place a hand on his arm, hoping to keep his attention for as long as I need him.

"Oh, I hardly interacted with her. My position on the board is quite nominal. The rest of the members don't involve me, for whatever reason, and Mathilde, well, I've never gotten the sense that she was grateful for the introductions I made for her. In any case, it's terrible what's happening now. I hope she's found soon, and alive. It's tricky for us to continue without her since she's an intangible artist. Without her person to perform the art, how will we make money? Great artists don't exist in vacuums, and there are many other livelihoods tied up with hers. Then again, what we do have will certainly be more valuable. Of course I hope she's alive."

Of course he's more worried about the foundation's future than he is about the actual human responsible for elevating his social status and bank account.

"She was always so disturbed, wasn't she? So afflicted. I can probably admit now that I found a great deal of her art tasteless, as well as deeply troubling. *He Is Risen*, for example. Salacious? Yes. Indicative of severe mental trauma? Yes. But was it really art?"

7

Amonth before the Biennale, my mom shook me awake.

"Your friend is on TV," she said. I threw on some sweatpants and joined her in the living room, groggily trying to understand what was being said on the news.

"The pope is calling for . . ."

"To be uninvited . . ."

"From the Biennale . . ."

"Ghastly . . ."

"To lose such an honor . . ."

"Would be devastating . . ."

"Church officials revolting . . ."

"Devil incarnate . . ."

"Expulsion from certain sites, maybe even the city . . ."

Slowly, I pieced things together. While in Rome, Mathilde had been going to confessionals and admitting to all kinds of horrible things. How she badly wanted to know the taste of older men. That she couldn't see vestments without her panties filling like a cannoli, the cream piped by her light pink, and as yet hairless, pussy. That she had a small figurine of Jesus that she rotated endlessly between her orifices.

When she could hear that the breathing on the other side of the confessional box had changed, she hurried out of her space, pulled the curtain aside, and took a picture of the priest's erection. She uploaded the photos onto a website, along with audio of her breathy fake confessions.

The work was called *He Is Risen*, though indeed it was she who rose, to the likes of acclaim usually reserved for the art world's men. The website launched Mathilde Wojnot-Cho's career as an impermanent structural artist of international renown.

The Venice Biennale issued an official statement. They were not in the practice of censoring art, so Mathilde's exhibit would proceed as planned. There was speculation everywhere online about her forthcoming piece. The buzz was palpable, even from sleepy Gainesville. I searched my phone for calls I might have missed, or texts I hadn't seen. Surely she had mentioned something or sent the website to me. Surely it was just the online buffer keeping us from each other. I tried to reach her a few times, but nothing went through. Mutual acquaintances kept texting, asking if I had known what she was doing in Italy. I left them all unanswered, unable to admit that, like everyone else, I had been in the dark.

Umbiblical closed the Biennale. A record number of attendees stood around the stage: a large rectangular platform that had been built in the middle of the room. It was empty, except for a black oval structure in the center. Was it a sculpture? An egg? Was

Mathilde crouched inside it, waiting to emerge? The oval was so dark and smooth, it yielded no answers. No one knew what to expect, and because of that, there was a frenzied energy in the crowd. People were craning their necks and stepping on each other's shoes to get a better look, even though they had no idea where the artist or art would materialize. A hush descended on the room as Mathilde appeared in a corner. She had cut off all her hair and wore only a simple black leotard. She made her way to the platform, and the audience silently parted to make a path. Her eyes were lowered in deference, or maybe fear, as she walked toward the stage, as if magnetized. She stopped walking when she was directly in front of the oval. The structure had looked to be stone, marble, or granite, but there must have been an opening or a softness that yielded from the top. Slowly, she lowered her hands and they disappeared into the oval. They resurfaced holding something oblong, unmistakably phallic. Mist shrouded the object and her body, and we heard something sliding into place. The oval was a refrigerator, and whatever she was holding, it was very cold. The oval began to retract into the ground, and once it was fully subsumed, Mathilde took its place, crouching on all fours at the center of the platform, and proceeded to fellate the object in her grasp. Drinking, sucking, and chewing greedily on it, reducing it in size until, at the center, something dark red, almost black, and rigid (later revealed to be an edible resin cast colored with beet and ume plum) started to show through. Viewers watched in horror, worried she was going to eat what many assumed to be a used tampon but was actually her umbilical cord. Although there was much grumbling and shushing in the audience, everyone stayed. As the object reduced in size, its psychological power seemed to grow. The crowd watched as something purely sexual became sensual, became unbearably sad. In the span of twenty minutes, Mathilde captured the whole spectrum of human emotion. The desperation and hunger of lovers, not unlike the desperation of children, and even the care and tenderness of a mother.

Tears rolled down her face, mixing with saliva as she choked, finally consuming the solid mass at the center. She looked up at the end of the performance, stunned. Many people in the audience were crying, some out of confusion, but most out of a feeling that they had just witnessed a journey to the emotional core of humanity. Sitting on the ground in front of hundreds of people, she began to cry. The audience eventually started to applaud, but she continued her high-pitched keening, crying out the names of her parents and mourning the last physical connection she had to them. People began to fall to their knees, and to add their own grief. Their voices found each other in a dissonant symphony of despair and release as they made their way onstage, laying hands on Mathilde and one another before the video cut out.

I wept after the low-res video's abrupt end on my computer, in awe of my friend and her lack of self-consciousness. Her ability to commit. Like everything Mathilde did in the art space, it was deeply moving. And even though it could be compared . . . was an obvious descendent of the chocolate and soap sculptures Janine Antoni created by licking in *Lick and Lather*, it managed to be wholly original for its emotional content. I watched it again and again. On my fifth watch, I recognized another reference. My own umbilical cords, which she had seen just a few months ago. I couldn't help but wonder if she would have made this work without having seen them. *You're an inspiration to me*, she had said. Could that have been more literal than I thought? Of course the concept and resulting works were totally different—the biggest difference being that she got to show her work at all, on one of the most visible stages in the world.

"Did you see it?" She sounded breathless on the phone.

"Of course. It was amazing . . . *You* were amazing."

"Thank you. I couldn't have done it without you. Anything, any of this. I'm so grateful for our friendship. You— Oh, they're calling me back for another interview. I'm sorry. I'll call back when I can."

. . .

"I just went to lunch with Marina. It was life-changing. I can't wait to tell you all about it. I can't talk now because I have a TV thing, but I miss you! I wish you were here."

. . .

"You'll never believe this, Enka. This guy who attended the Biennale is apparently filthy rich and he loved my work. *Umbiblical*, but also *He Is Risen*. He wants to start a Mathilde Wojnot-Cho Foundation with ten million dollars. Isn't that wild?"

"Wild. I mean, that's . . . What does that even mean?"

"I'm not sure. I have to get a lawyer, I think, or a manager. Anyway, how are you? We need to catch up . . . I want to hear how things are going with you, but I have to run for now. Meeting my new assistants!" She hung up before I could say goodbye.

I knew she wasn't bragging in our conversations, simply telling me what was going on in her life, but a chasm had opened. Maybe it had always been there.

She deserved every bit of her success and I'm sure there was a part of me that was happy for her, but I found myself answering her calls less and making excuses not to respond. Sometimes I just couldn't take another phone call where I served as the sole audience for Mathilde's Great and Prosperous Career.

8

kept watching videos about *Umbiblical*. Interviews, reactions, press coverage. I was fascinated by the work, but a part of me was also watching to see if she would mention me. Every time she failed to do so, I was irrationally upset. Why would she? The connection between our works was tenuous at best, but I couldn't deny a similarity and didn't see how she could. I kept watching, like picking at a fresh scab, until the exhibit soured for me. Mathilde's voice started to cause a physical response, a pressure that grew inside of me. I could feel it expanding my skin, stretching the knit fabric of my sleeve, my waistband growing tight. I took my sweater off, and then my bra and sweatpants and underwear. I was so claustrophobic, I would have peeled off my flesh if it were possible.

"And are you working on any new projects?"

"I'm not actively working on anything new yet," Mathilde said. "But I have something in mind and I'm looking for collaborators in the science and technology space. It would be amazing to work with Pathway Labs, for example."

"Pathway Labs . . . I'm not familiar. What do they do?" the interviewer asked.

"I think an easier question would be, what don't they do? Their work aims to use technology as a way of furthering human connection, something I'm naturally interested in exploring as an artist."

I felt a small, sharp pang at this sudden mention of her interest in technology—my medium. I paused the video and typed the name of the lab into a search engine. I clicked on the first result.

A young man appeared on-screen, his name, Logan Dahl, scrolling across the bottom. He raked a hand through his abundant blond hair while keeping his dark blue eyes focused on the woman in front of him. Listening intently to her questions, he seemed relaxed. Assured but not self-important.

"Is it true that you've had some success already?" the interviewer asked.

"Yes, it's true. We're very excited. The successes are mild so far, but enough to give us hope."

"And what do you want to do with this technology?"

"I don't think anyone will argue with me if I point out that, as a society, our empathic muscles have atrophied. The SCAFFOLD device, when widely implemented, will be revolutionary in the way it brings humanity together again."

"How does it differ from already existing technologies that promise empathy?"

"No offense to my fellow innovators in this space, but we've seen so many of these companies fail at genuinely connecting people with one another. Instead of building community, they aggregate and isolate us from each other. The SCAFFOLD is radical in that it's a device that literally puts you in someone else's mind. There's no possibility for misunderstanding."

"But it requires brain surgery, isn't that right? Which would be rather costly, wouldn't it? Are you worried that you might be commodifying empathy, making it something affordable for only a certain swath of people?"

"I wouldn't call it brain surgery—" he began.

"What would you call it?"

"If you think of the brain as a house, this is a light renovation, maybe an addition . . . and while the procedure would be costly, we envision a social business solution where those who can't afford it will be subsidized by those who can. We'll also be working with insurance companies to aggressively reduce out-of-pocket costs for consumers who would most benefit from the SCAFFOLD."

"I'm afraid that's all the time we have. Thank you for joining us today. We'll be following your work closely."

I paused the video before it could continue to the next one. Where had I seen his name before? I quickly typed it in a new window. Papers for *The New England Medical Journal of Medicine*, *Physical Review Letters*, and *Science*; degrees in neuroscience and artificial intelligence; owner of Pathway Labs, son of billionaire Richard Dahl and his philanthropist wife, Monika. Rich, famous, and intelligent. It wasn't until I saw a picture of his father with the dean of BCAD that I realized why the name had been so familiar. My scholarship . . . the thank-you letters I wrote every year to the person funding my education.

What did Mathilde want with Pathway Labs? I studied the pixelated face on my screen. Now that she had voiced her desire to work with them, it wouldn't be long until she was connected. Maybe this very moment, someone was sending his contact information to her. A thought passed from my mind to the rest of my body, its movement a kind of physical pain. Mathilde had never shown any interest in working with technology. Why now? And why didn't she consult me first? One of the reasons our friendship was devoid of the tensions that plagued other artistic relationships was because our chosen practices were so different. We pushed each other to go deeper in our separate fields. A collaboration with Pathway Labs made more sense for me and my line of work. How did she even know about them? She was always ten thousand steps ahead of everyone else. Incredibly and frustratingly so. I felt stupid for not knowing the powerful family behind my scholarship. Why hadn't I sought to examine the hand that fed me?

It couldn't hurt to reach out. Maybe we could all work together. If Mathilde was interested in the art technology space, it could only be from my influence. Who better to work with her than me?

I reached out to the BCAD gifts department: "I'd like to do something a little more thoughtful this year to show my appreciation. Can I be put in touch with my donors directly?" I gnawed on my nails for the hour it took to receive a courteous response that appreciated my initiative, "but out of respect for their privacy, we are not allowed to connect students with donors."

There were no other cards to play except maybe reaching out to the dean, but what would I say? *Hi, can you introduce me to this donor? I'm interested in meeting his son.* That wouldn't be creepy at all.

I searched the family members online, looking for alternative avenues of getting in touch. I had known that Richard Dahl was an architect. He used digital twin technology to predict how cities would be impacted by climate change, and then designed much-needed housing developments around those factors. It was estimated that he had saved the United States government $13 trillion in damage from natural disasters, not to mention countless lives. He then used the same digital twin technology to experiment with demographic criminology. He believed that everyone was dangerous, but only when activated by other people. What combinations of people become dangerous? With this question, he invented a new branch of research for integrative and holistic criminology. The federal government was convinced by his data and introduced buffers in order to drastically reduce crime. I had forgotten that the buffers had been a Dahl Corporation invention. By now, the silver sculptures were ubiquitous. Even though they were less than a decade old, I couldn't remember a time when they hadn't existed. I do recall the confusion of those first few weeks, when everyone was trying to figure out if they were being kept in or kicked out. A slightly different reality was depicted on each side of the sculpture via screens, which made it difficult to tell. Richard Dahl explained that it was a kindness not to see what you couldn't acquire. Those who had less would be free from the tyranny of desire, and those who had more would be free of their guilt.

It had been an extremely controversial project, and after several attempts on his life, Richard had receded from the public eye, explaining why I had forgotten about him. According to online news sources, he was now rumored to be working on his supersecret Project Naiad, which everyone speculated had to do with clones. Though I was somewhat familiar with Richard's name and career, I hadn't known anything about his wife, who was maybe even more impressive. As a neurobiologist, perfumer, and family-systems sociologist, Monika Dahl had combined her different fields to create scents that could successfully control mammalian behavior. There were whispers that she had bewitched Richard with one of her fragrant concoctions, though of course there was never any proof. She was politically active and philanthropic: a formidable presence on the arts scene, seemingly on the board of every museum and greenspace. An endorsement from her in any arena all but guaranteed success. Richard and Monika had one child: a son, Logan, who had clearly inherited their intelligence. He was a polymath, as gifted an economist as he was an engineer. He had been one of the youngest scholars in the history of the Institute for Advanced Study, but his intellectual achievements didn't take up all of his time. He had most recently been linked to a Scandinavian princess, and his handsome face was splashed across European tabloids. Certain aspects of the Dahls' lives, like those of other uber-rich families, were predictable. Yet, to me, they were fascinating. It wasn't just the wealth. It was the access their wealth gave them. I read a profile of Monika that contained a tour of her private art collection, including pieces she had acquired before her marriage. Considered the modern-day Peggy Guggenheim, she could thrust an artist into the discourse with an acquisition or the mere mention of a work. Flatteringly, her taste was similar to mine. If money had been no object for me, I would also be collecting Elaine de Kooning's portraits and Hannah Wilke's vulva sculptures. I would also eschew Pollock's showy cosmic splatter for Lee's esoteric and indecipherable iconography. Lee, who had apparently been a close friend of Monika's mother!

Scrolling through the pictures, I'd never wanted to be an enclaver more. The Dahls represented everything I'd always been denied: wealth, power, and influence. Now it was within my grasp, but only through technology. The Dahls' work in technology and their patronage of the arts gave me a kind of validity. Technology wasn't a lesser medium. It was just ahead of its time.

The coincidence was too great to ignore. What were the chances that the person Mathilde wanted to find was the son of the donor who facilitated my education and, subsequently, our friendship?

On the website for Pathway Labs, there was a contact page, but no email or physical address. Instead, a form with a bouncing smiley face asked the question: "Interested in the SCAFFOLD?"

I didn't have a clear idea of what I wanted out of a response from Pathway Labs, but I held my breath when checking my email for the next week. A dizzying rush of disappointment accompanied every refresh that yielded nothing. Another week passed. I tried to trick myself by forgetting my phone in certain places or forcing myself to leave it behind. All coping mechanisms I had exercised years ago, when I was waiting to hear from BCAD.

Until, finally, a response.

Ms. Enka Yui,

We are grateful for your interest. The SCAFFOLD is in its earliest phases of testing, and we are still looking for volunteers. Our current testing cycle begins in two days. If you are able to join us, you will need to fly to Argentina tomorrow. I've attached a plane ticket to this email in the event that you can make it. You may show it to any attendant at the JFK International Airport and they will know how to proceed. We sincerely hope you can join us, but understand if the time frame is too rushed. With your permission, we can put your name on a list for future tests.

Orik Carney
Head of Communications
Pathway Labs

I opened the attachment. The plane ticket made everything more real. I screamed so forcefully into my pillow that I almost threw up. By the time I stopped coughing, I had resolved to go.

"But why is it happening so abruptly?" My mom's brow furrowed with suspicion.

"There was a last-minute opening. It's really prestigious . . . and you know this industry is so time-sensitive and private."

"But why the secrecy? What are you going to be doing? I've never heard of this company."

I knew better than to mention Pathway's connection with Richard Dahl and his corporation.

"Relax, Dad. I'm just going to be a fly on the wall. Observing stuff for artistic inspiration."

"Well, who's going to be there? Who can we get in touch with if you don't call?"

"I'll call."

We had variations of the same argument all day as I packed. It was aggravating to me that they didn't understand how exciting this opportunity was. They were treating a free plane ticket to Argentina to work with a distinguished lab like it was something dangerous.

Exhausted from defending my decision, I was relieved to find myself alone on the way to the airport. But my own nervous thoughts began to surface. It had taken Pathway so long to respond, and yet, when they did, it was with such raised stakes. Wasn't that suspicious? I had filled out a basic form detailing my interest in the SCAFFOLD, and all of a sudden, I was flying to Argentina for brain surgery. It was a drastic and unexpected turn of events, but wasn't it exactly what I'd wanted? Surely I could change my mind if I wanted to, once I was there. If it didn't feel right. But deep down, I knew that even if it felt wrong, horribly so, I wouldn't refuse the surgery. Not when I was this close to being part of something historic. I picked at my right thumb cuticle until it bled, and sucked on it to stanch the flow.

When I arrived at the airport and showed one of the attendants my ticket, I was immediately whisked away.

"Follow me," she said. Her red lipstick was too bright and her hair too disciplined with gel for this time of day. We passed tired parents haggling with their children over sugary snacks. We passed couples in love, on their way to honeymoons or vacations together. A man played his guitar in a corner of the airport, a pencil between his teeth. We exited the airport, and she turned around, gesturing to the nearest plane.

A man briskly walked toward me and took my small carry-on. "This way, Ms. Yui. We're so glad you could join us."

As soon as I stepped onto the private plane, I was immediately ensconced in a fine leather seat and assaulted by servers asking what I would like to drink, did I want silk pajamas, would I be needing one or two cashmere blankets, and could they show me the massage settings for my seat? It took me a moment to realize they were serious, and I asked for a glass of water because it seemed rude not to ask for anything. The water arrived with a single-page form and a pen. "Standard-issue NDA regarding interactions with the Dahl Corporation," the server assured me.

From the window, I watched as a car rolled to a stop by the plane. The door opened, and a pair of cream-colored sneakers appeared. They were attached to Logan Dahl. I hadn't expected to see him so soon, if at all. Would we be traveling together? I watched as he thanked his driver through the open window before running to the trunk of the car to grab his suitcase. I followed his steps until he disappeared from my line of sight. On the plane, I listened as he greeted the staff and spoke with them for a long time, asking after family members and other news. After assuring them he didn't need anything, he finally walked over to me.

"Hi, I'm Logan. Very nice to meet you."

"Oh," I said, reaching to place my hand in his. A firm and dry handshake.

"Hope you don't mind if I join you. I thought it might be more convenient for us to go together. I promise I'm not kidnapping you," he said hurriedly.

I didn't know that I would mind if he kidnapped me. He had been generically handsome in the videos I watched online, but he was even more attractive in person. My cheeks were heating dangerously. "I'm the one who's grateful. I've heard so much about the SCAFFOLD and I really want to learn more."

"Enka . . ." He hesitated. "Am I saying your name right?"

I nodded, feeling oddly powerful for someone who was on the plane of a man they had never met. There was something about the way he was looking at me or, more precisely, avoiding my gaze. He brought a folder out of a zipped backpack and started riffling through some papers. I saw my picture and got a thrill out of the fact that he had been carrying it with him, on his person.

"It says on these application materials that you're a student at the Berkshire College of Art and Design. And that you're majoring in technology art with a scholarship from my father's company."

"You can see why I find the SCAFFOLD fascinating," I said.

"I can. It would have been a perfect fit, but because of your fellowship, there's an unfortunate conflict of interest."

He must have noticed my confusion.

"I'm really sorry. Honestly, we were excited to have a female test subject, and somehow details of the background check slipped through the cracks. I was just informed, on the way here, about your enrollment at BCAD. There was a large group of applicants for the SCAFFOLD, including many students from your school. Since you're the recipient of the Dahl scholarship, it would look too preferential for you to participate in the trial. At least for now. I hate that optics is such an important part of what I do, but that's the reality of it."

I stared at him, not completely understanding. What was I doing on the plane then? And why was he telling me in person when surely he had staff members who could have emailed or called?

"I have a proposal that I'm hoping you'll accept. It doesn't have to be a bad thing that you're a Dahl fellow, and in fact, it should be a good thing! We're looking for inventive ways to publicize the SCAFFOLD and wanted to know if you'd be interested in observing the first trials for a week, learning a bit more about the process, and creating a piece around it?"

For the rest of the flight, he sat on the opposite side of the plane, working. I closed my eyes, pretending to sleep, but watched him through the gaps between my eyelashes. He was on the phone for hours, troubleshooting different projects. He seemed thoughtful, attentive, and capable of great focus, speaking to everyone with curiosity and respect. My mind spun with the possibilities of what I would see, and how I could create an artistic response. Would the device itself be physically available for me to make something with it? I hadn't imagined I would actually be collaborating with Pathway, and this quickly. But of course this was the logical direction for my work as a technology artist. Working with different companies, especially those that were inventing the software and hardware that would shape the future of humanity. My works would serve as the necessary counterpoint: reflecting the human response, questioning the effectiveness and ethics, and broadening the conversations that were necessary for the invention of any new technology. Here, finally, was a way for me to stand apart and above the colleagues whose future successes already haunted me.

"I'm sorry to wake you, but I don't want you to miss this," Logan said.

I blinked and sat up, confused. We were still on the plane, but I must have actually fallen asleep. Our heads bent close together as he pointed out the window. It was almost the next morning, and the sun was rising over the Andes. As we got closer to the mountain range, the view of gold dust settling on the mountains expanded. My breath hitched and my fingers itched to render the scene with creamy oil pastels and flakes of gold leaf.

"Thank you," I whispered.

He fell asleep soon after, and I saw how the tiny hairs that clung to his arm came alive in the sun's glow. He was wiry but sturdy, his body promising an attractive level of capability. I felt a deep gratitude for the opportunity he had given me, but something more, too: a need to redirect my attention from his body and my increasing preoccupation with it. When we landed, we had breakfast together. I was nervous sitting across from him, being the recipient of such unbroken eye contact. He asked a few questions, about where I was from and what my parents did: things he surely knew from the background check. I answered vaguely, shifting the topic of conversation to his work as soon as I could. I didn't want to draw more attention to the fact of my being fringe, or to give the impression that I was one of the many who hated his father for what he'd done to fragment the country.

"I took over Pathway from my dad. Once they shut down his cloning pilot program, it essentially became a useless brain farm. We didn't want them to go to waste." He laughed at the expression on my face.

"What does that mean . . . 'brain farm'?"

"They were growing isolated brains by inducing pluripotent stem cells to become brain matter."

"That's exactly as bad as I thought it would be," I said, trying not to visibly shudder.

Logan laughed.

"What do you do with them?" I asked.

"Do you really want to know? It's not for the faint of heart."

His expression had changed. He was pale, and his eyes fearful. I held his gaze. "Try me."

"Working from one of von Neumann's unfinished manuscripts, I found a way to translate neural pathways into a programming language that can be uploaded onto an existing computer system. We use electrical stimulation to map a bunch of existing brains, from all kinds of species, then transcribe and upload them to computers before downloading them onto the empty brains with the SCAFFOLD."

He looked down, almost sheepish, waiting for a reaction that never came. I was having trouble grasping what he had just said. Downloading onto empty brains?

"Can you translate that for me . . . to English?"

He looked relieved. "Basically, we download full brains onto empty ones, using the SCAFFOLD device, which connects two entities."

"So the SCAFFOLD is like a bridge?"

"Exactly. Except the entities don't have to be physically connected."

"And what happens when you download the full brains onto empty ones?" I tried to imagine what that might feel like for either party, but I couldn't.

He glanced at me cautiously before looking away again, but I could see that his eyes had lit up. It was clear that he was passionate about his work, if also a little ashamed of it.

"The results are unbelievable. The easiest way to explain, I guess, is that when we press play on these empty brains, they live out the information they've downloaded from the full brains. They have the same memories and experiences that these animals and, in one instance, a human had. We've watched entire lives."

I was still listening, but in my mind, a dark gallery flashed with the neon activity of these brains living out the experiences of various creatures, maybe even the deceased, if their brains could be harvested.

"What are the, um, ramifications? I guess I mean, why is this worth pursuing? Besides it being so fascinating."

"All science is worth pursuing, even without an end goal. You never know how something will be used. In this instance, though, my hope is to deepen empathy between humans. So much of technology these days is focused on the creation of alternative intelligences. But how can we begin to steward another intelligence when we, ourselves, are such a mystery to one another? The SCAFFOLD will help us see and experience someone else's life. And it was primarily created with the idea of therapy in mind. Say you have a brother with PTSD. If you both get the device implanted, you'll be able to completely understand what he's going through. Now let's say he's having a particularly bad episode. Before he can shut down or self-harm, you can actually absorb some of the trauma. Your healthy amygdala, hippocampus, and prefrontal cortex can help relieve his traumatic responses."

"You mean we . . . can share the pain?"

"Exactly. It'd be like sucking the venom from his snakebite. You can be a massive part of his healing."

"That's incredible," I said slowly.

"Well, we're getting ahead of ourselves a bit. That's the goal, but for now, we still have to test what happens when we download onto an existing functioning brain."

"A full brain onto a full brain?"

"Right," Logan said.

"Like an animal of some kind?"

"We started with animals but found that only marginally useful for our data. We can't exactly ask the animal how it feels and expect a response. We have some idea of what's happening because we can see it being mapped on the brain, but the images are often overlapping or multiplied in a way that makes it difficult to understand."

"I see."

"That's where the trials come in. We're going to start simple, by downloading a sheep brain onto our first human volunteer's mind."

9

For the first couple of days in Argentina, Logan arranged for someone to take me sightseeing since I wasn't permitted to observe the final preparations for the first trial. I saw things I never imagined seeing in my lifetime. The massive elephant seals in the Valdes Peninsula. Stunning endangered jaguars in the Iberá wetlands. I stayed in a building by the lab, presumably with the volunteers and employees of Pathway. I loved my simple room with sturdy, elegant furnishings. At night, I threw open the windows so I could hear the foreign insects and language of this city intermingling below. I struggled to fall asleep, too stimulated by the sights of the day and the work I was here to do.

I got a thrill from texting Mathilde and other friends that I might not be reachable because of a project I was doing in Argentina at the invitation of Pathway Labs. I waited for a response from Mathilde. Maybe even a request for an introduction. But she must have been busy because I didn't hear from her.

On the days following those excursions, I stayed close to the lab, taking long walks in the beautiful rosehip farm behind it.

"I love it here, too," Logan said one day when he found me there, hunched over my sketchbook. "These rosehips were a gift from the most important man in my life."

"I've heard so much about your dad."

"Not my dad, actually. Toru Nakajima. Don't get me wrong. My dad's amazing, of course, and he's given so much to me and the world . . . but you know. He was really busy, which meant he wasn't around when I was growing up."

"I'm sorry, that must have been difficult."

"It might have been, if not for Toru. He was an agricultural genius in Japan before my dad plucked him from obscurity to lead a few of his initiatives. He's an amazing scientist. Taught me everything I know, but he was also my best friend and kind of a surrogate parent. He's still the person I consult the most about pretty much everything."

"Even over your dad?"

Logan was quiet for a moment. "I don't know if you've ever felt this way, but sometimes I think it's inevitable that I'm going to become my parents. My dad, especially."

"That wouldn't be a bad thing, would it?"

"Not bad. But it still terrifies me. I respect him, but we have very different beliefs. That's why it was great to spend so much of my childhood with Toru. He was a counterweight, of sorts."

"I understand that feeling," I said, almost too ashamed to admit it.

"You do?"

I thought of how my parents and their skepticism about art felt toxic, somehow strangling any promising future I had. Before I knew it, and no matter what I chose, I'd be back in Gainesville, teaching art once a week at the community center and working several other "real" jobs.

"I do."

Just then a breeze washed over us, breaking the seriousness of the moment. I raised my arms to feel the wind and laughed when I saw that he had done the same. We walked back to the building that contained our living quarters, and I excused myself, suddenly shy.

The fragrance of the rosehips seemed to change every hour, sweet and floral during the day, medicinal and bitter at night. I loved their tightly packed shape and their vibrant color. During these hours, I forgot about the SCAFFOLD and the work I was here to do, instead spending significant amounts of time sketching and painting the farm. Being so far away from school, I lost the constructs I had built for myself. Here, I wasn't Enka, the Dahl fellow. I could do what I wanted, which was to paint. I had missed the gentleness of brushes, the sound of water swirling, the sudden bloom of color like you had just slapped one of Botticelli's angels. I could never get the color of the rosehips right—the reds were always too tomato or marigold—and I remembered the satisfaction of being frustrated in the pursuit of an artistic ideal.

Painting in the field one day, I was startled to see Logan running toward me. His lab coat flapped wildly in the wind, and the veins on his face bulged with effort as the tall rosehip sprigs lashed him in the face. Behind him, other people appeared, running or watching, including a few of the security guards I had seen on the grounds. I watched Logan for a moment, wondering how he had found me. Then I realized he was chasing something. A man bar-

reled into me, knocking me flat on my back. I screamed as he tried
to stumble over me. His arms and legs locked, and he rolled over,
his eyelids twitching. Logan reached us and fell to his knees to
catch his breath. A thick yellowish drool began to pour from the
man's mouth, onto his neck, into his ear. I scrambled to get away
from him.

"It's OK, Enka. He won't hurt you," Logan panted.

"What's wrong with him?" I whispered, watching in horror as
he repeatedly lifted and thrashed his head to the ground.

"We went too far in the download. This particular sheep was
slaughtered—that's what he's experiencing now."

We watched wordlessly until the man's body stilled, and was
carried away by the medical unit. We walked back to the lab, the
sweet fragrance of the rosehips mocking us the whole way.

I JOINED LOGAN and his team for a tense dinner that night. I had
to bite my tongue a few times to stop from asking what had happened. What had gone so wrong? Everyone was understandably
distraught, and further testing was canceled. I was extremely
thankful that I had been disqualified from the trials. I could have
been the one in that field.

Someone finally broke the silence. "This wasn't our fault."

"Thom—" Logan said, his tone cautioning his colleague from
saying anything more.

"As soon as he started going through anything that painful, he
should have slipped back into his own consciousness or muted the
trauma. That's why we have the device!"

"I understand," Logan said quietly. "But that can't be our story.
A man is in a coma because of something we made. We have to

lie low and strategize how to move forward. This includes you," he said, looking over to me. "The media frenzy is already too intense. I'm afraid an artwork about Pathway would seem insensitive and inappropriate now. It appears we've dragged you out here for nothing."

A grim silence fell over the rest of the dinner. I wanted to speak with Logan alone, but he excused himself after the main course and didn't return. Selfishly, I was sad about my work. Argentina had lost much of its luster after what I saw, but I had been looking forward to showing off a collaboration with Pathway and was reluctant to go home empty-handed.

Logan knocked on my door as I was falling asleep. I let him in, and he crumpled in a chair by the bed.

"What a mess. Enka, I'm so sorry that you saw . . . that you came all this way for . . ."

"You couldn't have known," I said.

Was he crying? I got on my knees and awkwardly patted him on the back. He shifted toward me, and I took him into my arms while he quietly wept. I noted the light clean scent of his shirt and his hair, and the soft texture of each between my fingers. At some point, our breathing changed, both of us suddenly realizing where his head was positioned against my body. He finally pulled away, sniffling shyly, and heat coursed through me. The intensity of his stare was electric, charging the air around us. My muscles tensed, reluctant to let him go.

"I hope there will be chances for us to work together in the future," he said.

Stay. But he put a hand on my shoulder and left. The next morning, I went home.

———————

SCHOOL STARTED AGAIN, but everything was different. Since the previous year, our class had dwindled to half the size. Kimberlee, whose work was based on language, specifically the four Chinese tones, had left. The lapsed architecture major who drew under-drawings over finished paintings dropped out, as did Aurelia, taking her beautiful game theory art pieces with her. Yuki, who used ancient Japanese lacquerware to depict pop culture personas, stopped making items and focused on extracting sap from the urushi tree to make lacquer, essentially pivoting to supply. Andie, the music artist who composed electronic pieces that served as audio frames for native birdsong, had a case brought against her, and she was selling the synthesizers, turntables, and mics that had previously occupied every inch of her room to afford a lawyer. The art business department had been thrown into chaos, trying to figure out what they could and couldn't sell. How do you price something that's only meant to be looked at on a computer? Were they suddenly all in a new part of the film industry? BCAD was offering a new concentration in digital art, where people could create digital works for the Stochastic Archive. The very trolls who were taking everything from us were now getting degrees for it. There were new professors for these fields, as well as a horde of IP lawyers on retainer, though the laws around this sort of thing were still being written. There were rumors that BCAD was considering becoming a school that largely focused on art law and policy.

Overnight, the Stochastic Archive had effectively sorted and determined which of us were still artists and which of us were now irrelevant. The art world was halved into things that were safe from generative ideation and things that weren't. And while the two halves were emergent and murky, there were certain branches of art that seemed more tenable. Jono, whose obsession with framing slowly took over his painting (he could hear when a piece had the right frame), was safe because framing was evidently too banal to be considered weird art. This hurt his feelings deeply (and, he claimed, the feelings of his frames), so he framed everything in his room, including each individual key on his keyboard, and uploaded a diorama into the Stochastic Archive. Performance art was a promising area, but only if you were willing to let yourself be pushed to the fringes of that field. Mathilde was lucky in this way . . . Others had always classified her works as performance art. But even in this space, artists were being crowded out by provocateurs on the internet. We had very few choices in what we could create, and the loss of control was devastating.

I was barely hanging on in classes. I had stopped searching for things in the digital museum because I had stopped thinking about making art. It was like the advent of the buffers all over again, a forced mass separation.

I watched as my classmates tried to outdo the Stochastic Archive. Ben, who used to be a sculptor, was working with evolutionary scientists to de-age himself. He was mostly absent from classes, healing from the various surgeries that were reconstructing him as a Neanderthal. Claryssa, who was a graphic organic food artist, now made content of herself eating inedible things. Nuddi carved his skin to make keloid art and issued a call for others to join him in making violent and explicit body art to protest the new digital art world. He found himself alone, as no one was interested in a less urgent reprisal of Viennese Actionism. Clover was pursuing an inane new medium he called "internal plastic surgery" . . . a kind of cell renewal that promised to make you beautiful on the inside but yielded no perceptible exterior changes. Maybe it had been better when we were just trying to outdo one another. We had a chance then, at least. Now we had to constantly prove our exceptionalism, racing ahead of technology's ever-reaching grasp.

Even though my work was previously meant to act as a bridge between art and the internet, I'd hated the intrusiveness of it. Especially social media. My screen, that shiny black pool I longed to escape into again and again, even though it filled my mind with the black bile of jealousy and bitterness. The shrinkage. The side-by-side comparison. There was a cultural obsession with the possibility of multiverses, but to me, social media was proof enough of their existence. With a flick of a finger, you could see every life you could have had if only you'd been born smarter or luckier, or made better choices. The Stochastic Archive went a step further. Every work you could have made in a parallel life, every *you* you could have been, already existed, so what was the point? Everyone in the world had become, in a sense, an artist, and thus no one was. If I couldn't come up with a convincing exhibit idea by the time the Junior Exhibit rolled around, I would drop out.

The dynamic between Mathilde and me had changed, too, cooling on my end. She was absent for the first few weeks of the semester. Busy with her new career, no doubt. Too busy to respond to me about Pathway or be in touch in any meaningful way. Online, I saw pictures of her with talk show hosts, famous celebrities, and heads of state. When she finally showed up on campus, she looked like a different person. Her slender body had inflated, her lips, breasts, and backside buoyant, bubbling up beneath tank tops and barely held in by newly tight jeans. Where the lines of her body had once been as straight as uncooked pasta, now they were perfectly done, twisted around a fork, and begging for consumption. Her cherubic cheeks were even more ravishing, and suddenly, I'd even lost the one thing I always had over her: beauty. I didn't know how to relate to her anymore.

She tried a couple of times to start a conversation about the frost that abruptly coated our interactions, but I always brushed her off. It had exhausted me to be on the precipice of promising things that ultimately fell through, and I was too depressed to deal with anything else.

"Come to Paris," Mathilde said to me one day after barging into my studio where I had been napping. "Join the foundation."

I rubbed the sleep from my eyes and looked at her to see if she was being serious. "But we're still in school."

"This is the kind of opportunity that school is for, Enka. We get a chance to start earlier."

She was right except for one thing: I failed to see how this was an opportunity for me.

"Please, Enka. I can't do anything without you. This way, we can work together. Live together . . . have a real partnership."

I DIDN'T GO to Paris. I needed to discover who I was without Mathilde, to figure out my artistic voice. I knew that I had to confront the Stochastic Archive. Turn it on its head, reveal the hollowness of its promise. I just didn't know how. I considered physicalizing it. Making a structure, an ouroboros of combined works that gorged on itself. A mass of meaning made moot by its very existence. I was already in the planning stages when I found out that another artist at BCAD was already doing the same thing. I considered connecting found artworks and modifying them, maybe scoring them with music . . . only to find that several of my peers were doing that, as well. Next I thought about suing the inventors of the archive for damages on behalf of the entire industry as a performance art piece. But there were already so many artists around the world suing them, another suit would be meaningless, if even noticed.

A new industry of art had been birthed in response to the Stochastic Archive, and I was no longer the lone technology artist. Everywhere I looked, I was surrounded by works that did what I had hoped to do: works that reflected the human response, questioned technological promises, and broadened perspectives. Somehow I, who had been ahead of everyone in this new medium, was suddenly behind, too late to realize its possibilities.

I went home for winter break, flip-flops in December and a different holiday movie with my mom after dinner. To their credit, my parents tried to hide how delighted they were to see me contemplating another life path.

I couldn't sleep the first night back. The blank canvases in the back of my closet stared at me like expectant faces. Parched brush tips longing to be submerged in water—to be dipped, swirled, tapped, and swooshed. I finally got out of bed around three a.m. and collected all of it in a trash bag.

I had Googled my old art teacher, Ms. Liu, when I got my acceptance letter from BCAD. Like mine, her parents hadn't supported her dreams of being an artist, so she had taught me to save up money. We fell out of touch when she was able to move away, but I wanted to contact her about my acceptance to show her that I had been worthy of her time. *Look*, I would say. *We both got out.* I saw that she was in a small town in Maine, offering second-rate portraits for special occasions.

Her low-budget website, and its revelation of a career that had decayed before it even began, terrified me. I didn't end up contacting her, afraid that whatever had stopped her career in its tracks had a residue. That it could travel a landline. I decided I would succeed where she hadn't, for the both of us.

And yet here I was, in my childhood bedroom, contemplating letting go of a dream that had never really been within my grasp. Even now, I ached to capture the way moonbeams were wending across my room. Wanted to etch it all in graphite so you could feel the loneliness. The starkness of my shadow against the brightness of the moon was so indicative of my failure, my inability to succeed. I went back to the closet and retrieved the carefully preserved paintings. Looking at them was painful. I had been so proud of them, but now I hated that there was so much evidence of my mediocrity. I added the paintings to the trash bag and took it all behind the house, stuffing it in the garbage bin. Returned to bed and shut my eyes. It wouldn't be easy, but I would work hard to unlearn all the ways I had been taught to see.

THE NEXT MORNING, I imagined that I even looked different to my parents. Something so monumental had shifted within me that it was impossible to believe it wasn't visible. I made toast and drank a glass of milk. Sat down on the couch for another day of TV. Since I would no longer create, my job now was to consume.

A few days later, Mathilde asked if she could visit. It was the first time I had heard from her since she moved to Paris. I knew it was an olive branch, her version of a hand pressed against the window. I'd never even heard of anyone from an enclave visiting the fringe. But I was too numb to register anything. I didn't have a good reason to say no, so I just didn't respond. It seemed like the only power I had in the world was this: that I could withhold myself from someone who wanted to see me, even though I desperately wanted to see her, too.

10

received an email from Logan on the last day of winter break. Pathway Labs needed something to distract the media, which had latched on to the accident and wasn't letting go. Would I be interested in creating an exhibit? Something flashy. He would make himself and anything I might need available. My stomach twisted at the thought of seeing him. The email, which I read again and again, revived me from my dormancy. The decision to quit art hadn't been an easy one, but I felt that it was right and tried to stay firm. In the end, though, Logan's promise of availability and the media attention that would be redirected from his lab onto me was too tempting. At best, this could be the first real step in my artistic career. At worst, it was a chance to be back in the enclave, if only for a taste of what I would be missing.

I wrote back to Logan that I was interested, and from there began to conceptualize an exhibit. I remembered the image that had struck me when he first explained the SCAFFOLD procedure to me. A dark gallery flashing with neon lights that captured the

experiences and lives of other people. I began to make that idea
into reality. The power of Logan's family name was so strong, all
I had to do was whisper it to access anything I needed. I was able
to secure the loans of six brains that were being kept in the Mütter
Museum, the Wilder Brain Collection at Cornell, and the Musée
d'anatomie Delmas-Orfila-Rouvière. The six extraordinary brains
we chose had been preserved well enough that their neural net-
works were still intact—pristine, even. Logan had generously provided me with a car service and a private suite in New York City
during my time working on the exhibit, and I enjoyed how
hands-on I could be. It was my first time in such a major enclave,
and I gorged myself on the artistic institutions that had been denied me. The Noguchi Museum, the Guggenheim, MoMA. The
Frick, the Cloisters, the Neue Galerie. And the Met . . . Every day,
the Met. I couldn't express what it meant to walk around in the
places that had been so inaccessible and hallowed, they had become almost mythological to me.

My own exhibit would be taking place at the West 21st Street
Gagosian, and while the exhibit was conceptually mine, I lacked
the scientific training to realize it. I was there to receive every
brain delivery, but then I could only watch as the Pathway team
stimulated the brains electrically, mapping and translating the
data stored on each one. This data was then downloaded onto
empty brains from Pathway's farm using the SCAFFOLD device.
Six floor-to-ceiling boxes were constructed to house the brains, for
display and cryopreservation purposes, each of them kept at a
temperature of –130 degrees Celsius. Logan and I decided to keep
the lives that were downloaded and uploaded onto new brains a
secret until the opening. Therefore, reporters from different media
outlets in Europe and the States flocked to the Chelsea gallery to

cover the piece. Logan insisted on arriving at the Gagosian together. Upon entering the space, and recognizing so many of the art world's biggest critics and players, my heart thumped so quickly, I was afraid the beats would blur and flatline. I knew it was a one-off . . . that I wasn't technically represented by *the* Larry Gagosian, but even so, this was more exposure than I had ever dared to dream. I couldn't wait to see the public's reaction when my concept came, quite literally, to life.

Once everyone had more or less assembled inside, the lights were switched off. From deep in the recesses of the building, the Pathway team turned the brains on. It was so dark in the space, attendees couldn't even see their own reflection in the glass of the windows. For a few minutes, nothing happened. A pair of heels clicking and some murmuring—the crowd was beginning to lose patience. I stopped breathing. What if there had been a malfunction? Just as I was readying to run to the Pathway team, a dark orange blot appeared on one of the brains. Crimson oozed from another, and pale lavender spores bloomed on the one directly in front of me. The colors bled and blazed continuously, and I relished the gasps I heard around me. The audience was dazzled by the visual playback—memories and experiences of some of the greatest minds to have walked the earth, including Beethoven, Einstein, and Virginia Woolf.

Logan put an arm around my waist and whispered in my ear, "Thank you for doing this. I'm so proud to have worked with you." Photos of that moment flooded the internet within seconds.

As I watched, the crowd was loudly debating what it meant that Marilyn Monroe's brain flashed with more purple than the others. "It's bisexual lighting!" someone shrieked.

Mathilde's 9/11 work resurfaced in my mind. Early in the planning of *Neon Séance*, Logan had suggested including a pair of headphones that would play the distortion of Beethoven's deafness for listeners. I was afraid people would think the faint static was a malfunction of my work, so I declined. Now I regretted that decision, realizing how moving it would have been to hear through his ears, to be able to appreciate on a greater level the works he managed to write despite his deafness.

Standing there, I realized my exhibit gave nothing in terms of real meaning or emotion. In the publications that covered *Neon Séance*, glowing reviews accompanied pictures of the brains. They looked like glorified screen savers. Mathilde had made all of us experience the helplessness of not being able to bring her father back to life. I *had* brought people back to life, but not in a way that made anyone feel anything.

Still, *Neon Séance, a Collaboration with Pathway Labs* was a minor national sensation. A fantastic diversion, drowning all other media coverage of Pathway Labs. It was widely regarded as Logan Dahl's first foray into the Art World, no matter how hard he tried to redirect the attention and credit to me. I was the envy of all my colleagues, and even my professors. "A dark horse," Professor Wiedenboch called me in my *Wired* profile. The collaboration with Pathway Labs marked a turning point for the industry. The Stochastic Archive had pitted technology and art against each other, but *Neon Séance* showed a path forward for them as companions. There was even a small profile about the exhibit in the alumni magazine that called me "the savior of modern art."

There was one interview that didn't go as planned. Logan and I were on a live news segment together, discussing the new exhibit, when the reporter ambushed me.

"Enka, it must be quite surreal to have such success in a world that was denied to you. It's true that you were a fringe kid, right?"

I felt the blood draining rapidly from my face, pooling between my toes, and dissipating from my body.

"That's right," I said.

"So you wouldn't have been able to go to museums or have really . . . *any* cultural experiences. Yet here you are. How did you defy the odds, with no exposure to art? Some would say that your success is precisely the kind of thing Logan's father is trying to prevent."

Even Logan was shocked into silence by this line of questioning.

"Prevent? Don't be ridiculous." I lightly swatted the reporter's shoulder, trying to bring levity to the situation. "It's true that I didn't have the same access to the arts as enclave kids, but I had enough."

I gained confidence as I went on. I refused to be made a victim on live television, and I wouldn't be used in what seemed like this reporter's personal vendetta against Logan's father.

"To be honest, the buffer helped me. I am the original artist I am today because my mind isn't overrun with other influences. And I'm proof that the buffer isn't meant to separate or even enforce a certain lifestyle. The boundary is clearly more fluid than you think, otherwise how would I, a fringe kid, be sitting here with Logan Dahl?"

Ironically, it was this interview that cemented my status on the other side. Enclavers accepted me as one of their own, holding me up as an example of what was possible if you persisted. Even though what I said wasn't how I'd felt growing up, it was true to who I was becoming.

On the heels of *Neon Séance*'s success, Logan offered me the position of artist-in-residence at Pathway, hinting that eventually I could be considered for the same role on a bigger scale at the Dahl Corporation. I still had a year left at BCAD, but *this is the kind of opportunity that school is for, Enka.* So I accepted.

For the first few months of my new life, I was unmoored. It was hard to get my bearings because Logan wanted me to accompany him everywhere for research. We were in Argentina part of the week before going to New York or, more often, California for meetings. Sometimes we went to smaller labs in the Midwest for consultations, but we were rarely ever home. My little studio apartment in Argentina remained empty and unfurnished. The meetings were unintelligible to me. I didn't understand how I was supposed to get inspiration when I couldn't comprehend what was being said. Sometimes they wouldn't even let me in: certain labs and companies had proprietary materials that they were only comfortable sharing with Logan and his core team. I would wander around these small towns, wondering what my classmates were doing in school and how Mathilde was spending her time. I kept telling myself this was the life I had always wanted. The looks on my parents' faces when I called them from exotic locales and replenished their bank accounts almost convinced me.

One good thing about the incessant travel: getting to spend time with Logan. He was rich, handsome, and intelligent, not to mention the only constant in the sudden whirlwind of my life. It was how he treated me, too. He remembered the blanket I liked to use on the plane and how I took my coffee. I remarked once that I liked the sheets at a certain hotel, and he made sure they were everywhere we subsequently stayed. He took care of me in a way that I hadn't believed possible, and that I honestly found a little terrifying. I didn't feel like my actions or words were worthy of such attentiveness. I kept waiting for him to reveal another side of himself, but eventually, I became resigned to the fact that maybe the perfect man existed.

One day, we were looking at scans of a candidate's neural pathways and I told him they reminded me of Demuel Steiner's works. He photographed cities and painted over them with scenes from nature.

"Show me," he said.

I brought out my phone to show him examples, but his hand covered mine.

"In person."

A few hours later, we were in Denmark, strolling into the Louisiana. Steiner used a mixture of paint and acrylic crayons to draw over his photographs. A green slick of oil paint leading up to the Arc de Triomphe rendered a long tulip stem flowering in the middle of Paris. A night market in Taiwan was underwater, phosphorescent kelp and jellyfish glowing. Grass tendrils snaked toward us out of the sidewalks in New York's midtown, tickling children's sandaled feet.

"It's a simple idea, maybe even childish, but it gets to the heart of where we've been and where we're going. It questions whether humans have done the right thing by constantly building, progressing. But it's also beautiful to look at, and so tactile. I love the way the textural components draw me in."

Logan wasn't paying attention to the art.

"Look," I insisted, gesturing toward the piece.

"No," he said quietly. He took my face in his hands and kissed me. Quick, over before I had a chance to register it.

"If you're not interested, that will never happen again," he said.

"And if I am?"

I DIDN'T FALL in love so much as finally indulge in the feelings I had been pushing away for months. He confessed that he'd started having feelings for me in Argentina the first time, and that he'd found himself unable to let them go. These confessions were meant to make me feel secure in our relationship, but they made me wonder if the initial exhibit and residency were all a ruse for courtship. I couldn't decide if that was sweet or depressing. Maybe both. Three months after we officially started dating, we went to New York for a meeting with the manufacturers of the SCAF-FOLD device. I had just dropped my bags in the foyer of his building when he took my hand and rushed me to the elevator. The doors opened to a massive Steiner: Barcelona, ensnared by painted snapdragons and Venus flytraps. I stepped out of the elevator in awe.

"You bought one?"

"I did."

"I've never seen this piece."

"I commissioned it."

"What?" I turned to him in surprise and saw that a member of his staff had joined us.

He handed Logan a bouquet of flowers that matched the painting. One of the Venus flytraps tipped open to reveal a small velvet pouch inside. From a bed of blue velvet shone a diamond so large, you could skate across it. I looked at Logan, who was suddenly so much lower, having gotten down on one knee.

I said yes.

The ring was barely on my finger when Logan rushed me back outside. His parents were waiting for us, for a celebratory lunch. In the car, my heart began to pound. There hadn't been time to change or to check my appearance in the mirror. I was wearing an outfit I frequently traveled in, and despite habitual dry cleaning, it was slightly wrinkled, the colors faded. I had imagined a perfectly curated first meeting with his parents dozens of times, and now it was happening without any chance for me to plan or prepare. I tried to focus on the ring.

"It's so beautiful," I said over and over, relishing the snugness, the exactness of fit. Even if his parents disliked me, even if they could smell the fringes on me, it was too late.

THE RESTAURANT WAS in the vault of an old bank. Oak tables and paneling in a dim industrial environment where only one table was set. My future mother-in-law stood in a light blush dress and simple silver heels and waved us over. An Asian man was seated to her left, and there was no sign of Logan's father.

Monika kissed her son distractedly, keeping her eyes on me.

"Aren't you stunning?" she said, giving my cheeks a good peck each. I had been thinking the same thing about her. With her sleek copper strands and light gray eyes, she looked nothing like Logan.

"Come, sit."

She helped me into my seat, next to the man I didn't recognize. "Enka, this is Toru."

Of course.

"I've heard so much about you. What an honor to finally meet you both!"

"Finally? We're the ones who have been begging to meet you. Logan tells me you're the genius behind *Neon Séance*. You'll have to tell me all about your other work."

A moment of déjà vu. A rush to my head. All those months ago, wishing stupidly for someone like Monika to be my mother. And here she was.

"Oh, we're ready!" Monika raised her hand slightly, and a server whirled around so quickly, I was afraid he would snap his neck. "The crab cakes for everyone. Don't you think?" She scrunched her nose and looked around at the table. "Now that crabs are extinct, we have to get them when we can. And champagne. We're celebrating."

The server was already halfway to the kitchen by the time she finished speaking.

"My kind, thoughtful son," Monika said, ruffling his hair before turning her attention to me. "I'm so excited to finally meet the beautiful young woman you've somehow managed to trick into a lifetime with you."

I WAS PREPARED to tell Monika the usual lies about my upbringing, but to my surprise, she didn't seem interested in it at all. She asked me questions about my works, artists I liked, and my current artistic pursuits. Her eyes lit up and she squeezed my hand with hers when I told her that Helen Frankenthaler's soaked paintings brought me pure joy. She listened intently as I described my past works.

"One of the things I created for my submission to BCAD was a video . . . I modified my *Dance Dance Revolution*'s source code to change the texture files of arrows into words. Stereotypes and expectations I felt pressured to meet. In the video, I played this personalized game and it went so fast, I fell to the ground, literally collapsing under the weight of the model-minority myth."

She looked at me eagerly. "And?"

"And then I was accepted!"

Her expression twisted into confusion for a moment before it smoothed. "I see. Very impressive. I'm sure that was quite the piece to behold."

She continued to smile, but I felt distinctly that she had lost interest in me. This had been some kind of test, and evidently, I had failed. Pressure was building behind my eyes, but I willed myself not to cry.

"There was something else I was proud of," I blurted out.

"What was that?"

"I volunteered at a sanatorium during high school. One of my jobs was to collect the vomit from younger patients struggling with eating disorders. I melted down butterfly clips and used their plastic to encase the vomit in resin. I called these regurgithaliths *Girlhood*."

"That *is* interesting." She took a sip of her champagne before facing me again. "You know, I heard about a piece like that, once. From a friend who happens to be a professor at BCAD."

I began to sweat. Mathilde had been invited to attend BCAD, but she had submitted an application anyway, out of fairness and respect for the other students. *Girlhood* was part of that submission, and I had wrongly assumed that only a handful of people knew about it. "Well, there's nothing new under the sun. Isn't that the saying?"

"That's true. The art world is all artifice and kitsch now. The idea that something is just as good or should have merit because of how close it gets to the original . . . has never sat right with me."

Even though the air in the vault was frigid, I could feel sweat dripping down the sides of my dress now. My vision blurred, and the white gold bangles around her arms and neck suddenly reminded me of the buffers, coiling off her limbs and making their way toward me, trapping me in place.

"Your piece. It's the one I've heard of, isn't it?"

I stood before I had even made the decision to leave, mumbling something about needing the restroom.

I rinsed my hands in cold water and tried to slow my breathing. Why had I brought up *Girlhood* and pretended it was my own? The ring shone in the dim light of the bathroom, and I held my hand up, letting it put my mind at ease. There would be more chances to get it right, a lifetime of chances to impress Monika and to make her forget this conversation ever happened.

I returned to the table after a quick reapplication of my lipstick. I didn't want her to think that I had left out of humiliation, even though that was exactly what had happened. Logan squeezed my knee when I sat down.

"Mom had to run to another meeting, but she sends her deepest apologies."

I hid my relief at the news. Logan and Toru resumed their conversation about plant intelligence, and whether it was a disservice to the plants to try to graft human intelligence onto them. I tried to understand what they were saying. Something about automation or self-replication. Eventually, I gave up and tried to focus on ignoring the server, who was standing by the door, panting like a puppy, waiting for us to need him. I remembered, then, the strange rumors I'd read about Monika. That she could control mammalian behavior with her fragrant secretions. I was almost disappointed, upon meeting her, to realize her ability to control the world was just the usual combination of enormous wealth, privilege, and power. Another glance at the server reassured me: at least I wasn't alone in my desperate, appalling need to impress the Dahl family.

WE SET A date, and I busied myself with wedding planning. Everything was moving fast, but it felt right. And anyway, I was treading water in my career; getting married seemed like a good way to keep moving. To feel productive in a way that society recognized. Wedding planning, it turned out, was a wonderful way to distract myself from the disappointments in my life.

Monika made decisions about the venue, catering, and who I would wear, but I got to choose the particulars. Baroque or modern furnishings, squab with roasted butternut squash or pacu and heirloom tarwi bread? I flew to Giverny every few weeks to try custom dresses sewn with flowers from Monet's garden. The guest list was massive: not only friends and family but affiliates of Dahl Corp. Reading the names of celebrities and world leaders who would be at my wedding made me lightheaded. How had this become my life?

I had very few people to contribute to the list. A few friends from school I'd haphazardly kept in touch with, and some family members and their plus-ones. I wanted my parents to be at the wedding, of course, but the other person I couldn't imagine getting married without was Mathilde.

She and I hadn't spoken for nearly a year. I had been declining her calls, always texting right after with an excuse. For the first few months, she frequently sent me photos or messages about the things she ate, saw, or did, but when I wasn't responsive, she stopped reaching out. I still kept up with her life. It was impossible not to when everything she did was newsworthy. She'd had two major works in the last year. The first was a long-term exhibit/social experiment called *IncARTceration* where she bought three abandoned churches in different rural American states and turned them into private prisons. She kept the stained glass and pews, and made the cells as comfortable as possible, opting for the most humane way to do something she thought "completely inhumane." The work questioned the legitimacy of private prisons and whether you could truly want people to be rehabilitated if you depended on their imprisonment for profit. Her contract with the government gave her $75 per inmate per day, and what wasn't used for food and supplies was set aside for them to be given upon completion of their appointed sentence time. Her private prisons were so popular, the cells so chic, there was a surge in people who committed petty crimes just to have a chance of being in one.

THE OTHER WORK was an exhibit at the Kunsthalle. She had constructed copies of Renaissance sculptures out of layers of frayed and shredded denim. People were invited to take scraps of material with them, to sew into their clothing or to wear. Within a few hours of opening, the exhibit had been emptied by unhoused citizens who were then able to sell the pieces for exorbitant sums of money. The entire thing had been underwritten by the German division of Levi's as an exploration of ownership and whether it was possible to make "art for the people" that would actually benefit them. Both exhibits were considered massive successes, and Mathilde had quickly become one of the most well-known and exciting artists of our time. She was also one of the most controversial. There was a growing group of dissenters who complained that Mathilde's art wasn't art but commentary. What made it meaningful was how it engaged an audience, not the simple fact of its existence. They said that she wasn't making art from within but from without, grasping for opinions and controlling interpretations. At the other end of the spectrum, an artist collective of young women had begun going around and doing their best to replicate Mathilde's performances. I was enraged on her behalf, and shocked she didn't feel the same way. In an interview, Mathilde expressed excitement about their work. "It's so wonderful to see a new generation interested in exploring many of the same problems as I am, and collectively, our message will reach farther."

From a distance, her successes didn't sting as much as they had when we were students. I was proud of her, and I missed her presence in my life more than I cared to admit.

Time was running out for me to tell her that I was getting married and that I wanted—needed—her to be at the ceremony.

When she answered the phone, I could hear the surprise in her voice.

"Hey," I said weakly.

"Enka, hi. It's been a while . . . Everything OK?"

"Yeah, yes. Of course. It *has* been a while. How are you?"

"It's so good to hear your voice. I'm all right, just plugging away."

A long pause.

"I'm calling because . . . I'm getting married and I want you to be at the wedding," I blurted out.

"You are?"

"I am."

"Wow. I mean, Enka, that's amazing! Congratulations!" I could hear that she was struggling to sound happy for me.

"Thank you."

"Who . . . ? Who's the lucky person?"

"His name is Logan. Logan Dahl."

I wondered if she recognized his name, or if she was pretending not to know. By now, we were a staple in tabloids and online speculation websites.

"How long have you been dating?"

"What?"

"I just mean . . . I've never even heard you mention him before."

"Well, we haven't kept in touch . . ."

"*You* haven't kept in touch, Enka." She said it quietly but firmly.

"I'm sorry. It's all been such a whirlwind."

"Of course. And . . . I don't mean to make this about me. It just seems really fast, that's all. I'm surprised, but happy if you're happy."

"I *am* happy." I hated how my voice sounded. Petulant, like a child with something to prove. "I'll send you a save-the-date soon. It'll be in late summer, but maybe you can fly down earlier and stay? Or have a meal? We can come to you, too."

"Either would be lovely. Thank you for inviting me. I have

some . . . health factors that require constant monitoring. But I'll do everything I can to be there."

Oh.

"Are you OK? That sounds serious."

"I'll be OK. I should go back to resting now."

"Of course."

"Thanks for calling, Enka. I've really missed you."

After the phone call, I sank to the floor in shock. She had health factors I didn't know about. She needed constant monitoring and had to rest after five minutes on the phone? I wanted to call her back. Apologize for not being more available, no, for *making* myself unavailable to punish her. I was seized with the impulse to fly to Paris. Who was taking care of her now? Who was in her life? How could I have been so stupid? To think that distance could be one-sided? Of course our relationship had changed for her, too.

I was back on the outside with a palm to her window, begging to be let in.

11

A light tinkling sound interrupts my thoughts, and I look up to see Monika climbing onto the small stage that has been set up for the evening. Two especially slimy Bosq pieces hover menacingly over her shoulders.

"Welcome, everyone. I can't express how wonderful it is to see so many beloved faces in the audience tonight. Thank you for coming to celebrate the new partnership between the Dahl Corporation and the LORA. Thank you especially to our sponsor tonight, my dear husband." She claps, and the crowd parts around Richard as a beam of light shakily hovers over his body.

"And of course let's not forget the woman of the evening, Enka, my wonderful daughter-in-law. You have transformed our family with your beauty and given us the greatest gift in Bastian and Roy."

Polite applause and too many eyes directed at me.

"In fact, Enka, why don't you come up?"

The spotlight jerks its way across the atrium to land on me.

Blinded, I make my way up to the podium where she's standing. Monika receives me onstage like I'm the one who has been missing.

"Isn't she beautiful?" She puts her palms together, leading the audience in an awkward slow clap.

"Speech, speech, speech!" they chant at me, and as I look out, still dazed by the light, I imagine they're all foaming at the mouth, with pitchforks in their grip. Monika reaches for my hands, which are clenched by my side, pries one open, and forces the microphone into it.

I raise it to my lips and the crowd quiets.

That's when I see her. In the corner, holding a stemmed glass and talking with her favorite teacher, Professor Abara. She looks exactly the way she did when I dropped her off at the airport, when she was leaving for Paris before our junior year. I remember being so surprised that she was moving to a foreign country with just one small suitcase. She wore jeans and a baggy T-shirt, and her shaved head was growing out, hair curling at the ends. The small mass of cowlicks turned her into an adorable Medusa. We tried to make the best of the goodbye, but we both knew that my decision had changed things between us. In her eyes, sadness and frustration. She didn't understand why I wasn't coming with her. Truthfully, I didn't understand either. I just knew it wasn't something I could survive.

But then I remember that Mathilde hasn't had short hair in years. I blink and see that Professor Abara is talking with one of the servers.

"Say something," Monika hisses at me. The crowd is waiting.

"Thank you, everyone, for being here. I'm so honored to have this new addition named after me. It's everything I ever dreamed of."

I stop speaking to wipe the sweat from my palms. The smile is slipping from my face. This isn't my dream. I've never wanted my name on art museums and institutions . . . I want my name inside them, next to my works.

"I'd like to thank my mother-in-law, Monika, for everything she does for the art industry. My father-in-law for constantly pushing the boundaries of human knowledge. My wonderful husband, Logan. The kindest soul. And, of course, every artist who has ever inspired me. Especially—"

I have to stop and catch my breath, ripping at the restrictive bodice of my dress. I can't help it. The tears start to fall, and I'm nowhere near the bathroom. I hand Monika the microphone and stumble down the stairs as fast as possible.

I vaguely hear her speaking as I hug the back wall, trying to make my way outside. As I exit the building, I crash into Professor Abara, who wraps his arms around me and lets me sob wordlessly into his jacket.

He lowers me onto a bench and gives me his handkerchief.

"Look at me, Enka." He places both hands on my shoulders, applying a pressure that grounds me. "She will turn up. Don't give up on her."

"Everyone is already talking about her like . . ."

"Wherever she is, there's likely a very good reason."

I hiccup and take a few deep breaths. "It's refreshing to see someone else who's worried about her."

He nods toward the gathering inside and tsks with his mouth. "I always forget what these functions are like . . . Everyone in there is probably happy she's gone. They're so jealous."

"I had the same thought earlier."

"I'm glad to see that you're not like the others. It can be hard, being friends with someone like Mathilde."

"What do you mean?" I ask, even though I know.

"Her career, the way it took off when you were both students. And the way she leaned on you . . . I often wondered if it took a toll on you."

His comment makes me feel self-conscious. "Did it look like it took a toll on me?"

"It's funny. People respond to jealousy in so many different ways. Some people use it as fuel or ammunition. They get more competitive, and they can become very successful with the engine that jealousy gives them. Others aren't so lucky, and they get mired in pettiness and toxicity. These are often people who feel a good amount of entitlement. There are also those who can't handle it at all. They withdraw slowly, depressed, unwilling or unable to find a space for themselves. In actuality, there is room for everyone, but the market benefits from an illusion of scarcity."

"So which one was I?"

"When Mathilde experienced a great success, no one was prouder of her than you. But I always sensed that it cost you something to be that way. You had a way of smiling that looked like an open wound on your face."

I want to cry again. "Do you think she could tell? That it hurt sometimes?"

"No, Enka. I think Mathilde could only feel the immense love you have for her."

"Well, that's good, at least."

"It is. And you always surprised me by finding a way to continue. Being her friend, as well as being an artist. I've always deeply admired you for that."

I let those words sink in, feeling pride, if only for a moment.

"Do you really believe there's space for everyone?"

"I do. Maybe not in the market or in the industry. But I believe that every person is capable of art that meaningfully connects with others in the world."

"I've always felt that I wasn't as gifted as other people."

"Ah-ah. Like I always say in my first lecture to every new class, there is no gifted. Only the gift of being fully oneself, and expressing oneself to the utmost."

I smile at that memory. I wanted, and still want, that to be true.

"Come, let's conjure a happy memory of Mathilde before we go inside and join the others. When did you last see her?"

A strong gust of wind lifts the hair from my face, and I let it take me back two years.

12

Months of planning vanished in what felt like seconds, and suddenly, it was the weekend of my wedding. Even though it was my big day, all anyone could talk about was Mathilde's imminent arrival. It turned out that she hadn't just been evading me but the art world at large.

I was relieved she was able to come. There had been no further mention of her health; in fact, she had even announced a new exhibit. Details were scant, but it was expected to open in six months.

Before the rehearsal dinner, I waited for her nervously in my private suite. I'd opened a bottle of rosé to calm my nerves, but it wasn't sitting well. Bubbles rose unevenly, as if my stomach were a bog. Despite how clammy and nauseated I felt, the person who looked back at me in the bathroom mirror was lovely. My long black hair hung down my back like a single sheet of silk, and my skin was as clear and unblemished as the sky. I washed my hands and plopped onto the bed, wondering if a tiny nap would ruin my makeup, which had just been professionally done.

A soft knock. I opened the door a crack and saw dark brown eyes, thick black eyelashes that extended straight out, and the beauty mark between her collarbones. Every detail that had once been so dear and familiar, in front of me again.

For a moment, neither of us said anything.

"Are you going to let me in?" she finally asked.

I opened the door and held my arms out awkwardly to embrace her. "Of course. I'm sorry . . . I was just surprised. Are you . . . ?" I looked from her face to her stomach.

Mathilde's eyes widened with fear as she nodded, pulling a hand protectively over the swell of her belly. "I am. It's part of the exhibit I've been working on in Switzerland," she said.

I was shocked. Preposterously, I also felt envy . . . for the child and the life it would live, the genius it would surely inherit from its mother. But Mathilde had disappeared from the art world for over a year, and for her great return, she chose motherhood? It was a cliché. Domesticity as spectacle. Motherhood as artistic practice. It would have been feminist and surprising maybe a few decades ago. What happened to her impermanent structures? Nothing is more permanent than lineage. I wanted to know who the father was, if he would be an equal partner, or if the insemination had been anonymous. Instead, I asked how she was feeling.

Mathilde seemed to withdraw into herself. "I'm really scared. I've never been so scared in my life. But I've also never wanted anything more." She took a deep breath. "And if I fuck up, there's no one else to blame."

So she was going to do it alone. I supposed that was a little more interesting, artistically. Single-motherhood. I put a hand on Mathilde's shoulder and squeezed. "You're going to be a wonderful mother."

Mathilde looked up at me. "I know. Everything I know about love and care, I learned from you." She pulled me into her arms, and I relaxed, breathing in her scent of neroli, cream, and spice.

Mathilde was late to the rehearsal dinner that night. My dad was in the middle of his speech when I saw her, leaning against the doorframe.

"We're so proud of everything you've accomplished. We always believed in you and knew you would find your way."

I focused on looking at Mathilde to keep the annoyance from curdling into anger. Always believed in me? They never lifted a finger to help me with my career. And what accomplishment was he talking about, exactly? Marrying rich? Now he was babbling on about how he hoped this was the beginning of one big family. I stopped listening, too embarrassed by how he looked over at Richard every few words, as if for approval. Mathilde's hands were laced sweetly over the slice of skin that peeked out from between her cashmere sweater and silk skirt. A dark curly tendril swept across her face. We caught eyes and I smiled, beckoning her to join. Anything to interrupt the verbal train wreck hurtling from my dad's mouth.

She came toward us, taking small steps in the tiniest heels, and everyone turned to look at her.

"Is that . . . ?" My future mother-in-law gripped her chair.

"Mathilde Wojnot-Cho. She's a close friend," I said. By now, I was sure she had forgotten the *Girlhood* incident.

"I'd love an introduction."

"Of course."

Mathilde's subtle glances and eye rolls made the rest of the speeches much easier to stomach. After the dinner, I introduced her to everyone, beginning with Logan. I was uneasy watching them meet. I couldn't help noticing how beautiful they were together. She was shorter than me, which optically made for a better physical fit. She had to tilt her head up to speak with him. As she did, her thick chin-length hair fell away, revealing a long languid neck. I suddenly realized why I had never mentioned either of them to the other. Logan thought I was the most creative person he had ever met, but my point of view was only fascinating because he had little to compare it to. Maybe I had deliberately kept them separate, afraid that her beauty and brilliance would diminish mine.

"I'm so sorry to interrupt, but you're Mathilde, aren't you? I've been trying to reach your representation for months. Absolute kismet to meet you here!" Monika had charged over. I had never seen her so enthusiastic, not even when discussing wedding dress designs. She was very familiar with Mathilde's previous work and rapidly drew her away, hogging her for the rest of the evening. I felt a twinge of jealousy at the interest Monika had never shown my work. But she would soon be family, a reminder that consoled me.

THE NEXT MORNING, Mathilde and I had a private breakfast before joining my other bridesmaids in their shared suite.

"Morning sickness," she said, suppressing a small gag. "Also why I was late last night."

"You arrived at exactly the perfect time."

She grinned as I shut my eyes against the memory of my dad's speech. "Monika is . . . interesting."

"How so?"

"She's really interested in fertility. I thought I was, but she's . . . almost obsessive about it. I guess Logan was born really late?"

"That's right." I didn't want to admit that she knew something about my future husband that I hadn't known.

"She wants to get involved with my foundation, actually. Or at least my upcoming exhibit."

"That's amazing," I said.

"I'm not so sure. I can't figure out what the appeal would be for her," Mathilde said, squeezing a lemon slice into her sparkling water.

"Are you serious? Who wouldn't want to support you? You're doing such amazing work."

"Don't you think it's an odd fit? My work is irreconcilable with everything the Dahls stand for. Sorry . . . Logan seemed nice. But you know what I mean. The buffers, the cloning rumors . . . they're predatory. I can't tell if she's interested in the foundation as a way of gaining credibility or feeling less guilty. I don't know. What do you think?"

"I think you're overthinking things. I'm sure she's just interested in supporting a young woman artist she respects."

"Does she work with other young women artists?"

"Oh, absolutely. Many of them and . . . obviously the timing would have to be right, but she's told me countless times that she wants to be more involved with my work," I said, mostly because I wanted to be done talking about Monika.

WHEN WE GOT to the suite, Mathilde was immediately swarmed by Polina, Mona, and the other bridesmaids. I smiled as I went to get her a matching silk robe. Normally, I might have been envious of the attention, but I was feeling generous. It was my wedding day, my best friend had flown all the way from Europe to attend, and her massive comeback wasn't as terrifyingly brilliant as I had thought it would be. If anything, I was disappointed.

I approached the gaggle of women who were passing around a stack of photos and discussing Mathilde's upcoming exhibit. Raving about it, wildly.

"This is going to change the world."

"Has anyone signed up?"

"What's it made of?"

"Mostly plasma, mucus, water . . . It was surprisingly simple. Just very time-consuming. I'm amazed it hasn't been tried before. The biggest challenge was creating seminiferous tubules for the injection of testosterone," Mathilde said.

"Can anyone do it? Are there any requirements?"

"Anyone can do it, and we'll have it set up for that purpose at the exhibit. There will be a lot of paperwork that goes along with it, though . . . waiving me of any responsibility, monetary or otherwise!" Mathilde responded.

"That makes sense," Polina cooed.

They'd all lost their minds. Yes, obviously, motherhood was amazing. Yes, in a way, it was art. But it wasn't exactly original.

Mathilde was beckoning for me to look at the stack of photos in her hand. I flipped through pictures of what looked like delicate, extremely fragile ice sculptures. As if milk had been frozen and stretched, braided and woven into fantastic shapes that ran the length of white walls. Flowing water frozen in time.

"Enka inspired it all," Mathilde said. "I was really struggling, considering ending my life. But she cared for me in this incredible way that changed how I think of female community and mother-hood."

The last photo was of a pipette, with a diamond-encrusted rubber head.

"What am I looking at?" I asked.

Mathilde glanced down at her hands shyly. "It's a textile I made with the help of a lab in Switzerland. Maybe it's more like a recipe? I call it Specialized Plasma Exempting the Requirement of Men. Or, you know, SPERM for short."

I looked at Mathilde's stomach, remembering what she had said earlier.

If I fuck up, there's no one else to blame.

I don't remember leaving the hotel or arriving at the Metropol-itan Museum of Art. Nor do I remember walking up the aisle or anything that was said by Toru, who was officiating. My veil was so heavy, I wanted to faint. I couldn't remember the point of hav-ing a veil made from shattered white iPhones. I supposed I had been thinking of my wedding as another exhibit. It had seemed important to make a statement against other kinds of connection, to show that what technology offered was limited compared to true love. It was stupid and, worse, ugly. And in terms of impor-tance or an actual fucking contribution to humanity, it was leagues below the innovation of creating sperm without men. Of produc-ing an insertable textile and open-sourcing the recipe so that any woman could have a child who was hers alone.

"Enka?"

Everyone was waiting for me to say something.

"I do," I said.

My new husband smiled with relief. His hands were warm as they enclosed mine.

"You've made me the happiest man in the world," he whispered, looking at me with the same steady gaze that had been reserved for me since the night we met. I started to cry. Not because I was happy, but because it felt, as always, like everyone else was looking at Mathilde.

13

When Professor Abara and I rejoin the crowd, Richard is finishing a short and reluctant speech that Monika no doubt wrote and required him to read.

". . . is because I believe in bringing about the next phases of human evolution. In order to survive the crises we've wrought, we need to be better equipped. Science's only goal must now be to preserve and protect humanity and its diverse cultures."

The crowd toasts to science and claps effusively as he walks offstage. Bosq, wearing an aromatic gown constructed from foraged banana peels, climbs onto the platform with the help of his latest assistant/girlfriend and grabs the microphone from the stand. Feedback shrieks, causing many of us to cover our ears. When it doesn't stop, we realize it's not feedback but Bosq, crying hysterically into the microphone. Monika tries to gently take it away from him, but he refuses to let go. She gives up and we experience an agonizing few minutes.

"As you all know," he finally says, "Mathilde Wojnot-Cho, one of my closest friends and dearest mentees, is still missing tonight. And the latest update? That she might no longer be with us. I'm sure I speak for everyone when I say that I'm devastated. This was supposed to be one of the most important nights of my career; instead, it will forever be a night of trauma and grief. I dedicate every work you see here tonight to the memory of Mathilde."

He pauses to wipe his face. Mentee? Dedicating everything to Mathilde? She would have seen right through these works and deemed them cheap and extractive. This is the problem with being missing or dead. Mathilde is already being co-opted by other artists. Bosq was exaggerating their association in the same exact way he had done with his Ketumbe ancestors. I'm repulsed by his display, yet jealous that he's able to feel so deeply and so publicly. I've always wondered if my aversion to this kind of performance is why I've never been a good enough artist. I hold back, possessed by self-consciousness, which erects a barrier between me and my audience. But when have women been allowed to be hysterical? Especially in public?

"Can you believe it?" Bosq continues. "Presumed dead!" A ripple of gasps across the crowd. It's a thousand times worse, hearing it said aloud at this volume. Logan appears by my side, and I slump into his arms.

"If you have any leads. If you know anything about where she might be—" Bosq breaks off with a wail.

He appears to be wielding a small object of some kind. He points it behind him, and a giant screen slowly descends. On it, Mathilde's lesioned face appears. The unnaturally high-pitched sound of her laughter and the eerie thwumping of something behind her make me want to plug my ears. Her rank, greasy hair and the bloody, frayed rope that hangs from her frail wrist make her look so vulnerable. So close to death. It had been bad enough on Polina's phone, but now it's ten times the size and utterly unbearable. But with more screen, there is more information. Behind Mathilde, an afterthought. Something shimmering slightly out of frame. Raised and skewered. A tower? My body remembers the snaking circular structures before my mind does, before I remember those drawings I saw years ago. The words come to me last. *This part of my life is just for me.*

Suddenly, I know where Mathilde is.

MIDDLE STYLE

1

Outside, the cold air pricks my skin. Logan, I know, would help me get to Mathilde quickly, but he could involve Monika. It would be a betrayal to lead anyone Mathilde might be avoiding straight to her. I look back toward the atrium, and even from a distance, I can see that most of the guests are drunk. My absence won't go unnoticed forever, but by the time anyone starts looking for me, I'll be well on my way. I walk toward the curb and lift an arm. The screen on the buffer shows an empty calm night, but I can hear the voices. I'm sure that beyond what I can see is a crowd of people protesting the event. A taxi sidles up alongside me, and I get in. We drive for many miles before we escape the shadow of the Dahl name, which is sculpted atop the new museum wing.

At LaGuardia, I wait an hour for my first flight. In one of the airport shops, I search for the most nondescript clothing, and still end up with a shirt and sweatpants that declare a psychotic level of love for New York. Strangers look at me with the special hostility reserved for tourists. It's been so long since I have flown with other people, I'm surprised to realize that part of me has missed the constant negotiation for space and attention that comes from being in public spaces. Looking at my fellow travelers, I wonder where they're coming from and where they're going. How different their lives must be from mine. Because of Logan and his family, we have been insulated from the many changes that have occurred in New York, and the world. If you have enough of it, money can keep the unseemly from happening to you, and the unsightly from view.

Exhausted, I sleep through eleven hours and two groggy connections before landing in El Paso for the last stretch: a three-hour drive to the abandoned Cho Cactus Sanctuary. Logan has tried to contact me numerous times. I quickly send him a message—"Finding Mathilde, need privacy"—and then switch my phone to airplane mode. I need to preserve what's left of my battery, and I don't want to be tracked.

The sun has almost set when I finally get a dusty rental car and start driving. I have never been anywhere like this. The world stretches so far. I don't recognize any of the plants that sprout up from the reddish earth or the alien rock structures that occasionally tower over the road from either side. The sky burns slowly, oranges and reds smoldering until everything is extinguished by a lowering black screen.

At the airport and on the planes, I had been too tired and distracted by other people to think about anything. But now I'm alone with my thoughts, and I can't remember the last time I've had this much time to myself. A deep wrenching in my gut as I realize how much I miss the boys. Another twist, and a different pain, at the realization that *this is nice*. This silence, this solitude.

The last two years have been a constant blur of travel and drastic life changes. Exhausting, exhilarating, and with hardly a moment for me to process any of it. Everything feels beyond my control . . . The responsibilities of running a household and living with an exacting mother-in-law require so much energy. So does being a good wife and mother, whatever that means. I often dream that I'm chasing my life, which is unraveling in front of me. I always wake before I can catch up to it.

I had assumed that our married life would be a continuation of our life before: Logan and I would be creative companions. But he is infinitely more important—any artistic component of his work a minuscule speck compared to his actual responsibilities. He is in charge of Pathway Labs, but he is also a professor, responsible for guiding some of the most brilliant young minds of our time. I was tired of traveling with him and being shut out of conversations. Though I had been somewhat respected or tolerated when I was his artist-in-residence, I was met with disdain or even hostility when I entered a room as his wife. If I had imagined doors were closed to me before, I found them all firmly shut now.

It was a relief when I became too pregnant to travel with him. When we had to drop the ruse that I was any kind of equal partner, I threw myself into preparing for motherhood. All of a sudden, our lives looked like every example I'd seen and promised myself I would avoid.

After the wedding, Mathilde and I lost touch. *Immaculate Conception* was an international phenomenon. I read about the birth of Beatrice Wojnot-Cho, the first baby born without chromosomes from a man. I saw the photos of Mathilde's ravishing face, dewy and flushed, smiling coyly from a hospital bed next to the small bundle that was Beatrice.

I waded through the many articles, comments, and responses to the news. A shocking number of people opted to inseminate themselves at the exhibit. Overnight, Mathilde had become an icon for lesbians, who could now have children without, as one commenter stated, "the inconvenience of man." One woman uploaded a video of herself sobbing because she had raced to the exhibit as quickly as she could, but was still behind the hundreds of people who had gotten there before her. In the comments for her video, there are the usual men volunteering their own sperm with a promise of zero fatherly claim or involvement. Other women who inseminated themselves on a whim or a dare were now distressed, bound to something they were sure was a mistake. Someone was threatening to sue because "it was just a stop on the scavenger hunt for the bachelorette party. I didn't think it was real!"

The Vatican, which has always denounced Mathilde's work, claimed her baby was not alive because it never truly existed, being an abomination of God, while the Satanic Temple welcomed Beatrice's soul, as did Mathilde's many loyal fans, for whom she could do no wrong.

The Lancet, one of the world's most prestigious medical journals, showcased Beatrice's growth and development on the landing page of their website. I kept tabs on Mathilde and Beatrice this way, occasionally checking on them from the distance of a screen.

Meanwhile, everything about my external life changed. I now had access to an obscene amount of wealth. Anything I wanted was within reach. A few weeks after the wedding, my dusty unused belongings in Argentina were packed into a few boxes and shipped to New York. Logan went to Argentina from our honeymoon, leaving me to move into our new home in the city alone. A car was waiting for me at the airport, and after a congested drive, we stopped in front of an abandoned field of yellowed grass, littered with crushed cans and broken bottles. The driver helped me out of the car, and I looked around, confused. He saw the bewilderment on my face as I stepped gingerly to avoid walking in decaying matter.

"Don't worry, it's not real," he said.

I walked behind him a little farther until he abruptly stopped.

"This is your entrance. Always look for these rocks." He pointed to a pair of boulders placed next to each other.

The landscape in front of me split in half, and I realized it was a screen. Through this crease in the universe, I saw where we really were: still on the Upper East Side, in front of the home Logan had just purchased for our new life together. Though it was six stories and took up the entire block, it was completely hidden from view by a private buffer . . . something I hadn't known existed. Like all buffers, this one was covered in microelectromechanical systems, millions of micro-mirrors paired to microscopic silicon actuators. Impulses of electricity cause them to change positions constantly so that they can reflect whatever light is necessary to look transparent at all times. Our buffer projected a wasteland so convincing that passersby averted their gaze or crossed the street so as not to get too close. It was an incredible security system.

WEEKS WENT BY before I stopped getting lost in my new home. I didn't go anywhere without a bodyguard. I had drivers, a live-in resident manager, twenty-four-hour concierge service, doormen, and even an in-house dry cleaner. Most of the exquisite furniture in the home had been embedded with OLED nanodots, every surface a potential screen. There was no need for me to install, connect, or even carry devices anywhere. My drawers had been prefilled with extravagant jewelry pieces and other accessories. I was invited to fashion shows all over the world, with entire collections sent ahead of time. Every meal was cooked in a second kitchen on the basement floor that rotated up-and-coming chefs. I wasn't just the envy of my classmates anymore; I was the envy of the entire world.

I BOUGHT MY parents new cars and a massive home on the other side of the buffer, in what would have been our old neighborhood. They reunited with friends they hadn't seen in years, all of whom pretended nothing had happened. Soon they were pillars of their new community. Endless dinner parties, country club events, and nights out at fancy restaurants. My mom found a group of women who loved to play mah-jongg as much as she did, and my father began playing golf. My parents were grateful to me, and now that they could afford to support my interests, they tried their best. My dad even started taking art appreciation courses at the museum. But I couldn't let go of my lingering resentment and threw money at them as a way of absolving myself from spending time together, something I had learned from other rich people. I suppose I also wanted to rub it in—how well I'd managed without them. In spite of them.

Although I was perfectly dressed and coiffed, I sank into a puzzling kind of grief. It took almost a year to realize what was wrong. My fellow classmates had gone on to make and show new

works. Their achievements were even more impressive now—
school awards merely paving the way for Duchamp Prizes and
National Medals of Arts—while I kept getting further away from
my dream. What an unbelievable scam it is to get everything
you've been told to want.

WHEN I STEP out of the car now, my breath hitches at the number
and clarity of the stars. From a bed of blackest night, prehistoric
plasma glitters like hundreds of eyes, all of them trained on me.

Although the temperature is rapidly cooling, it is still stiflingly
hot. When I exhale, it feels as if my breath might ignite. I check
my phone's offline map and walk in what I hope is the correct
direction. Ahead is a large structure, a wall of some kind.

A peculiar smell in my nostrils. When I reach the wall, I see
that it is made of overlapping layers of cacti. The spikes protrude
far above me, trying to impale the stars. I check my phone again.
It's almost dead, but I'm headed the right way, so I turn it off and
begin walking alongside the wall, looking for an opening. Within
a few minutes, I happen upon a break I can barely squeeze through
and find myself in the middle of an immense maze. The silence is
unsettling; only my footsteps and the occasional soft tear of my
clothing from a stray spike are audible. I turn abruptly to catch a
shooting star in my periphery, causing an especially sharp stake to
dig deep into the flesh above my hip. I press a hand to the wound
and hold my palm up to my face. The starlight illuminates a dark
smudge of blood. It isn't deep or painful. I wipe the blood on my
pants and keep walking.

My legs are becoming tired. A fly starts to nag at me, its buzz echoing in the vast space. It hovers around my wound, so I cover it with one hand and wave the fly away with the other. A few minutes pass, and another fly appears, the hum disorienting and aggressive, amplified by the desert's natural surround sound. The path is gradually narrowing, and more spines prick me, drawing blood. The smell intensifies, becoming a rot that is more unbearable with every step. My instincts tell me to follow it. The walls have become alarmingly tall, as if I'm walking between the coils of a slumbering serpent, fangs covering every surface.

Gradually, the path begins to widen again, leading to a clearing where I can see movement ahead of me. The sand is getting deeper, burying my ankles with every step, and my legs are aching. The stars hang low in the sky, coming in and out of focus, and it takes a moment to realize that it's a murmuration of starlings, expanding and contracting in dizzying fells and swoops. The smell is so overbearing, it's now impossible to breathe through my nose. I gasp through a small opening in my mouth and walk faster to escape the flies that are accumulating around my wounds. I'm certain that Mathilde is here, in the grip of some mythical wasteland beast.

I turn the corner, and another, and another, until ahead of me, a dark undulating void is silhouetted against the starlight. I've found her. Even in the middle of nowhere, Mathilde is beautiful. Her eyes are locked on something I can't see, but they shine competitively against the stars. She's dressed in a gown with a train, every inch of her body covered with what look like giant violet sea stars, each larger than my palm. I become aware of how I look: sweaty and tired, my outfit torn and pasted to my sticky body, while still insisting, absurdly, on how much I love New York. I can't even try to be dignified, necessary as it is for me to plug my nose childishly.

With every step toward Mathilde, I see some new gruesome detail that horrifies me. The skin on her face is ruined, even more chapped and lesioned than in the video. Her lips a raw gash over a chasm of red flakes stitched together. What I'd believed, from a distance, to be a murmuration is actually a horde of flies. They are mostly concentrated on a pile of shrub and wood a short distance away from Mathilde, but a cluster of them dive in and out of the dark purple folds on her body.

"How did you find me?" Mathilde asks without looking at me.

"I guessed." I can barely hear myself over the buzzing.

She is silent for a long time, eyes closed and arms opened wide as if to receive the flies, which dive greedily around her, rendering her nearly invisible. A few of them land on the open lesions of her face, and I run to close the distance between us, trying to swat them away. I can't imagine how many diseases the swarm around us is carrying. Only then does Mathilde open her eyes to look at me.

"You should leave."

Now with my nose uncovered, I vomit the ham-and-mayonnaise sandwich I'd been served on the plane. My senses are being violated by the putrid scent clinging to every opening of my skin, and I want to scream.

"I won't leave without you."

"I don't intend to leave."

I try to grab her arm, but she recoils.

"Mathilde, we have to go. Now."

"I can't."

"Why?"

Mathilde looks helpless. I imagine a sinkhole forming beneath her, pulling us under.

"I don't want her to be alone."

"Who are you talking about?"

"Beatrice." Mathilde's face cracks at the utterance. "She needs me."

Mathilde lets out a cry and runs to the pile of wood, lifting something from it. A rusted cloth bundle, covered in flies.

Only then do I realize the trauma my friend has endured. This must have been the cause. The break Polina had failed to mention. My arms ache for my children. Their loss is a grief I have often imagined, if only because it would be unimaginable. Unendurable.

I remember the last time she looked this way, her arms filled with the carving of her father. Now, at the edge of the earth, tipping into somewhere else, she holds the corpse of her daughter.

"She's gone, Mathilde. You know that, right? Please. I know you can hear me." I look into her eyes, searching for someone I hope is still there.

Mathilde looks at the clump in her hands with deep sorrow. "I know," she whispers quietly. Saying the words seems to take everything from her.

I seize her hands and speak with as much force as I can. "Mathilde, it's time to say goodbye."

She looks at me and nods. "Goodbye, Enka."

I shake my head, tamping down the revulsion that repeatedly threatens to surface. "No. Goodbye to Beatrice. I can help you. Whatever you need."

Mathilde tries to smile at me. "I don't need anything from you. The flies will take care of us."

I begin to breathe deeply, trying to acclimate to the smell. Every part of me wants to run away, yet I move even closer, putting a hand on either side of Mathilde's face. The flies scatter beneath my touch, rushing to populate other orifices. Clouds of them roil against the night sky, blotting out the stars and surging around us. The sound is deafening, a subway whooshing toward us the moment before impact.

You breathe in and I breathe out.
You breathe in and I breathe out.
You breathe in and I breathe out.
You breathe in and I breathe out.
You breathe in and I breathe out.
You breathe in and I breathe out.
You breathe in and I breathe out.
You breathe in and I breathe out.
You breathe in and I breathe out.
You breathe in and I breathe out.
You breathe in and I breathe out.
You breathe in and I breathe out.
You breathe in and I breathe out.
You breathe in and I breathe out.
You breathe in and I breathe out.
You breathe in and I breathe out.
You breathe in and I breathe out.
You breathe in and I breathe out.
You breathe in and I breathe out.
You breathe in and I breathe out.

You breathe in and I breathe out.
You breathe in and I breathe out.
You breathe in and I breathe out.
You breathe in and I breathe out.
You breathe in and I breathe out.
You breathe in and I breathe out.
You breathe in and I breathe out.
You breathe in and I breathe out.
You breathe in and I breathe out.
You breathe in and I breathe out.
You breathe in and I breathe out.
You breathe in and I breathe out.
You breathe in and I breathe out.
You breathe in and I breathe out.
You breathe in and I breathe out.
You breathe in and I breathe out.
You breathe in and I breathe out.
You breathe in and I breathe out.
You breathe in and I breathe out.
You breathe in and I breathe out.
You breathe in and I breathe out.
You breathe in and I breathe out.
You breathe in and I breathe out.

I repeat the words until Mathilde starts to weep softly. We collapse together on the sand, and even when she begins to wail, I do not waver. I continue to say the words that had once brought her back to me, hoping the spell has magic left to bind us together.

WHEN THE SOBS ease and she has cried herself empty, I stand and pull her up with me. Resigned, she lets me strip her of each fetid flower, trying my best not to hurt her already ravaged body. Not once do I look in the direction of Beatrice's body, but there is no escape from the smell of rotting flesh and crumbling bone.

I do not have the heart to watch as Mathilde slowly moves to forage what sagebrush and artemisia, germander and lamb's ears she can find, using a rotting wooden branch to grind the herbs against a large stone along with Beatrice's remains.

I have limitations to what I can do, and as I watch Mathilde's unflinching face, making a putrefying paste out of that which she loves most in the world, I wonder if these limitations are simultaneously what keep me from being a great artist and from going insane. At Mathilde's request, I search for tree bark. I come back with scattered scraps, mostly large twigs, and Mathilde grinds the tree bark. When she is finished, her hands are bloody and splintered from the makeshift mortar and pestle. I'm having trouble breathing and start to convulse as Mathilde combines the two pastes with her bare hands. Then, an eternity of spitting. Both of us muster what liquid we have in our dehydrated states to wet the rough pulp. Mathilde shapes it into a large cone, careful to leave a hollow center. The sun is rising when we finish, and the little water we have contributed evaporates immediately. From the soiled cloth that once held Beatrice, Mathilde lifts a small matchbook.

"Enka . . . I promise I'll be right behind you, but I need time alone with her."

I hesitate, unsure if I can trust Mathilde in her state.

Mathilde grasps my hands and holds them tightly with her own. I flinch at the splinters that drive into my palms.

"She was mine and mine alone, and I need to say goodbye to her."

I nod and begin to walk away, the guilt and sadness on my friend's face too much to bear. I hear the hiss of the match and the furious roar as it catches on the large incense cone we built together. I begin to walk faster, afraid of potential fire, surrounded as we are by a wicked lace of tinder.

When at last I emerge from the maze, there's a surprise in the distance. My rental car is surrounded by many others. In a daze, and in the unyielding brightness of an already too-hot morning, I start to walk toward them. When people notice me, they begin to run. I recognize the uniforms of police officers and the large cameras and microphones of reporters. Officers rush to my side, but the reporters move past me. I look back, confused about where they could be going. They have hurried to catch the woman emerging, naked and filthy, from a cavern of smoke.

2

Mathilde is disoriented by the sight of the reporters and their flashing cameras. She sways on her feet for a few moments before collapsing, and is rushed to a hospital in Dallas. I stay with her for two anguished nights, waiting for her to stabilize. Whether from grief, or complete exhaustion, Mathilde doesn't speak to anyone as she recovers. Not even . . . or maybe *especially* not me. Her eyes remain unfocused and glassy as I explain to her that I had nothing to do with the cameras. I apologize for the unintended betrayal: I hadn't meant for everyone to find her when I did. But I'm not sorry I found her, and will gladly bear any resentment or anger she has toward me.

Logan had grown frantic when it became clear that I was no longer at the gala. He told Monika I was missing before seeing my message, and things spiraled from there, the gala ending abruptly with everyone on high alert. Bosq insinuated there was someone kidnapping artists and that he was likely next. Logan traced my whereabouts first to the airport, then to Dallas, and lastly to the outskirts of Marfa, Texas. My message about going to find Mathilde eased his worries, and he shared it with other people to quell their anxiety, but Monika and the rest of the board desperately wanted to find Mathilde and hoped I would lead them straight to her.

They alerted the media, and a small number of photographers and local reporters arrived at the site of my rental car within an hour of Logan. They were very lucky, surely getting amounts of money they hadn't anticipated for capturing Mathilde Wojnot-Cho's forced return to the public eye. Some of them had called in reinforcements when they realized what was going on, and the media outlets that were able to drop everything and helicopter to the site were rewarded with stunning visuals.

THE MOST MEMORABLE photos are aerial views of a lone figure traversing a labyrinth of smoke, returning after defeating that Minotaur, grief. For weeks, newspapers and websites publish these pictures and accompanying articles about Mathilde's revelatory depiction of grief as a maze you can get lost in, smoke shrouding everything. Mathilde's discarded gown of fly-pollinated hoodia cactus flowers is reconstructed and displayed, its rotten stench causing riots in museums. A line is traced from Julian of Norwich to Mathilde, who is thought to be the continuation of feminist mysticism after Simone Weil. One journalist calls it "a remarkable feat of penance," a phrase that gathers steam until it becomes the unofficial name of the work. Even at her most desperate, Mathilde cannot help but be a creative genius. I might have been jealous in a previous lifetime, but now I only feel relief that she is alive.

MATHILDE NEEDS LONG-TERM professional care, but I don't trust any of the organizations that want to provide it for her. The lab in Switzerland, for example, where she had been a willing guinea pig, sends repeated requests to manage her care, making new promises each time. Eventually, they demand, for intellectual property reasons, that she be returned to them. I swarm them with Dahl Corp's lawyers instead. With ample photographic evidence of her recent mental health crisis, Mathilde's foundation board takes the necessary steps to become a conservatorship. They have full monetary and bodily control, and want to ship her off to an ashram/medicinal retreat in Kerala, where they can monitor her spiritual and physical healing. But I want to keep her close, and surprisingly, so does Monika. She convinces the rest of the board to let me take the reins for her recovery in the short-term while they research other options. When Mathilde is released from a hospital in Dallas, she moves into the building Logan and I share with Monika and the kids.

We make appointments with all the best doctors to check and treat her for the bodily harm she has done to herself. The flies in the labyrinth that pollinated her hoodia flower garment, the constant proximity to decay after keeping Beatrice's decomposing body with her for weeks, and the other inventive ways she punished herself for failing to keep Beatrice alive—all of it needs to be addressed.

We also set her up with critical mental health care. After months of analysis, her team of psychiatrists believe they've unearthed an original psychic wound: unspecified early-childhood trauma that caused severe mental deterioration. This, they can't discuss with me or Monika, but they can share that the more recent events involving the deaths of her parents and Beatrice have wreaked more havoc, splintering Mathilde's understanding of the real and unreal.

The first thing her new conservatorship does is to put her on a very restricted diet. She takes a strong sleeping pill every night for the first two months, and I'm only allowed to see her as the pill is kicking in. I sit by her bed as she drifts off to sleep, searching for any signs that she might be getting better.

Monika takes Mathilde's care very seriously, conferring with different doctors and analysts daily and making changes to her various treatments based on their suggestions. Members of Mathilde's foundation stop by, and I hear them chittering away with Monika behind heavy doors about the necessity of holding the public's interest, plotting exhibits Mathilde hasn't approved. Having had my own experiences with Monika and her obsession with control, I despair at the complete power she now seems to have over Mathilde's life and body. As member after member slips out of her office, I wonder if there are other reasons for the diet and the pills, if maybe there are advantages for the foundation if Mathilde remains weak and drugged.

But before these suspicions can amount to anything, Mathilde begins to heal. She starts to make eye contact with the people around her, and to listen with comprehension. Finally, one day, I walk into her room and find her sitting up in her hospital bed. Her feet swing at a rapid pace as she talks with one of her psychiatrists. She pauses mid-sentence and turns to see who's entered the room. Her face breaks into a smile as our eyes lock, and my heart wrenches with hope. Is she truly back? Can she really be happy to see me? I had been worried that as she became fully conscious again, she would be angry that I had found her and brought her here. But her expression at seeing me again can only be interpreted as one of joy.

Mathilde's presence in the house brings me pleasure, but it also brings joy to everyone else. I had been worried about her being near the children, afraid it would remind her too much of her loss, but Mathilde seems happiest when she is with the twins. If Mathilde isn't in her room, I know to go to the boys' floor. There, I'll find her on all fours braying like a donkey or crashing around like an elephant, with Bastian and Roy on her back. Unlike me, Mathilde is free to spend as much time as she wants with them. I allow myself only a small pang of jealousy at Monika's approval of Mathilde being with the children. Is it because she has a Guggenheim fellowship? Or can everyone see that I'm an unnatural mother in some way that I can't? I swallow these feelings because I'm grateful for Mathilde's creative influence on the children. Part of me had been afraid that the boys would inherit my artistic struggles. When I see them building train sets or drawing with Mathilde, I feel the same creative inadequacy she has always inspired in me. How does Mathilde know, for instance, how to play? I hadn't realized that it wouldn't be intuitive. Never have I felt more of a dearth of creativity than when I am alone with my children and they ask me to play with them. How? With what? Is my inability to *play* related to my inability to be a great artist?

One afternoon, we are finger-painting with the twins. Before I've even tentatively dipped a finger into the paint, Mathilde has lazily smudged a dozen pages. She throws her arms around me from behind, puts her hands over mine and dips them, making a mess on the construction paper and the carpet. She boops my nose blue before the twins lunge to finish painting both of us. The four of us collapse on the floor in giggles and a myriad of colors. Monika walks in and joins us, even allowing a single fingerprint from each twin on an arm. She nods proudly at Mathilde.

"I was just reading a book on how important mess is for children's development. This is wonderful."

I have a sudden urge to pelt Monika with the twins' wooden toys. If Mathilde hadn't been here, Monika would have been deeply upset by the mess. She would have collected the finger paints and papers and confiscated them to prevent further abuse. She has done this with countless toys and activities I have introduced, and yet, because Mathilde the genius has sanctioned something, it has unquestionable value.

Most of the time, though, I feel a great calm watching Mathilde with Bastian and Roy. They are getting a better start to life than I had, with my own dull childhood. Early exposure to an artistic mind like Mathilde's is the best possible arts education. If the twins want to pursue art, their last name and time with Mathilde will ensure an easy path. Once, I even feel a twinge of relief that Mathilde no longer has a child of her own.

3

n a way, Mathilde was responsible for the twins. Her pregnancy made me realize I wanted children of my own. Every night on my honeymoon, no matter how tired or full Logan was, I forced myself onto him. Sat on him, wriggling and writhing until he had no choice but to give in to my pleasure and his own.

A few months later, we had dinner with Logan's parents to let them know that a grandchild was on the way. Monika arrived at our residence the next morning and moved in. With her commanding presence, she easily co-opted the security and household staff and used them to enforce new house rules. During gestation, I was to be carefully monitored. I would want for nothing in terms of approved food or drink by the many nutritionists and prenatal dietitians Monika hired, and I wouldn't be allowed to work or lift a finger for the duration of my pregnancy. Any print media, music, or technology I wanted to interact with had to be signed off by Monika. I passed my time with a strict diet of art house films and obscure European novels by dead men. An in-house string quartet was hired to play Bach chorales and Mozart's chamber works for five hours a day. She instated mandatory prenatal stretching every morning and a fifteen-minute afternoon walk. All other physical activity was banned. "Your most important job now is to rest. My grandchild needs every bit of your precious energy." Monika told me she had secretly been worried I was too frail to conceive and that she was overjoyed to have been wrong. She seemed to be reacting to that joy with the rigorous control of someone who was afraid of losing it. I tried repeatedly in a multitude of ways to express my frustration to Logan, but he was busy with the SCAFFOLD, and reluctant to see anything besides the utmost care and thoughtfulness in his mother's decisions.

WHEN BASTIAN AND Roy were born, I first saw them lifted over a sea of outstretched hands. The extreme pain and claustrophobia of being surrounded by so many naturopaths, doulas, midwives, and doctors clamoring for Monika's approval and my attention melted when they landed in my arms. The smell that emanated from the tops of their heads was intoxicating, as was their weight on my chest. I was immediately delirious with joy. A tiny hand found its way to my mouth, which was opened wide with awe, and thrust itself inside. I cried at the intimacy, at the knowledge that these perfect creatures had been made by me, had just emerged from me, and with the solace that my house arrest would be over.

One of the boys opened his eyes, and I was shocked to see a color so different from my own. Only when I saw the thick black tufts floating around their heads, so unlike their father's golden wisps, was I reassured that there was no undoing my involvement in their lives.

———————

LOGAN WAS BARELY home, pausing his incessant travels for only the first week of the twins' lives. I was upset when he left but too tired to protest convincingly. An hour later, I received a knock on my bedroom door and opened it to find Toru.

He bowed deeply and congratulated me on the birth of two beautiful children.

"Thank you, Toru. What brings you here? Logan is away, I'm afraid. Argentina this week."

"Yes, of course. He asked me to look in on the twins occasionally in his absence. I wanted to make sure that would be something you're comfortable with, and thought it might be best to ask you in person."

"That's very generous of you, of course you can look in on them."

What else could I say? I knew that Logan wanted the twins to have a relationship with the person who had raised him, but I was furious at him for outsourcing fatherhood. Eventually, I grew to love Toru's gentle and playful presence in the home. I realized, too, that Logan was frightened by fatherhood. "I don't know what I'm doing," he whispered when I first handed him one of his children. "Is this OK? Am I holding him right?"

As much as I wanted Logan to be with me, I didn't need him as a co-parent. There were multiple night nurses, live-in lactation consultants, and early-childhood education experts on rotation— not to mention the maids, chauffeurs, and general help who had populated my life since my marriage into the Dahl family.

My parents came to meet their grandchildren a month after they were born. I was surprised by how happy I was to see them.

Surrounded by Logan's family, friends, colleagues, and staff, I found it refreshing and necessary to have people nearby that I could claim as my own. They arrived on a hot Tuesday afternoon and I barely recognized them. The way they dressed, carried themselves, and even spoke was completely different. They gawked at the home, and the amount of help I had, but paid little attention to Bastian and Roy. I had assumed they would stay for a while, but they left after a few days. They had settled into their lives and didn't want to miss too much by being away.

"You understand, don't you?" my mom pleaded in the direction of my stony face as I watched them pack. "We were denied so much before . . . We just want to enjoy our lives as much as we can. We're getting older . . . It isn't ideal for us to care for anyone else. Besides, it doesn't seem like you need our help." I seethed with rage at their hasty return to a lifestyle I provided for them.

Monika had the opposite reaction to becoming a grandparent. She transferred her pervasive surveillance to the twins, which meant I was largely free to do what I pleased with my days. But all I wanted was to be with my children, and it seemed as if everyone conspired to involve me less and less. When the twins woke in the night, a staff member deftly turned up the volume on the multiple white noise machines in my bedroom while a night nurse was deployed to comfort them. When I wanted to see the boys in the morning, to feed them and play with them, I would be told that I shouldn't disturb the regulated playtime being led by play-learning specialists. When I tried to visit them during the day, I might be told that they were at the park or feeding ducks or meeting with early-development consultants who were working wonders on their fine motor skills. At night, I would try to read them bedtime stories and tuck them in, only to find that the best voice

actors and a third-generation puppeteer had just left, having en-
tertained the children so much that they fell asleep promptly after
three stories.

One morning, I passed Monika's door, which was slightly ajar.
As I considered whether or not to ask her, again, for more time
with the boys, I overheard a well-meaning nurse telling her that,
if she was being honest, my milk supply was not as bountiful as it
could be, and that the twins sometimes had trouble latching.

"And is that because . . ." Monika's voice dropped to a whisper.
"I've always suspected that Asian nipples are insufficient. Is that
why they're having trouble?"

My eyes fluttered wide at the question, catching the nurse's
shocked expression.

"Say no more," Monika said to her firmly, pressing a finger to
the other woman's open mouth.

The next day, I was introduced to a team of young women
Monika had assembled, all of them Eastern European immigrants
who had just given birth. Presumably, these women did what I
could not: gushed creamy white high-quality milk from philanthropic breasts perfectly constructed for motherhood.

I want my sons to have the best of everything, so I was grateful
for the help and tried to console myself with the knowledge that
their sprouting teeth would no longer draw blood from my tender-
est flesh. But as I watched my boys bounce from breast to ample
breast, I felt like I had utterly failed at something that should have
been intrinsic to me.

CONTINUING MY ROLE as artist-in-residence for Pathway Labs had
not been up for discussion when I became pregnant, and it was

somehow even less possible after the kids were born. I know how lucky I am, to have all the help I do and to be where I am in the world, but I can't shake the feeling of profound loss that meets me every morning. I spend my days like a ghost, haunting the halls of my own home.

The constant scrutiny and control make me more alone than if the house were empty. A lack of agency fills me with a depression and rage so crushing, I often want to scream, if just to hear myself.

Mathilde's presence is the only thing that gives me any consolation. She listens to me complain about my mother-in-law, has her own complaints, and always knows how to distract Monika when I want extra time with my children. I can't help but think that, in many ways, Mathilde is rehabilitating me. Now being denied the right to mother my own children, I am relieved to have Mathilde as a vessel for the immense love I have to offer, the love I am afraid will suffocate me if I can't find anyone to receive it.

4

When the boys have gone to bed, Monika makes herself scarce, and Mathilde and I steal away together. I love spending nights with her, alone and uninterrupted, discussing artists of the past. How many of them would have been able to be artists today, we wonder aloud, in the age of the Stochastic Archive?

"It didn't seem like there was any point," I tell her candidly one night. "Everything I did . . . everything I wanted to do. All of it had been done."

Mathilde doesn't think the Stochastic Archive has changed anything. "OK, legally, yes, it changes things. But in terms of actually making art . . . we've always known there's nothing new under the sun. I don't think of myself as some great original . . . and we place too much value in originality of concept."

"But Mathilde, you *are* original. You have so many awards for innovation."

She rolls her eyes and blows a raspberry with her tongue. "Nothing I've done is original. I've commemorated the loss of loved ones through sculpture and modeling. I've made works that challenge patriarchal and authoritative religious structures. These are all things that have been done a thousand different ways, going back to the beginning of our species.

"Don't hold originality up on some pedestal, Enka. Who does originality actually serve? Not the public. The public needs to be shocked and reminded of their own feelings, which everything else in the world seeks to numb. Whatever the purpose of art is, it isn't to be original for originality's sake."

I shrug and pour another glass of wine for each of us. This discussion would have been interesting years ago, when the Stochastic Archive was just beginning. I could have positioned myself as someone actively working against it, taken a stance or a side. Now, with the ongoing collapse of the internet brought on by the invisible buffers and the transition of everyone living in their own virtual reality bubbles, it would be futile to try to make art for a collective public. Humanity had chosen individualization.

But Mathilde's presence loosens some thread in me that I had kept tightly coiled. Every minute with her unravels it further until my old ways of thinking and seeing begin to surface.

We often spend our evenings on the fourth floor in one of the boys' many unused playrooms. Bastian and Roy are only three, but they already prefer the other spaces that are AR-compatible. Another reminder that the world around us has traded in the tactile for the virtual. But a renowned child psychologist had designed their playrooms, each with a different theme, and I didn't want them to go to waste. The spaces offer as many encounters with different textures as possible and are meant to foster a love for the natural world. In the garden room, Mathilde and I drink wine and snack on beds of different grasses that are grown indoors. In the coast room, we sink beneath sand or splash in the shallow saltwater pools. Everything in the playrooms is made with materials for sensory simulation: the furniture is made of mushroom concrete, the wooden toys are whittled from fallen and collected old-growth redwood trees, and the textiles are a special composite of spun barrier reef and pulverized oyster shells.

Mathilde and I joke about the rooms being our version of a man cave. Instead of hunting trophies and vinyl records, we have the textural and the natural. "It's almost like an exhibit," Mathilde says one day while running through the baby olive grove we'd sourced from Crete for the mythology room. "The path not taken by humanity, all that we've forgotten and forsaken."

Starting with everything in the playrooms, we compile a list of what has lost value. Objects we miss and experiences humanity has destroyed.

"You know what I miss about paint?"

"What?" Mathilde asks.

"The daubiness. The globs of texture that cake the tube and smush together and dry."

"And the tube that would somehow end up at the bottom of your bag and ruin everything in it."

"And all of your clothing. Until the next tube."

"And how it glistens. There's no comparison with all this digital stuff. Something is lost without the texture. Remember the way Mona used to wash every canvas with soil first?"

"The texture she got with that imprimatura was incredible."

"I miss that kind of thing. The methods, the processes, the tools. The way we experimented and looked for something new to relate humanity's oldest feelings."

The list grows longer, day by day. We add to it with increasing frenzy. Something will occur to me as my teeth or hair are brushed by my Living Vanity appliances and I'll run to her room to tell her. I'll wake up in the morning to a message projected on my wall of all the things she dreamed. For the next few months, every moment we spend together is one where we reminisce and indulge in a nostalgia we feel is ours alone. We don't even realize what we're doing until it's done, but of course Mathilde was right. It is an exhibit. One that, as she said, the public needs in order to be reminded of their own feelings, which everything else in the world seeks to numb.

MNEMOSYNE OPENS AT the LORA almost a year later. Once we'd made the list, it was just a question of acquisition, design, and placement. Guests step off the elevator on the second floor and into a dark structure of branches and hair. A life-size nest laden with cracked eggshells. To continue, you have to part with a few strands of your own hair. Only then can you tumble from the nest onto a carpet of edible Icelandic cotton candy moss to reach the rest of the exhibit. From there, everything is meant to be touched, licked, and interacted with. At different junctures, scents from endangered terroirs are piped in, with heavenly or repulsive scents. Dancers and actors brush up against you, barrel through you, hold intimate or hostile eye contact with you. Beneath the carpet, there is sand or water, surprising guests who lose their footing or find themselves afloat.

Mnemosyne by Enka Yui-Dahl

This is a work of anti-curation. Life used to be full of dis-comforts and annoyances, but those with money can buy their way out of friction and curate a specialized life. As soon as curation was commodified, curation as an act of art died. This is a celebration of the power of unexpected encounter. An ode to interruption and the way it expands our minds. The first of a series of explorations questioning what we lose when we only get what we want.

A STAGGERING NUMBER of people come to see the exhibit on opening night. It was a gamble to have a purely physical exhibit, but people are evidently intrigued by the idea of something that can't be accessed virtually. It's Mathilde's first public appearance since *Penance*, but everyone is so disarmed by the exhibit's offer-ings that even the people who expressly came to see her forget to gawk.

Ira comes to congratulate me, remarking that not even Bosq got as many heads at his recent opening, including virtual guests. Beneath his gracious and admiring veneer, I sense a little jealousy at the fact that *Mnemosyne* is more successful than any of the ex-hibits that have happened under his purview as LORA's head cu-rator. Monika, who has always made it crystal clear to me that she in no way sees me as an artist, suddenly wants to introduce me to her friends. And not as her beautiful daughter-in-law, but as the talented artist who happens to be part of her family. I almost for-get to be upset that Logan isn't here, needing to be in Argentina for urgent SCAFFOLD-related work. I look around for Mathilde amid the men and women climbing the walls and licking the ground, pairing off with actors in separate corners. At last, I spot her flushed cheeks and gleaming eyes, pointing in my direction. Exalting my work to someone who doesn't seem to know or care who she is.

When we get home afterward, we're giddy with leftover adrenaline and stumble into Bastian and Roy's bedroom, drunkenly kissing their sleeping heads. I take a bottle of champagne to the planetarium, and we sit under a sea of projected stars. What we've done feels revolutionary. Our first collaboration, so real and messy, challenging people's ideas of an optimized and idealized life.

"I feel on top of the world right now," I tell her.

"Really? I feel so small."

I change the settings of the planetarium to have fewer stars. "Is that better?"

"Oh, I mean . . . I like feeling small."

I change it back.

My head spins from the alcohol and I don't know where to start. But we have to capitalize on the momentum, the interest. We have to think of something, ideally in the next few weeks, to present to Ira. A continuation of this work that somehow builds on it or collapses it entirely or, or—I can feel my eyes beginning to close.

"I spoke to Monika tonight. She's so proud of you," Mathilde says.

"She is, right?" I make a Sisyphean effort to raise my eyelids. "I still don't understand why you didn't want your name on it. The work is just as much yours as it is mine." I had been worried that she was ashamed of being publicly linked to me, but now that it was such a success, maybe she will change her mind.

"I think attention, good or bad, would be a distraction to my healing. I'm doing so much better. I wouldn't want to jeopardize that. Monika agrees. She said the board would help me look for my own place soon."

A jolt of alarm creaks down my spine before the sludge of alcohol suppresses all feeling again. "What?"

"I think it's time. It's been over a year of me draining your energy and your resources. And I'm really doing so much better."

"Are you, though? Just a few days ago, you were inconsolable." *The New England Journal of Medicine* published a commemorative obituary of Beatrice that detailed how parthenogenesis caused an unusual expression of recessive genes as birth defects and other organ malformations that led her body to fail. Her cause of death had not been revealed to the public until now, and I'd found Mathilde in bed, sobbing, after reading the nasty comments directed at her.

"Mathilde! What's wrong? What's happened?" I'd asked, hurrying to comfort her.

"They're right . . ." she shrieked. "I *am* a monster. I didn't realize the consequences . . . It was unethical, what I did . . . She wasn't art, she was alive. And the pain I caused her! The suffering she endured because of me!"

It had taken hours for her to stop crying.

"I still have days consumed by grief. But I think that's the new normal. I'll never not miss her."

I want to throw my arms around her, but my body grows heavy, relenting to gravity. I collapse on the sand beneath me, crushing Mathilde's shadow. In my dreams, Mathilde is crying again, and I shrink her down until she fits in my palm. I wrap her in a peony petal and tuck her safely in my pocket where nothing can hurt her anymore. Where neither of us will ever have to be alone, and where she won't be able to leave me.

5

The next day, I wake with a pounding headache that rips through my body. Ignoring the pain, I tap one of the windows, igniting the nanodots that allow it to be used as a screen, and search for my name in recent headlines. I magnify the glowing reviews of the "whimsical and deeply felt exhibit by Enka Yui-Dahl" so that they blanket the entire room and I can bathe in the words. *Hyperallergic* titles their review "A Radical Encounter with Love and Memory." *Juxtapoz* writes that "Enka Yui-Dahl dazzled the world with works that speak about the seriousness of a lost time with a devastatingly light touch. Though the sensory experiences of last night were ephemeral, the impact of the exhibit continues to reverberate in my mind."

"I wouldn't be surprised if many exhibits soon copy this model now that the public's insatiable thirst for works created to be seen in real life, rather than through a screen or other interface, has been revealed," *Artforum* predicts. A *New York Times* reviewer writes, "I passed the evening in a state of childlike ecstasy. Laughing, drinking, tasting, and touching. Enjoying myself tremendously until I left the exhibit. As soon as I set foot outside of the LORA, I was struck with a deep sense of loss, knowing that so many of those experiences now only exist in the space I just left."

It's my first time seeing my name as more than a footnote to my family or friends. In my message centers, so many people have reached out to praise me. People I haven't seen or spoken to in years, and people I've admired for just as long, have all sent their congratulations. My heart pulls out of my chest, it's thundering so hard. I flick back to the reviews. A publication that has only ever referred to me as "Logan Dahl's trophy wife" has put out a profile with a timeline of my art career titled "Who Is Enka Yui-Dahl?"

But in every article, the things visitors and critics appreciate the most are parts of the exhibit that Mathilde came up with alone. I read about their love of the Gravity Dispenser, the straw-like apparatus we attached to the side of the building that sucks people up or spits them out three stories below. The desire to have a Snuzzler of their own or to walk through Canoodler Row every day. In fact, the nest and the carpet were her ideas, too, as was the goal that everything be edible. I kick off the covers, suddenly hot and itchy. The words stitch into my skin. My name is all over the exhibit, but how much of it is really mine? Really, I had been nothing more than a sounding board for Mathilde these last several months, as she shaped my incoherent thoughts into an experience of nostalgia with universal resonance.

I switch the screen back into a window and take the stairs down to breakfast, hoping the slight physical activity will help with my headache. In the kitchen, Monika sits alone, reading the same reviews I just read, projected on the island.

"There she is, my talented daughter-in-law," she says, smiling.

"Hi, Monika. Has Mathilde been down yet?"

"She took Bastian and Roy to the park with Finola. You just missed them."

"When?" I'm a little annoyed to be stuck with Monika alone, when all I want is to read through the reviews with Mathilde, to see if the responses trigger inspiration for a next work. A kind of claustrophobia sets in at the idea that she might be moving: my breaths are rapid and shallow, and my throat feels as if it's swelling. I have to take advantage of our proximity while I can.

"They'll be back soon. Why don't you come sit," she says, patting the chair next to her. "Look at these reviews. I had Grant fetch real copies of everything, poor thing, he's been at the printers all morning. But these are so fantastic, I think we should frame them, don't you? And I've been thinking . . . you don't have a manager or an agency, do you? That seems like a big oversight. Thank goodness Logan reserved the LORA floor exclusively for you."

Is she pouring a cup of coffee for me?

I smile at her nervously. I'm used to being on the defensive with Monika; now I'm not quite sure how to respond.

"This series of continuing explorations. How far along are you with the next phase?"

"It's coming along," I say. In the art world, that could mean anything from two weeks to twenty years.

"We should definitely make sure you have representation by then. If I had known the scale of the event last night, I would have helped you more."

I should be excited by Monika's response. Instead, dread makes its way up from my toes, locking my limbs in place.

"Between you and me," she says in a hushed whisper, "has

Mathilde been distracting you from your work? We've started looking for places she can move into that will provide the care she needs. Should I ask the board to ramp up the search?"

My heart quickens, remembering what Mathilde said last night.

"Not at all. If anything, she's been so helpful and collaborative—"

"Collaborative?" Monika's face freezes as she angles it toward me. I can't tell if I'm imagining the accusatory lilt in her voice.

"Not *actually* collaborative. I just mean that it's been so great to bounce ideas off of her . . . It's really been more for her. In fact, this entire exhibit idea began as a way for me to keep her engaged—to distract her from grief."

"So you don't mind if the search takes a little longer? She does seem to be doing much better."

"I wouldn't be so sure about that. Just the other day, I found her sobbing and . . . I worried . . . that she might self-harm again."

I want to take the words back as soon as I say them.

Monika gasps. "Really?"

"You know the media. They can be so brutal about Beatrice. Not allowing her to grieve because they don't believe the baby was real in the first place . . . Reading that kind of thing takes a toll."

"But she told me, and the rest of the conservatorship for that matter, that she feels almost a hundred percent. That she's ready to move. We were excited, of course. We need her to heal to be productive. You've known Mathilde for a long time. Have you known her to be dishonest?"

My head moves up and down a few times before I realize what I'm doing and stop.

"I don't feel well," I say, abruptly rising and exiting the kitchen. When I reach my room, I close the door and lock it. All morning,

I had wanted nothing more than to see Mathilde and to talk to her. Now I'm not sure I could face her.

Self-harm? Where had that come from? Why couldn't I have just been honest? Told her that Mathilde is indispensable to me, as my muse and my companion, and that it's better for both of us if she continues to stay here. But is that even true? If Mathilde is trying to convince people that she's better, maybe she wants to leave. Heat rushes through my body so fast, I don't register it as anger at first. But I am angry. Why can't Mathilde see how much I've done for her? How good we are for each other?

I head for the kitchen again, determined to confront Mathilde. It's dark outside and, with a pang, I realize I've missed the whole day, including dinner and bedtime with the kids. When I get to the first floor, I hear voices and pause to listen at the door. Mathilde and Monika, arguing heatedly.

"We aren't a charity, Mathilde. Many of us rely on you financially. We've been very patient with you over the course of your career, but we need certain guarantees if this is to continue working for us."

"Why won't you believe me when I tell you that I'm feeling so much better?" Mathilde asks this softly, a desperate edge to her plea. The guilt is immediate and heavy, as if lead is being poured on me.

"We need quantifiable proof that you're better before you can live on your own. You're lucky I'm in a position to order these tests for you. It's not like anyone can just walk off the street and get these done. What are you so afraid of?"

"Nothing. I'm better. You'll see." Her voice is hollow but determined.

I sneak up the stairs quietly. Better to speak with her another time.

THE NEXT MORNING, Mathilde knocks on my door and surprises me with a mug of tea and breakfast on a tray.

"Where were you yesterday?"

"I was too hungover to get out of bed. What did you get up to? I looked for you in the morning, but Monika said you were out with the boys."

Her face crumples at the mention of my mother-in-law.

"She doesn't believe me, Enka. She . . . The board wants me to take these tests next week. They're preparing them now."

"What kinds of tests?"

"They're, I guess, trauma scans. They want to make sure I'm not 'irretrievably damaged.' They need to guarantee that I'll be able to keep contributing to their fortunes."

"I'm so sorry."

"I just wish she would believe me. I'm better."

The guilt is like an anchor in my throat, slowly lowering into the pit of my stomach. I know all too well what it's like not to be believed by Monika. But if Mathilde is improving, the tests won't necessarily be a bad thing.

"I should be getting my own place, not burdening you any longer."

"Wait, is that why you want to leave? Because you think you're a burden?"

"I know you would never ask me to repay anything . . . but this imbalance in our relationship makes me worry. I can't always depend on you to bring me back—" Her voice catches and she clears it before continuing. "What do you even get out of helping me like this?"

I'm shocked to see embarrassment in her face.

"Are you serious? I get to spend time with the greatest and most inspiring person I know. Don't worry about me."

She smiles at me thinly.

"It's not just that I'm worried about being a burden. You know I love Bastian and Roy. They're amazing, but sometimes it's difficult to be around them. I find myself wondering what she would have been like at their age. Would she have liked this toy? That video? And before I know it, I'm right back there, losing her all over again."

6

A week later, we watch as the city slowly drains from the car window. The sky bruises, buildings shrink, and apartment complexes are snatched away by distance as we speed into greener and wilder spaces. The surrounding cars desert us and bright highway lights blink on, reminiscent of a Seurat, blurring into the loose freehand of a Munch landscape as we approach the secluded forest.

The boys are excited for the trip, hoping to catch another glimpse of the "ghost" they saw on their last visit: a man with a half-burned face who wanders the property. Unlike them, I've never been to their grandfather's thirty-seven-acre compound in Westchester County, known to all as the Dahlhouse.

The twins fall asleep between Mathilde and me, their warm sleepy bodies a comfort. Mathilde fidgets with a ring around her first finger as she stares into space, and I wish I could tell what she's thinking. It's late evening when we veer off the main road. The moon is a pale yellow smudge hovering nervously between the trees, more and more of them, until the sky is blotted out entirely. The unmarked exit takes us to an outer gate that's nearly undetectable under a veil of vines. The car slows to a crawl to navigate the gravel road. The dense foliage is so low, the leaves seem to be brushing the vehicle for fingerprints. Mathilde is ghostly pale in the backseat, watching the large black leaves press against the window before the car scrapes forward. I have the irrational thought that if I were to open the window, the leaves would wrap her up and take her. The trees begin to recede, and finally, we reach a clearing. I can tell from Mathilde's face that she's equally relieved to be out of the oppressive wilderness. The car stops beneath giant winged sculptures. I recognize them to be Magdalena Abakanowicz's *Birds of Knowledge of Good and Evil*, formerly a public installation that Richard Dahl had plucked for his own private collection.

As soon as the car doors open, Bastian and Roy run to look for their Uncle Toru, leaving Mathilde and me to contend with the imposing structure in front of us. A hulking black mass, silhouetted against the sky, makes the darkness around us seem bright in comparison. There are no windows and no door. Nothing that resembles a place of entry. We might as well be trying to enter an ancient mountain range. Just when I'm certain we're in the wrong place, an abyss yawns before us and a pale hand flits out. An older woman with shoulder-length white hair slowly emerges from the shadows. "Welcome to the Dahlhouse. My name is Frances and I'm the head of staff. I'll show you to your rooms."

She leads Mathilde and me through the door, and I have to blink to make sure my eyes are open. Slowly, they adjust to the lack of light.

"We keep things very dark in here to preserve the art," Frances says, noticing my surprise. I look around at the walls of dark charcoal stone, occasionally sliced with ochre. I can't make out the ground at all, and every step is taken with a fear that I'll fall through. We grope our way up a set of stairs and start down a long hallway. She turns into a room on the left, and I'm relieved to see that it's lit with the softest lamplight. More a suggestion of warmth than actual illumination. A bed of blue velvets and linens is supported by an ocean of layered navy carpets. Mathilde's room is down the hall, and I watch her and Frances disappear into the encroaching darkness beyond the door.

I change into a simple black dress and go down to find the formal dining room. I turn left at the bottom of the stairs, and my hand runs into something spiky. A dried bouquet of black protea, preserved in a cold ceramic vessel I can't see. I pass by a room that must function as a kind of hanging gallery. Faces float en masse on the wall, each of them beheaded and glowing green.

I feel a weight on my shoulder and jump. It's Frances, guiding me out of the space.

"Richard collects paintings of the saints from the thirteenth century. He prefers when the red cochineal pigment has decayed and the green underpainting is all that's left."

A disembodied face catches my eye, and I startle at my own appearance in the mirror. Frances appears beside me, her white hair a shock in the dark. For a split second, her blue eyes almost glow.

"This way," she says, steering me past the mirror. Our footsteps make no sound on the carpets, and I can't see my own limbs when I glance down. So little in this home affirms my existence.

"There are no windows," I say, only just noticing the lack of view.

"That's correct. Most of the main living quarters do not have windows. Natural views can't be controlled, and Richard likes to keep a strict handle on the aesthetics displayed in the home. Here we are."

A freestanding slab of concrete dominates the dining room, set with oozing candles, wax melting freely between the gleaming silver tableware. A dark crimson wall is crowded with paintings. They almost seem to touch, the blood-red shoes in a Penny Goring stomping on the narrow-faced Modigliani below, which connects to a tortured mass of Schiele limbs. I take a seat beneath a ghastly smiling dis-figure by Soutine, knowing I won't have an appetite if I can see the painting. The subject's bloated red lips smear outward toward their flesh, which in turn dissolves into the background. It's reminiscent of Van Gogh's *Starry Night*, but the swirling strokes that so beautifully evoke nature are convulsive, diabolical when applied to portraiture.

Beneath the wall of bodies, Frances puts finishing touches on the table settings with the rest of her staff.

Mathilde appears to my left and smiles nervously at Frances.

Monika and an older, more tanned and wrinkled version of my husband walk into the room. She claps a hand around Frances while looking at us.

"Hi, Richard," Mathilde says.

"Please, call me Dick. It's so nice to see you, Mathilde. A pleasure to have you here. Take a seat."

"Thank you. It's a beautiful home," she says, glancing around before sitting down in one of the medieval iron chairs.

"It is, isn't it? We keep everything simple, to feature the art better."

"And dark," I say.

"Of course. We can't chance any of these precious works being ruined by the sun. Speaking of precious works, this is a big week for you, Mathilde. We're all very excited."

A crack appears in the darkness behind him, and that seam widens to show three silhouettes bearing something massive into the room. As they approach the table, I can see them better. Three young women, with snow-blond hair and light blue eyes. Their skin is so colorless, I wonder if they've ever been outdoors. The triplets uncover the platter, revealing a giant boar. They slide it onto the center of the table, the snout inching precariously toward me.

Dick stands and carves the meat quickly, with great blustering breaths. Dark streams of red-black blood collect into pools at the bottom of the plate and the edge of his knife, which he sucks clean before each new cut.

I remember that when asked in a recent interview why one of the world's richest men was heavily investing in cloned meat, Dick Dahl had answered that it was to ensure he always had game to hunt. It wasn't an investment in cloned meat, but the design of controlled ambitions.

He serves everyone generous portions, and the women return with different sides. Brussels sprouts with soy glaze and crispy bacon. Green beans slathered with maple syrup and crusted in almonds. Aromatic rice threaded with saffron strands. When the triplets lean over to place the dishes on the table, the candlelight illuminates their strange identical features. Bloodless skin, slightly upturned noses, and light silver eyebrows and lashes.

They look at Dick and he nods, dismissing them before taking his seat at the head of the table.

"I was so sorry to hear about Beatrice."

I can feel Mathilde tense beside me.

"Monika filled me in on the particulars, and I read about it, of course. I happen to be quite knowledgeable about parthenogenesis . . . Which autoimmunes did she have?"

Mathilde begins to tremble, but Dick doesn't seem to register her discomfort. Or if he does, he doesn't care.

"Was it an option to introduce a later fertilization? Or a way to edit the genes that were recessive? I know Fritz well from my time in Geneva. I'd considered hiring him in the past, but after your debacle, I'm glad I went with someone else. Why did you go with him? And what exactly was the aim? Was it really just to have a child that was yours alone? There are so many other options, after all."

"Like adoption?" Mathilde finally speaks back.

"Well, yes, of course. And many other less pedestrian choices a woman of your means and fame can certainly access." He points a fork at her and narrows his eyes. "We should talk before you try again. Monika and I would love to be more involved. From what I understand, you didn't exactly keep your board informed about the work. A pity because Monika and I could have given you considerable support."

"I don't think I'll be trying again."

Dick leans forward, looking at her with astonishment. The hunger in his eyes, the animal expression on his face. In this moment, he doesn't look anything like his son. "But lineage is everything."

Mathilde shakes her head. "Maybe not. I've always specialized in impermanence, and it seems fate wants to keep it that way. It was arrogant of me to think I could make something that isn't touched or disfigured by death."

Dick laughs. "Fate has been proven obsolete by science. What's the real reason?"

Mathilde hesitates. "It was painful."

"Well, you wouldn't have the same outcome."

"That's not guaranteed," she says quietly.

"I assure you, I can guarantee it."

Monika lays a hand on her husband's arm. "Why don't we walk Mathilde through the procedure for this week? I'm sure you have so many questions."

Visible relief floods Mathilde's body. "I'd like that. It's just a scan, right? A trauma scan?"

Richard scratches his chin for a moment before answering. "That's a reductive way to describe what's going to happen. You might as well call Basquiat a scribbler. We'll initially take a scan, yes, in order to construct digital twins. And then we'll compare them."

"Digital . . . what?"

"A lot of people have them. I know a monk who has a digital twin who meditates for him while he sleeps."

"But what is it?"

"A simplified replication of your brain. We won't do anything to *you*, but we can have some fun on the twins. With one brain, we'll pinpoint any trauma we perceive in the amygdala, snip it out, and let the brain keep running. We'll leave the other as is for the Monte Carlo simulations. Both the scan and the twin will run at hyperspeed, projecting your future for, let's say, one hundred years. By the end of tomorrow, we'll be able to measure the twins against each other. We'll see the likelihood of full mental recovery from trauma versus not having the trauma to begin with, and how that affects levels of joy and creativity."

Mathilde puts her fork down on a napkin.

"What about therapy? What if the scan, I mean, what if I . . .

get better from treatments? You can't predict how that will impact the future."

"Of course we can. We'll obviously input the maximum recoverability by biological and social means into the equation for the scan."

She pushes back slightly from the table, as if she might stand. "I'm sorry, I agreed to a trauma scan. This seems quite a bit more extreme."

"Don't you want to see what your life would be, untethered from some of the more negative things that have happened to you?"

"Interesting. I think a lot of people would insist that trauma is what makes me an artist. Or that the filter of trauma through which I make art is what makes it mine."

"Well, now, watch out. It sounds like you might be glorifying pain and trauma. By that standard, this boar would be the most incredible artist. If anyone wants trauma art, I can resurrect him!" He points to the pieces of sinew and bone on his plate. "I thought you would be excited. You're going to be in great hands. The team of specialists working on you has been handpicked and vetted by yours truly. It usually takes two months for a digital twin to be constructed. We've figured out how to do it in a few hours. Then they'll study which specific calcium-permeable proteins to isolate and which PKM-protecting proteins to localize. Once they successfully remove the proteins connected to traumatic memories, they'll target associative synaptic memories without affecting nonassociative ones."

Mathilde's face slowly pales, either understanding very little or too much. Her eyes are unfocused, resting on the boar in front of her. I reach for her hand beneath the table and squeeze. It's cold and limp.

Mathilde excuses herself before dessert, and I'm left alone to stab at the mediocre cheesecake Dick orders all the way from a diner in the East Village while he and Monika chat about their recent acquisitions: islands, castles, new staff, and sought-after artists. None of whom are more coveted than Mathilde, of course. I escape as soon as the tiny bejeweled dessert plates are cleared, exhausted and ready for sleep.

I'VE ALREADY CHANGED into my nightclothes when I realize I can't find my purse. My luggage was brought up shortly after my arrival, but my purse isn't among my things. I open the door onto the dark hallway and let myself be absorbed by the inkiness outside. Even though I'm a guest here, walking alone makes me feel like a trespasser. I step quietly down the stairs and make my way toward the abstract torso by Gormley. I had placed my purse on its plinth earlier, and see it now, slumped on the floor behind the sculpture. The stone floor of the main entrance is cold beneath my feet, and I shiver when I see a light reflected in the darkness. I whirl around, looking for the source.

Behind the stairs, through a partially open door, I see three gleaming white heads. I recognize the servers from before, their heads tilted toward one another like a bizarre bouquet. I wait a moment to see what they're doing, but they don't move. I take a few steps closer and clear my throat. But their eyes are closed, and they seem to be asleep, though standing. I'm almost next to them now, breathing on top of them. I look at their chests for any indication that they're breathing, too, and detect a faint repetitive movement. Still, there's something strange about the way they're sleeping. Gently, I stroke the one nearest to me. Her milky skin is so soft, so translucent, I almost expect my hand to pass through. She opens an eye, and I jump back at the sight of her lid peeling up to reveal an abnormal blue glow. I blink and the eye has dulled.

A soft male voice calls out. "Eve?"

I back away, startled by the voice, and look around for its source. The server closest to me begins to move.

The man calls out again, and the awakened server turns away from her sisters toward me. I open my mouth to explain myself, my presence and my touch, but she doesn't seem to register me. I shuffle out of her way and watch as she slips wraithlike into the darkness. I look at the remaining two sisters, spectral in the void, and unchanged by her absence or my presence. Their eyes suddenly open, glowing blue. This time, they look directly at me. I run as quickly as I can upstairs. Shut the door, lock it, and muffle a scream with my arm. For the next hour, I'm immobilized under the covers. I keep hearing footsteps outside my door, but perhaps I am mistaking my loud heartbeats for something else.

7

leep comes to me in fragments, and when I finally drop off, a rapid knock wakes me. I open the door to Mathilde, barely visible in the near darkness.

"I couldn't sleep."

Wordlessly, we take up our old positions. She crawls into bed, and I lie by her side, running a hand up and down her arm.

"Can you . . . ?" she whispers.

"I breathe in, you breathe out," I repeat until she drifts off. I'm not able to do the same. When I close my eyes, I see the triplets. The blue glow. Surely that was a dream? A kinetic sculpture? To distract myself, I mentally sketch Mathilde, revising and rubbing charcoal as the pale sun pronounces the shadows of her eyelashes and nose, dim gold rivers melting and filling the hollows of her cheeks. Watching the sun cradle her face, I have the sudden impulse to pray for her, but to whom?

Frances comes upstairs to collect Mathilde, and I go with her. We're both still in our monogrammed pajamas, one of Monika's obsessions. Frances comes upstairs to collect Mathilde, and I go with her.

Outside, the air is still cool, and long stalks of grass flirt with our ankles, darting between our toes. My vision fills with so much green, I almost feel dizzy, and I begin to comprehend why people might want to live outside the city.

Mathilde grabs my hand.

"I do kind of wonder," she says.

"What?"

"Who I would be without trauma. How much of who I am is a reaction to my circumstances."

"We're all reactions to our circumstances."

"I just wonder who I would have been. Now that this version of me is possible, it feels like I would be abandoning myself not to give her life."

"Her?"

"My digital twin. Maybe I can learn from her. I'm thinking of it as an artwork. Maybe I'll even propose that it be exhibited. The impermanent structure of the body. The beginning of an out-of-body of work. In a way, my entire career has been leading up to this."

A glass, steel, and wood structure abruptly comes into view.

A nervous-looking young man paces outside the door. "Hi, I'm Gunter. I'll be the main technician operating on you today," he says to Mathilde.

"Operating?" I ask in confusion.

"Gunny, what have we said about inflammatory language?" Frances admonishes him.

"Right, sorry. Not operating but administering. Follow me."

Everything is white and steel, displaying a fanaticism toward sanitation. We sit in a small waiting area on a white sectional that looks like an outcropping of marshmallows. From this room, we can see into another. The glistening chrome instruments and white leather straps on a steel raised bed make me think that it must be the operating—no, administering—room.

"Would you like some water?"

Mathilde nods, and he gives her a small ceramic cup as he goes into the other room, readying tools.

"When you're done with your water, you can come in."

Mathilde rises and places the cup on a white tray. I follow her into the other room.

"You don't need to undress for this, just lie down," he says, gesturing to the bed.

She sits at the edge tentatively, and he briskly straps her ankles together before moving upward to her calves, and then her thighs. He gently pushes her to lie back.

"Is this really necessary?" I ask.

"The first thing we'll be doing today is injecting her with a few different dyes, all of which will search for and show us different memories."

"Like a map?"

"Exactly. We'll see the topography of her experiences and emotions, and this is the scan that will be used to construct the digital twin. The dyes, being highly reactive, can cause movements among the patients. We strap everyone in so they won't inadvertently harm themselves while they're under."

Patients? Under?

He must see the questioning look in my eye. "We have to put everyone under anesthesia in case the dyes trigger unwanted memories."

"What happens after you dye my brain?" Mathilde asks.

"We create the twins, edit the trauma from one, and leave the other. Let them run. Once they're done, the scans develop in a solution for an hour.

"Like a photograph?" she asks.

"Yes, or an X-ray. But unlike those, these scans have no need for a fixing solution. Simply removing them from the developing solution will instantly fix them through oxidation.

"You can loosen your grip now," Gunter instructs, looking at my hand where it holds on to Mathilde. Her grip, as well as her jaw, has slackened. He must see the anxiety on my face. "I'll be here the whole time," he says as Frances steers me out of the room.

At the main house, I'm too distracted to eat, so I grab a mug of coffee and take the twins outside. I enjoy watching them run around and make up games to play. This is what I was trying to simulate with the playrooms, which were so expensive and still don't compare with the real thing. Why don't we go to parks more often? Why do we spend so much time cooped up in our building?

Sprinkled around the compound, there are art-storage facilities kept at controlled temperatures. A small gallery cycles through the art in Dick Dahl's extensive collection. I take the boys to see the current show. A collection of line drawings. I've seen these works at a museum before, but to see them among the glass and the green, contextualized as an extension of the nature around us, is a new experience. The space activates the lines differently, making them more expressive, almost dangerous. My heart begins that slow and heavy pounding that signals a love and yearning to make something. We leave before that desire can be twisted by deprivation.

I let the boys play hide-and-seek in the Serra sculpture park, getting lost in a few of the spirals and ellipses myself. The concert hall is next, oxblood seats and dark wood creating a sacred spiritual space in which the boys can take turns banging on the piano. In the Zen garden, they play on maglev rocks and rake the sand before flinging fistfuls of it at one another. Last but not least, we visit the ecological exhibit on view at the compound. Xugxie made exact renderings of the melting ice caps out of Carrara marble. She lives in one of the many guest cabins and chips away at her works every day to reflect the changes indicated by daily data readouts. According to the data when she had first conceived of this work, the ice caps would have towered over the guest cabins. Now there are fewer, and they are the same height as the twins. I look up and take in the negative space where they used to be. Roy tugs at my hand, pointing at something farther afield. A disruption in the ceaseless green around us. I follow it with my eyes, the image cohering as a naked figure slinking into the woods. Chalk-white skin and hair trailing from her head and between her legs.

Bastian giggles. "She's naked!"

"Hey!" I yell. The sound comes out hoarse, strangled by the wind. The figure doesn't respond or even look back, receding into the forest, as if eaten by the foliage.

There's no sign of anyone else nearby. I tell the kids to run back to the main house, and they finally do when I promise them an extra portion of dessert after lunch. Wanting to hear a comforting voice, I call Logan as I walk.

"Hi," he says, picking up after the first ring. In the background, I hear the soft hum of his car.

"Just wondering where you are," I say.

"I'm on my way to you. Traffic isn't great, but I'll make it there before dinner. How are things going with Mathilde?"

"Good. I think. They're injecting her with dyes now."

"Who's working on her? Gunny? Malin?"

"Gunter. He's very . . . young?"

"He looks younger than he is, don't worry. He was best in his class at Johns Hopkins before they failed him."

Before . . . what?

"Failed? What do you mean?"

"Don't worry . . . He has all the expertise, but he had to fail. They all do . . . The nature of what Dahl Corp does is too experimental. Dad requires a specific kind of practitioner."

"I . . . see." I wonder if Logan can hear the confusion in my voice.

"Listen, I need to hop on another call now. I'll see you very soon. Love you."

"Love you, too."

GUNTER SEEMS ANNOYED when he opens the door for me. I'm more than an hour early, but I want to make sure I'm here when she awakens. I follow him into the administering room. Mathilde looks like she's sleeping. Her deep breaths calm me.

"How's it going?" I ask.

"So far, so good." He smiles abruptly. "Here they are."

He walks over to a large container full of a shallow silvery liquid where two photographs are submerged.

"As is"—he points to the left—"and the edited twin," he says, pointing to the right. "I've never seen creativity or recovery from trauma this strong. She might be the only person I've encountered who's better unedited. We'll have to wait until it fully develops, of course, but the renderings being etched are already pretty astonishing."

My heart thumps quickly. I had almost forgotten how swift, how dizzying, envy could be.

"Everything OK?"

I swallow the feeling that rises like bile in my throat. "Yeah, I'm just relieved, I guess."

The two photos float lazily in the liquid. They come in and out of focus, and I can see each one gaining definition. On the left side of the scan, Mathilde's promising future rapidly solidifies with every second. I'm mesmerized by the black lines strengthening and spreading . . . a virulent labyrinth of artistic possibility. On the right, a grayish color moves sluggishly, struggling to keep up with the other scan.

"I mean, look at this." Gunter points out the deepening lines on the left. "I don't know if I've ever witnessed a more exceptional mind," he whispers.

I turn to him suddenly. "I meant to ask . . . I saw something weird earlier—"

The blood drains from his face. "What did you see?"

"A woman outside. She was naked."

"Alone?"

"I think so."

"Shit."

He snaps his gloves off and runs out, leaving me with Mathilde. I look at her face; her mouth is slightly open, but otherwise she is at peace. I watch the two scans drifting in the fluid, their distinct futures being inked moment by moment. My hand reaches for the photo on the left and lifts it out of the solution for a few seconds before dropping it back in.

8

back away from Mathilde and return to the main house, fighting the instinct to run with every step, and even though I wipe my fingers on my pants the whole way, they still feel wet.

"You're shivering!" Logan says, coming to sit beside me. "What are you doing in bed?"

I wrap the comforter tighter around me. "Just tired. I must have fallen asleep. Is . . . Mathilde back?"

"She was deposited in her room a couple of hours ago. She is still resting, but she should be waking up soon."

Logan tenderly strokes my head a few times. "I'll get the boys ready for dinner. Take your time meeting us down there, OK?"

When I hear his steps echoing far enough down the hall, I steal out of bed and attempt to de-rumple my clothes. Run my fingers through the snarls in my hair. The door swings open soundlessly, and I tiptoe to the next room, turning the knob as quietly as I can. In the dim room, I vaguely make out Mathilde's figure, engulfed in a blaze of scarlet bedding. Only her dark curls and a sliver of pale skin are visible. I watch for a few moments, wanting—needing—to make sure she's still breathing. The slightest movement on the bed sends a wave of relief through my body. She must be in a deep sleep, but as I close the door and walk away, I think I've just seen the corpse of a holy figure.

THE REST OF the family is already seated when I join them for dinner. I try to smile at Logan as I slide into a seat between the twins. One of the serving girls appears, placing a plate in front of me, while another brings me utensils. Even though they're fully clothed, my gaze wanders between their legs, searching for long white hair. A few bites through the second course of heirloom vegetables and steamed rainbow trout, Mathilde appears in the doorway. Her hair is disheveled and her cheeks rosy and feverish from her nap, as if the bedsheets had somehow deposited their color onto her.

No one is very talkative except for Dick.

"How do you feel?" he asks, spearing a cherry tomato.

Mathilde nods meekly in response.

He frowns, looking at her. "You should feel fine."

"I do, just groggy, I guess."

"How did you like Gunter? I hired him over Fritz. He would be the one overseeing your next conception."

I freeze in discomfort and glance quickly at Mathilde, who looks too tired to respond. Frances enters the room. "Apologies for interrupting your meal, but the data from this afternoon is ready."

Already? My stomach drops, and an awful pressure builds behind my temples. Dick plucks the sheaf of papers from Frances's hands, and Monika scrambles to his side to peer over his shoulder.

Dick's face remains expressionless, giving nothing away. To my right, Mathilde grips the edge of her chair. I can almost feel the sweat dripping down the back of her neck on my own. He passes the papers to Logan. Even the twins glance at them. Mathilde and I are the last to see the results.

The data confirms what Monika and the board had suspected. Mathilde's brain is not healing. It has an alarming proclivity toward stagnation, whereas her edited brain is fertile, capable of creative growth.

The rest of the dinner is quiet. Monika excuses herself sweetly, moments after a dessert of cloying peach cobbler, no doubt going to call the other members of the board. Dick tells a story about hunting ducks in Japan, not realizing or caring that no one is listening.

"Thank you," Mathilde says to one of the servers as they clear her uneaten dessert. She slowly rises from her chair, and I do the same, discreetly communicating to Logan to put the boys to bed without me.

Once we close the door to her room, she begins to pace.

"I don't know what I was expecting. Now that I think about it. Would I have been happy if trauma was somehow the thing that made me great? Has anything changed now that I know it's done the opposite?"

"It doesn't have to change or define anything. You can create and train new neural pathways," I say, trying to make her feel better by parroting things I've overheard from Logan and his technicians.

"It factors in therapy and all of that stuff, remember?" She starts beating on the bed with her fists. "Why did I let them do this? What have I done, Enka? What are they going to do?"

I return to my room once Mathilde has exhausted herself. I'm unable to rest. Her words keep echoing in my mind. *What have I done?* I'd only taken the scan out for a few seconds, *if* that long. I run down to the dining room, to look for Monika or Richard . . . whoever I can find that will let me take another look at the results. But the room is dark and deserted, our uneaten food left on the table. I spot the crumpled sheaf of papers between two half-full plates and seize them. One of the scans is unfamiliar to me, having developed another hour after I'd seen it. The other, I recognize as my work. It has the exact pattern and depth of line as the moment I lifted it from the developing fluid, a movement as conclusive as putting the brush down at the end of a painting.

As soon as the sun peeks over the horizon, I go to Mathilde's room, sick with guilt, and find it empty. Downstairs, I resist the boys' attempts to bring me outside. I see her on the back porch with a mug of coffee and join her. She is pale, her cheeks hollow, and purple veins spider beneath her eyes.

"They've scheduled a meeting for this afternoon," she says quietly.

"Who?"

"The board. They're all flying in."

She drains her cup of coffee and sets it down. She steps off the porch, and the twins flock to either side of her as she begins to run.

Logan comes down the stairs now, looking like the only person who got any sleep. He glances around quizzically.

"They're with Mathilde. I think she wants to forget everything for a few hours."

He takes my hand and pulls me gently into his arms.

"Let's try and enjoy the day. Come on, I haven't seen Toru yet."

IT ALWAYS MAKES me happy to see the way Logan and Toru greet each other. Toru, warm but restrained with everyone else, is incapable of hiding his pure and total joy with Logan. I remember that for all its advantages, an upbringing at the Dahlhouse was intensely isolated. Toru was one of the only friends Logan had growing up, and even then, he was an employee.

"How are the kids?" Logan asks.

By now, I know "the kids" is what Toru calls the acres of different green tea and rice varietals he grows. For the last few decades, he has been experimenting with how to teach plants to adapt more quickly to survive extreme weather changes. Logan spent most of his childhood outside with Toru, helping him tend the fields.

Toru, seated on a small wooden stool opposite us, rubs his chin with a calloused hand.

"They could be better. Your father has requested my attention be diverted for some time now. I find it difficult to change tracks. My plants were just learning to adapt at a rate that we could see. It was remarkable. But I fear your father has always had this new track in mind. To integrate these self-educational systems into other intelligences."

He drains the rest of his tea.

"Would you like to see them?"

I walk a few paces behind them in the fields, as much to give them time alone together as to let my anxious mind run freely.

"Is this supposed to be happening?" I finally call out to Toru. I point to the strands of leaves that have trailed behind him, though somehow not Logan, and which almost trip me with every step. As soon as I stop moving, one of the vines crawls onto my shoe, and I let out a little shriek of surprise.

Toru laughs a little and puts a hand behind his head.

"I taught this varietal to crave human contact. Neat, huh?"

I bend down and tentatively put a finger on the leaf, relieved that it stops creeping up my leg as soon as I touch it.

We head to the melting-ice-cap sculptures, and I watch Logan circle them quietly. I know that his mind is running a thousand miles per minute, trying to calculate how he can save them or turn back time. How did I get so lucky? To have found the one wonderful man who isn't interested in anything besides helping humanity? Logan is so unlike other billionaires who are all bogged down by their swollen egos. Of course he's relatively young. There's still time for him to become his father.

I leave Logan and Toru to a game of Go, and head back to the main house before the meeting. I want to make myself available to Mathilde, in case she needs support. A surprising number of board members have shown up for the meeting in person. Otto and Klaus, as well as newer members I've never met. Professor Abara has been replaced by Kenny Lowen, the head of Quant Media Lab, who now wanders the living room barefoot, mumbling to a pastry in his right hand. Myranda Stockton-Hardaway, the heiress to a fertilizer company, has replaced Polina. She traipses in right on time, followed by her three mastiffs and Kurt Trausch, the famous extinction economist.

It's a closed meeting, but they accept Mathilde's request for me to join. The board members only speak with each other, barely acknowledging Mathilde's presence in the room. We might as well not be here.

"Based on the results, there's really only one option to consider.

She should get the exact edits that were performed on her digital twin," Kenny is saying.

"I agree. It would be like facilitated adaptation, which is quite common in the field of conservation," says Kurt. "We're attempting it on many avian populations that are in danger of extinction. It's a way of preserving biodiversity."

"Exactly. Every artist, every person really, is in danger of extinction," says Otto. "If only Naiad were further along in the legalities. Then we could *realize* the twin."

"And what if I don't want to?" Mathilde speaks for the first time. All eyes swivel toward her, as if they've just noticed she's in the room. "I'm not the only one. So many artists go 'crazy' or make bad works because of their trauma. Their careers are often better for it. Markets always change."

"I agree with you in theory," Monika says sympathetically. "Markets change all the time, but misogyny doesn't. In our industry, men are still the only ones who are allowed to succeed when they fail. Trauma seems to add to their allure as geniuses. It's never really about their works."

"We're just going through the options, Mathilde. But we do hope you'll consider it," Myranda says, reaching out a stiff arm to pat Mathilde on the shoulder. "I mean, don't you think it would be so much better than staying yourself? You can't seriously want to remain this way." She holds up copies of the two scans, each one projecting one of Mathilde's possible futures: one that is artistically developed and the other forever stunted by my impulsive action.

"We are asking out of courtesy," Monika says slowly. "But if we all agree that you should go through with the procedure, our hands are tied. The conservatorship's purpose is to do what's best for you."

9

can't believe they want . . . to erase Beatrice," Mathilde says when we're finally alone. The board talked for so long that it is now evening. I can hear crickets outside, their desperation mirroring what I see in Mathilde's face.

"Well, just your memories of her," I say gently.

"No one else knew her the way I did. If my memories don't exist, it's like she won't have existed at all."

I gently place my arms around her, and she takes a deep breath.

"How are they so sure?" she asks. "I know the trauma makes up a lot of who I am now. I know that isn't convenient or whatever for production. Maybe it would be for some people. But they don't know what I was like before Beatrice. How much she added to my life. I would choose her over any world or life where she didn't exist. This grief I carry is so entangled with my love for her. How do they know that the love won't one day outweigh the trauma of losing her?"

During the board meeting, I had fantasized thousands of ways to casually bring up the fact that I had interfered with the procedure. But if I confessed, people would want to know why I did it . . . *Mathilde* would want to know, and I wouldn't have an answer. The procedure was expensive, and dangerous, and everyone had flown in to discuss the results. Why *had* I lifted it? What Gunter said about Mathilde's mind being the most exceptional had brought on a moment of baseness, a primal jealousy. I hadn't lifted it. It was some monster I had watched from inside my body.

Guilt is gnawing at my stomach hungrily, and I need to figure out a way to convince the board not to go through with the trauma editing before it eats through me.

Mathilde returns to her room to shower, and I do the same.

"Late to be working, isn't it?" I ask when I see Logan sprawled across the bed, frowning at something on his laptop.

"I was just finishing up some projections for the SCAFFOLD while waiting for you. How did things go with the board?"

"They want her to get the trauma edits."

"That's not a surprise," he says, shrugging. "I figured they would. What does Mathilde think about that?"

"She's upset, understandably," I say. "She doesn't want to forget Beatrice."

Logan sighs. "I can understand that. Trauma editing has been invaluable for a lot of survivors of PTSD, but some of them regret it. They can't remember exactly what it is they regret losing, but the sense of loss is pervasive enough that it seems like a substitution of one grief for another."

"So . . . is it even worth it?"

Logan taps his temple in thought. "You know . . . the SCAFFOLD could be an option here. It's proven to be much more successful, at least with veterans."

I shudder as images from Argentina flash through my mind.

"I know what you're thinking. But he's been perfectly fine for years now. And we've had that much time to refine the technology. Even the transcranial devices are half the size they used to be. Hypothetically, whoever Mathilde chose as a companion could use the SCAFFOLD to drop into her mental space and, from there, monitor her trauma and pain. In moments of excessive pain, the companion could relieve Mathilde by absorbing as much as they deem necessary . . . sort of a choose-your-own-empathy situation."

"How do they absorb it?"

"I've never experienced it, so I can only relay what our users have said, but the traumatic spaces are darker in color. Gray, sometimes even black. And if your observer interacts with that darker matter—"

"Interacts how? And what do you mean, 'observer'?"

"Our users say that when they're in someone else's brain . . . they aren't themselves anymore. They retain their own memories and experiences, but they aren't as strong, which makes room for them to be an observer of the other person's memories, experiences, and pain. Touching the dark matter can transfer the trauma from the inhabited to the inhabiting observer."

"But does taking someone else's trauma cause the observer pain?"

"It does, but far less, because they don't share the associated memories and all experiences are secondhand. Except in rare and peculiarly violent situations, the trauma isn't as visceral. It would be like watching a movie or reading a story that moves you and causes you to feel. The SCAFFOLD would allow the companion to continue making new works for them, something the board might be very interested in. And Mathilde would get to stay unchanged . . . for the most part. The SCAFFOLD's therapeutic benefits mean that over time, with someone else to help her off-load her trauma, her amygdala, hippocampus, and prefrontal cortex would relearn how to regulate themselves. She might feel a not-unpleasant numbness, at times, similar to a strong antidepressant, that could help her turn the corner mentally. She would never forget Beatrice this way, but her trauma would slowly lose its debilitating power. All she would need is a volunteer."

"For brain surgery."

"Light brain surgery."

10

"Mathilde?"

A sob comes from inside the room, a sound that punctures my heart. I open the door and run to her side. Her pillow is wet from hours of crying, and seeing her familiar features distorted by grief makes me want to dissolve.

"There's another way, Mathilde. A way for you to remain yourself."

"But the board—"

"This way, you and the board both get what you want. I'd explain it to you, but Logan will do a better job."

LOGAN'S FACE CHANGES when he sees Mathilde looking so bereft. A fury and raw anger I've never seen before, never even guessed he was capable of feeling.

"I'm so sorry, Mathilde," he says bitterly. "My parents . . . they've never understood the value people have outside of the products they create. I can't imagine what you're going through, but I'll do everything in my power to help."

Mathilde looks up at Logan, relief carved into every part of her face.

"I'm sure Enka has told you that I've been working for a number of years on a technology called the SCAFFOLD. I know what it sounds like . . . another procedure . . . but it isn't as drastic. You wouldn't have to give up your memories of Beatrice. You would just need to find a volunteer."

"A volunteer."

"The volunteer has access to all of you. Your creativity, with which they can make art to keep the board happy. And your trauma, which is like a snakebite. A volunteer could suck the venom out of you—it wouldn't harm them nearly as much as the initial bite harmed you. It's not a perfect analogy, but it's close. This way, you'd get to keep your memories, heal from them, and the board would get to profit from your brain's creations."

Mathilde seems to consider it for a moment before a hopeless look falls on her face.

"There are things that have happened to me . . . that I haven't told anyone. It would be cruel to give them to someone else."

This must be the early-childhood trauma unearthed by the psychiatrists after Beatrice's passing.

"The trauma they experience won't be as visceral because it'll be secondhand. And the volunteer can control the extent to which they 'inhabit' you. That's what we call it when they leave their consciousness for yours. Unless they're a masochist, it's unlikely they'll be in real pain."

She looks at me helplessly. "Even so, I don't . . . I'm not comfortable with the idea of someone . . . I mean, 'inhabiting'? That's such an invasive word. I hate to think of someone poking around in my mind."

"Of course. I won't deny it's a very intimate thing. That's why consent is an important part of the SCAFFOLD procedure. The person in your role has to be the one to choose who will inhabit them."

Mathilde is silent for a moment, looking down at her hands.

When Logan speaks again, I'm surprised by how gentle he sounds. A tone of voice usually reserved for me or our children. "Take some time to think it over. It's a big decision, and it may not be necessary or right for you. I just wanted to give you another option."

Mathilde smiles weakly. "Thank you . . . I appreciate it. And I *will* think about it. I just can't even think of anyone I could ask, except for . . ." She trails off, taking another breath, her eyes darting in my direction for a brief moment.

My turn to take a breath, a sharp, shallow one of surprise. "Mathilde, I can . . . if you want, I mean."

As I say the words, a realization pushes its way into my brain like a balloon slowly filling with air: this is the perfect way to atone for my terrible mistake.

Her face breaks into a pained smile and she looks at me. "You would do that for me?"

Her eyes warp with tears when I nod.

"But . . . even if it's you, it's still so much of myself to share. I don't know if I'm comfortable. I'll think about it."

"Mathilde, please. Let me do this for you. I promise we'll do everything together. I won't go anywhere in here," I say, gently touching a hand to the side of her head, "without your express permission."

She blinks at me for a few seconds as my smile strains my face. "You promise."

"Yes," I say, trying not to sound exasperated. Why can't she see that this is the best and only option?

"I don't know. I need to think about it."

"It's this or lose Beatrice forever. You heard the board. They're not going to listen to you . . . they'll rip her from you without a second thought."

"I guess you're right."

I can hear the reluctance and defeat in her voice. "You'll see. This is the right decision, Mathilde. I know it. The only one."

She nods, slowly at first, but eventually with more confidence.

I raise a hand up toward her, our silent gesture from all those years ago. Tentatively, she lifts her hand and presses it to mine.

"I breathe in," she says.

"I breathe out," I respond.

11

can barely eat at dinner. Lost in thoughts of the imminent future, I spill my wine twice and sweat runs down my face, as if wrung from my hair. All the board members have decided to stay for a meal, so Mathilde doesn't join. She doesn't want to be seen by them, and her face is too swollen from crying, anyway. I listen to Monika and the others gossip and chitchat as if they hadn't spent the afternoon debating how to best strip someone of their agency. They are all despicable. The twins start to yawn, and I feel so grateful for the excuse to put them to bed.

I go through the motions, barely present as I read the twins a few stories and tuck them in. Then I go for a walk, alone, to think.

Logan had explained that I'd have access to Mathilde's memories, that I could slip into her past or present at any time. The technicians would give me a unique access code, a series of improbable gestures that people wouldn't naturally think of. When I imagined these movements in a specific order, I'd be able to drop into her mind or get back to my own. Unless I told Mathilde, she wouldn't even know if or when I was inhabiting.

Her board will have the final say, but even the possibility of being paired with Mathilde is thrilling. And terrifying. I push the recurring images from Argentina out of my mind by looking up at the stars. A chance at relevance . . . at brilliance. A way to keep collaborating indefinitely. This is what I've always wanted, right?

LOGAN IS ALREADY in bed when I slip into our room. Desire has seldom visited me these last few years, but seeing his curved body tonight ignites something in mine. The appetite that has been suppressed by my daily anxieties falls away, and I undress quickly, reaching for him. He's sound asleep and unresponsive. His skin, which is cool, stays cold beneath my touch, and when I try to turn him over, his eyes are open, blank and unblinking. I shake him, but his body is rigid.

The door to our room opens, and Toru runs in. He stifles my screaming, a hand clasped firmly to my mouth. The dull sound at the edge of my consciousness stops.

"Enka, I need you to calm down. It's OK, it's all going to be OK."

"He's d—" I can't bring myself to say it.

"He's fine. I'm going to let go now, if you can be quiet. Can you do that for me? We don't want to wake the whole house."

We don't?

I nod.

He lifts his hand from my mouth and struggles to scoop Logan into his arms.

"He's fine."

I kiss the graying skin at Logan's temples and squeeze the wooden flesh of his hand. "He's not," I say. "He's dead . . ."

"No, Enka. He's alive, I promise. But I need to take him now. Get dressed and meet me in my cabin."

THE TEARS ON my face dry as I run through the dark cold house and the grain fields until I'm in front of Toru's modest cabin. I can see him through a window, his face gentle and focused. A fire crackles on the other side of his home, casting warm light and large flickering shadows on the walls. Where he sits, fluorescent grow lights wash him out.

Logan is seated across from Toru, perfectly upright and still. Toru looks up and sees me on the path. He rises and comes out to meet me.

"I don't understand," I say, still looking inside at Logan.

"I can explain." We go inside together, and he helps me sit down. He hands me a teacup and I almost cry again, this time with gratitude when I take a sip and taste whiskey. The burn at the back of my throat revives me. Logan is still sitting, as if sleeping peacefully on his chair. I can tell by the gentle rise and fall of his chest that he's breathing, alive.

"Logan . . . ? What's wrong with him?"

Toru grabs my hands and looks me in the eye, getting on his knees.

"There's nothing wrong with him. A slight malfunction from a change I made yesterday. I . . . wondered if this day would come, and I'm sorry I wasn't more proactive. Logan, your husband, is . . .

and I can't stress this enough . . . a real person. He's also the first prototype for Project Naiad."

"What?" My pulse accelerates again.

"He's the first—"

"No, I heard you. I just don't understand . . ."

"I've been the project lead for the last forty years, ever since Richard recruited me."

I can barely hear Toru over the hooves of my heart, thrashing against my rib cage. "I thought you worked with plants."

"My work began with bioengineering plants, but the intention was always the eventual programming of self-educational and sustaining systems in created intelligences."

"So what . . . Logan . . ."

"He's a created intelligence."

"What does that mean?" He can tell that I'm getting frustrated with his weird terminology.

"I think you would understand it better with the word 'clone.'"

"I'm sorry, that's . . . impossible. You're—" I look at the man in front of me, who sounds calm and completely rational, and I feel sorry for him. He clearly isn't in his right mind.

"Your husband is a clone."

I can't help it. I start to laugh. Is this a joke he and Logan have concocted together? But Logan gives no indication that he can hear me. I stop laughing and look from his blank expression to Toru's face.

"This isn't a joke then? Please tell me this is a joke." I begin to panic.

"No, Enka. Logan is a clone of his father."

"But that's not possible."

"It is possible, I assure you."

"But . . . I would know. He's my husband, I would know." I hate how childish and whiny I sound.

"It was my job to make sure you wouldn't." He pauses. "Monika and Richard tried for decades to conceive, but nothing worked. They were heartbroken when every conventional avenue for children failed. Monika wanted so badly to be a mother, of course, and Richard needed an heir. Initially, I was just brought in for Logan. The making of one child. But once it was successful, we realized that this kind of replication would have far-reaching consequences for everyone, which is why we began Project Naiad, Richard's pilot cloning program. Logan, for example, is a way for Richard to ensure that the trajectory of his company goes exactly as planned."

I begin pacing the room. "My husband is my father-in-law . . . for business reasons?"

"It's less absurd when you remember that hundreds of billions of dollars and no less than the future of humanity are at stake. The Dahl Corporation is more than a business. It'll soon be its own franchise . . . It functions as its own government and is an arm of the nation's governance. Companies are kingdoms, and dynasties have always left nothing to chance. These families have always been genetically engineered. What Richard is doing is the logical end point for our society's continued obsession with worldly control and dominance.

"I should mention"—Toru softens—"that, genetics aside, Logan is his own person. I know because I raised him. Nurture, in this instance, was more powerful than nature."

"But there is no nature. He's never been in a womb."

"And that's a formative experience you remember?" He sighs. "It's a lot to take in, I can imagine."

"Roy and Bastian . . ."

I look at my husband's face, a peaceful expression plastered on it.

I did give birth, right?

"Enka, you have two beautiful healthy boys."

"Nothing out of the ordinary about them?"

"That's right," he says firmly.

I reach out to touch Logan's arm, the skin I've stroked thousands of times. "Is he OK?"

"He's fine. Like I said, I made some changes yesterday during a regular checkup, and his system froze. Evidently, I went too far."

"So, what, you just press a button after and he wakes up?" My eyes move over his body, something I had assumed held no secrets from me.

"Nothing about his body differs from that of any other human. There are a few controls, for his safety or emergencies, but none that are physical. They're all remotely accessed."

"Does Logan know?"

"He does not. And I can't stress enough how important it is that he doesn't find out. Imagine if you found that out about yourself." He is silent for a moment. "You can't, right? It's an unimaginable thing. At best, it would cause confusion and pain. A lot of pain. Because remember, he is a real human being. His thoughts, his feelings, his love for you. All of that is real."

"At worst?"

"Catastrophe."

12

After some convincing, the board approves the SCAFFOLD procedure for Mathilde. News of my willingness to be Mathilde's volunteer, my selflessness, spreads through the art and technology industries. I find myself saying "thank you" over and over again when friends and reporters applaud my sacrifice.

I don't admit that I want to do this for myself, too. The idea that none of what happens next can occur without me—that Mathilde will be completely dependent on me—is intoxicating. Now I lose myself in fantasies of slipping into Mathilde's brain, of having complete and total access. I'll be a co-creator . . . so much more than a collaborator.

The device will be inserted in three months, giving the lab ample time to run additional tests and to set everything up with an abundance of caution. My brain needs to be analyzed to make sure I have capacity for the SCAFFOLD.

Time slips by too quickly and drags on too long. After Toru's revelation, I don't know how to be around Logan. I watch him constantly, looking for signs of what I've been told. He's confused by this new attention. "Everything OK?" he asks one day when he notices me staring at his arms, looking at the spacing between his arm hairs. If my father-in-law were here, would they be identical? Ostensibly, yes, but I can't imagine it.

One morning a couple of days after my conversation with Toru, I was still asleep when he reached for me. It was early, and my brain was sleepy enough that I forgot everything for a few blissful moments and gave myself over to him. I've always loved the way he grabs me, kisses me, pleasures me. I opened my eyes to better glimpse him between my thighs, and in his winking face saw such a resemblance to his father's that I froze. He paused, noticing a different kind of tension. "Is this OK?"

I leapt out of bed. The realization that I've been sleeping with my father-in-law all these years sent me running for the nearest toilet.

I was most uncomfortable when Logan and his father were to-gether. At a luncheon that the New York Botanical Garden held to honor Monika's charitable work in their conservation department, they were seated next to each other. I watched my father-in-law and his own act of conservation next to him. The way they cut their steaks and folded their napkins, even the little gap between incisor and canine—it matched: both had a piece of gristle lodged there. Richard caught me looking and winked. A memory forced its way to the top of my mind, of the first time we met. He winked and congratulated Logan. I had disliked him immediately . . . the way he looked at me like he was appraising a piece of art, gauging its value and place in his collection. Now I realize he had looked at me like I was a conquest, one of his own.

Watchfulness becomes disgust. I begin to shudder around Logan, and to avoid him as much as possible. I yank myself from his touch, only enduring contact with him in front of the kids. Even watching him touch Bastian and Roy fills me with unease.

Thankfully, we're both busy during this time, as he's working on the impending procedure, and I'm preparing for it.

"I'm just nervous about the surgery," I say whenever he asks me what's wrong.

I'm introduced to the doctors and technicians involved in the procedure. The actual implantation will take very little time, usually an hour or just under, but the adjustment period can be quite long. I'm given the access code: a series of movements to think in my mind. Throwing a ball into the air with my left hand, catching it in my right, watching it become a sparrow, and letting it fly away. I'll have to memorize these movements and practice thinking of them quickly enough to slip in and out of my own and Mathilde's minds. Separate from the access code, Mathilde and I have to choose a password together for the unlikely instance when one of us will need to override the hardware of the other, something only we will know. They also teach me how to navigate her mind. Any word I think or speak with focus will conjure a matrix of memories involving the subject matter. I should be able to move through them as I please. I'll have to get used to the idea of being a ghost or a silent observer while inhabiting her consciousness.

One month before the surgery, I'm not allowed to have much visual stimuli. I spend my days with a black cloth over my eyes, lying supine on the couch or bed, listening to meditative music and imagining the artworks Mathilde and I will make together. What will I discover in her mind? A file cabinet of curiosities? A computer with a search bar where I can riffle through my friend's experiences? Or maybe everything will be organized in various rooms, Mathilde my very own Bluebeard. And if memories are allocated their own spaces or floors, what dark cellar or dusty attic will I find myself housed in? What forbidden altar will there be for Beatrice?

An operations specialist I don't recognize pulls me aside one day, gently unhooking me from the machines and leading me to another room. I notice that his hands are shaking.

"I want to show you something," he says.

A video plays on a computer screen.

"I just want to make sure you understand what you're getting into." He pauses the video at a certain juncture to point at a large green splotch.

"This is the moment she loses Beatrice."

He presses play again and I watch the green spread. "Now let me play it from the beginning," he says. "There—" He points at the screen. "Did something happen? When she was a child?"

"Her parents died," I say, explaining an earlier bloom of vivid green.

"This would have been earlier, when she was eight or nine. There was no mention of an incident around this time in any of her interviews. I was hoping you had more information."

I bite my lip, remembering that Mathilde had alluded to something when we were discussing the possibility of the SCAFFOLD.

We watch the video again. I notice how prevalent the color green is, lining every groove of Mathilde's brain.

"I'm showing you this because . . . there have been some recent incidents regarding assimilation. Two of our longer-term companions were subjected to so much trauma, they lost the ability to mute it."

"My husband assured me that secondhand trauma has no long-term effect."

"Yes, and he's correct in most instances. But like I said, there have been two recent inhabitants who have needed psychiatric care because of the trauma they endured."

His forehead is beading with sweat. He is clearly taking a risk by telling me this without his superior's knowledge.

"Why are you telling me this? If my own husband didn't think it was worth mentioning . . . why you?"

"It wouldn't feel right," he stammers.

"I see. Thanks, I guess."

He flushes with relief.

"So, just to be clear. Her brain can influence my body?" I ask.

"We believe so, yes. And your brain."

"But I thought I would be able to heal her."

"Yes, but her levels of trauma are unusually high, compared with other patients we've had. There's an equal chance she could corrupt you."

FORTY-EIGHT HOURS BEFORE the surgery, I arrive at the Dahlhouse to stay overnight. They'll make a large incision at the hairline, the whole length of my forehead, before peeling my skin flap forward and implanting the SCAFFOLD. I had handled it a few weeks ago, before it had been through the necessary sanitation cycles, and found it surprisingly light, utterly unremarkable to hold and behold. It reminded me of the thin wire headbands sold in bulk at convenience stores, except that it widened considerably at the base where it would sit behind my ears. Once the transcranial device is inserted, they'll make sure it's synced and running before sewing the skin back to my hairline. The scarring should be minimal.

THE MORNING OF the surgery, Mathilde, Logan, and I walk over together from the house. Gunter, Dr. Hari, and a few other specialists are waiting to receive me at a facility that looks like Gunter's lab except bigger. Once I'm strapped in, Mathilde takes hold of one hand, and Logan grasps the other. A small Band-Aid covers a spot on her right temple where her pairing device was inserted a few weeks ago. Monika is here, too, and Frances, with a direct line to Richard, who is in Luxembourg.

As I fall asleep, the heavy laryngeal mask spewing anesthesia, I feel Mathilde squeezing my hand. She is saying something, and my consciousness strains against the drowsiness to hear.

"You breathe in, I breathe out."

WHEN I FEEL myself waking, I frantically think of the movements to access Mathilde's mind. I want to see if I can wake up in her mind. A sudden sound, a distorted crunching like bone against bone. I reflexively switch back into my own brain. Violently, maybe protectively. I can feel that one of my limbs has lashed out. Gritting my teeth, I try again. I need to know if the procedure was successful.

I AM SHOCKED when it works. A cold numbness seeps through my body. I am no longer Enka. Triggered by this realization, hundreds of images and memories of Enka flutter to life in Mathilde's mind. This is so different, so unexpected, from the files or rooms Enka had imagined. The experiences and memories are more like a flock of birds taking off at the mention of Enka's name. A sort of double consciousness occurs, a fracturing that allows Enka to observe herself.

This observer flits through and between these images and sees that the Enka recorded in this mind is at odds with the one Enka knows herself to be. This Enka is wise, powerful, and calm. This Enka is intelligent, thoughtful, and wildly creative. And where Enka has always thought of Mathilde as a bird at great height, soaring ever farther away from her, the observer now sees that Mathilde believes Enka to be just as mysterious. A sunk stone in the depths of the ocean that she longs to uncover, holding her breath longer to dive deeper each time.

And there is, beneath that layer of love that is mostly for Enka, something else. The observer feels that she can traverse it. Can climb down, following a path in the crevices of the brain, lifting the folds as she goes, as if they are thatched eaves of flesh dripping above her. The more she descends, the more difficult it becomes to breathe. As she comes closer to the tenderness, she can feel that it is swollen and quaking, and suddenly she realizes that this must be Beatrice. She retracts the graying hand she had briefly outstretched and climbs upward because she can, because she isn't just Mathilde anymore, but Enka-as-Mathilde, and, together, they are stronger.

LATE STYLE

1

They told me I kicked myself awake. The first thing I remember seeing when my eyes opened was a pair of legs juddering in front of me. It took a few moments for me to realize the legs were connected to my body.

"She's settling in. A lot to get used to."

The voice is coming from the man next to me, Dr. Hari, who supervised the procedure. The other physicians are gathered around, looking at me expectantly. Beyond them, I notice a window. Through it, Mathilde. I start choking when I try to sit up from the table. My legs spasm and my arms tremble. My body is communicating the need to see her, the urge I have to close the space between us. To be as connected physically as we are psychically.

The doctors hurry to stabilize me. Mathilde rushes into the room, and I grasp her face, violently pulling it toward my own.

My voice is hoarse when I begin to speak, the words struggling to rise from what feels like an unfamiliar throat. "She was beautiful," I say. "Beatrice. I saw her. I know her . . . She was so beautiful."

Mathilde starts to cry when she realizes what I mean. We cling to each other and sob, snot and tears mixing and running down our faces and arms as we mourn Beatrice together. The grief, now shared, becomes almost joyous.

remain at the Dahlhouse for a week of on-site monitoring. When I'm allowed to return home, I find that the building has been equipped with machines that will track my assimilation for ongoing research. From what I can tell, the integration has been smooth.

The first few months are difficult. The cognitive dissonance is so great, I'm constantly disoriented. I can only inhabit Mathilde's mind for fifteen minutes a day, and my body needs to be at rest, in a safe and soft space during habitation. By week three, I'm able to bear a half hour a day. Once I can comfortably spend an hour in her consciousness, Dr. Hari works with me on being able to maintain control of my body while inhabiting Mathilde's mind. I'm encouraged to vary daily activities as much as possible while occupying her mind. I have breakfast as Mathilde one day, and I can't figure out if I'm eating *as* her or *with* her. I brush our hair the next day. It's one thing to hear that your mind will have to learn a new body, and a different thing to experience it. Her mind isn't used to my inner ears and the specific way they relate to gravity and motion. It often takes the whole hour just to regain a sense of balance.

THE BOYS NOTICE when I'm inhabiting my body and Mathilde's mind simultaneously. Logan and I agreed to tell them I was recovering from a procedure, but we withheld the nature of the operation.

"Mommy isn't speaking right," or "Mommy is moving weird," they say. And it's true. Inhabiting Mathilde's consciousness affects the way I speak, gesture, and walk. It unsettles them to see my skin stuffed with a stranger.

Another thing that takes getting used to is the trauma. Accessing the darker matter of traumatic memories leaves a kind of residue. A soot that clings to me. When I reemerge in my own consciousness, I often find my mood affected, darkened by her despair.

There are pleasant surprises, too. As Mathilde, I remember music I've never heard before, and these songs are accompanied by strong emotions. How had I never heard Szymanowski's shimmering piano works? Why hadn't she introduced me to *Seven Pillars*, Sandbox Percussion's euphoric album? A melody or rhythm will bring feelings of intense anger, regret, or even sorrow to the point of nausea. I never knew how affected Mathilde is by music or the dimensional quality it adds to her work. Music has always been something I've enjoyed peripherally, but so much of her art is directly related to what she hears or chooses to listen to while she works. I feel as if I've happened upon a secret language, each of her works encoded. Beatrice's gestation accompanied by the Verona Quartet's sublime recording of Beethoven's late quartets, the blind scraping of the silverfish conceptualized while listening to Caroline Shaw's otherworldly compositions. The making of her father to the slow movement of Mahler's Ninth Symphony, the piece of music that most wrestles with death's inexorable power. I lose hours listening to music as Mathilde.

She and I are instructed to limit our in-person interactions for the first six months, until we're both used to the SCAFFOLD. This way, there won't be too much confusion or overlap. We talk once a week and keep our conversations short. Focused on our upcoming exhibit. I want to ask how she is and how she's feeling, but we've been told explicitly to avoid any talk of emotions. At least I can drop into her present. I feel that she misses me, but that she's keeping herself busy. Planning exhibits and thinking about new works. Cooking, reading, and going out for the occasional lunch with a mutual friend. Beneath the neat layer of routine, I can sense that she's worried about me and, surprisingly, somewhat afraid of me.

COMMUNION, THE FIRST joint exhibit by Mathilde Wojnot-Cho and Enka Yui-Dahl, opens nine months after assimilation. The procedure, my awakening, and the emotional reunion with Mathilde had been captured on video. They are blown up and projected on a giant screen at the LORA, confronting attendees as soon as they enter the space. The show is a modification of the idea Mathilde had before her scan. One that shows "the impermanent structure of the body. The beginning of an out-of-body of work."

For opening night, a special performance. A small stage had been set up with two easels, a canvas on each. The attendees picked a subject matter to be painted: a vase containing three tulips. I was to paint one as myself and the other as Mathilde.

I painted a blue-and-white vase with three dark purple tulips, each with a bright yellow streak. Enka-as-Mathilde painted an abstract of black and white stripes with neon orange smears that somehow conveyed the joy of encountering tulips rather than merely representing them. The drastic difference between our interpretations convinced everyone of the two different women now inhabiting one body.

The exhibit was a critical smash. The projected brain scans "functioned as a disco ball in the space, lighting everything with buoyant technicolor chaos. The joy of empathy, fully realized." The curtain that rose to reveal me to the audience was done with "such tantalizing slowness, one can almost imagine what a caveman must have felt in front of the universe's first lifted skirt." A life-size replica of Mathilde had been made, and from it, I emerged, clawing through the synthetic skin and stepping out of the husk of her body. *ARTnews* wrote that it was like watching "the unveiling of a bride in an exhibit where Mathilde gave herself away."

CERTAIN REVIEWS LEAVE me conflicted. They speak of the second painting so glowingly in contrast to the first that I can't help but take offense. I console myself with the fact that, technically, I did both paintings, and none of this would be possible without me.

Privately, I'm unimpressed by the exhibit. It's conceptually strong but visually weak. While the science of the SCAFFOLD is interesting, translating it to art is impossible. Those who can't switch into Mathilde's brain aren't able to be gratified in any real way. They can only see in two dimensions what I feel in three.

3

At the one-year mark, I can comfortably inhabit Mathilde's mind for two hours at a time. There are still mismatched expectations between brain and body, but they have become less frequent, and I'm expected to master it soon. The recovery takes all my time and focus, as well as Logan's. Sometimes I'm able to forget what I know about him. But moments of shared tenderness and joy and even the drudgery of shared parental duties become impossible when I remember, and I wish I didn't know.

During the hours that I inhabit Mathilde, I tend to stay in my studio, drawing and painting. I'm testing the waters, flexing the skills burrowed in her brain, wondering if they are as unlimited as I'd always imagined. Was it really as Helen Frankenthaler said? That technique determines aesthetic as much as aesthetic determines a new medium? With Mathilde's technique "applied" by my body, could I now unlock the mystery of her taste?

I'm continually in awe of the arm that is mine and not mine.

The first time I hold a pencil and put it to paper as Mathilde, I write the name "Enka Yui-Dahl" over and over again. Not only does the script look different, but the action of writing feels unfamiliar. Within those lines, a new grace and gestural pull. A tendency toward the middles of letters. Each stroke proof of our shared existence, all of it transference, her mind and my body yoked together. And yet, when I write Mathilde's name and compare it with Mathilde's handwriting, the names don't look as if they were written by the same person. It's close, but not quite. A subtle aberration or slight distortion. Could it be that part of me doesn't want to be subsumed? Or is Mathilde's muscle memory somehow resistant to being shared? This possibility devastates me. I want to be authentic.

Out of an abundance of caution, I continue to limit the time I spend with her in real life. I know from being in her mind that this decision confuses her, but verbally, she's understanding. I take her at her word and hope that she's content to speak over the phone once a week or so. The few times we saw each other in the flesh, it was too jarring to be confronted with her body, something I've begun to view as mine.

Even once I can inhabit without difficulty, I'm reluctant to look too deeply into Mathilde's memories. There is the trauma, of course, but I'm also worried what the memories might reveal about our relationship. The idea of perceiving our friendship from her perspective has begun to terrify me. "Invasive" had been the word Mathilde used when first introduced to the SCAFFOLD procedure.

Curiosity goads me until I finally give in. I wait for an afternoon when Logan is in Argentina, and the twins are with their grandfather, so that I can explore our connection undisturbed. In

Mathilde's mind, I utter my name, the equivalent of running a search. Immediately, seeds or pollen, each one a different thought or memory, begin to fall, accompanied by a vague hum. I sift through it all for something that can be called the beginning, the chaos becoming chorus as I search. The more recent memories and experiences make chords when they are summoned, each previous memory changing the next by adding a new strand or note. The most recent interactions are massive—symphonic in their many layers and accumulated meanings. I begin to look, or rather listen, for the sparsest melodic fragments, knowing that these will bring me to the events most deeply hidden in the past.

By this method, I find a group of memories from Mathilde's earliest days at BCAD. I'm amazed to learn that even before we'd formally met, I had cut a presence in Mathilde's mind. There was Enka in a newspaper article, a self-conscious smile on her face next to the *Dance Dance Revolution* experiment that was part of her application. There was the first sighting of Enka in real life, at the library. Even lovelier than everyone had been saying. Her long blue-black hair fell over a shoulder as she looked through books on Agnes Martin with an expression of deep focus. There was Enka's face, dark eyes sparkling as she carefully considered Joan Mitchell's *Edrita Fried*. Riding her bike across campus, jacket billowing, headphones tangled in the hair streaming behind her. At the farmers' market grabbing beetroots to dye with and stuffing them into a tote already full of fluffy carrot tops.

As Mathilde, I see the look of frantic concern on Enka's face as she tries to revive my slumped body when she finds me collapsed in the bathroom stall. The determination with which she presses a hand to my small studio window every day, the only view I have outside of the grief under which I am buried. I feel how that repeated action builds meaning, rupturing the wall of sorrow that fate built, and which I dutifully maintained. I hear the whispered words Enka shares with the sculpture of my father. Feel the wind getting knocked out of me when Enka hugs me immediately afterward. The slow tug and eventual release of my heart when she lies down beside him.

Unable to bear it any longer, I dive back into my own mind. My face is wet, and I am completely overcome, overwhelmed. I have never seen myself like this before.

I had not meant the same to Mathilde. Maybe, I meant more.

4

onika and the rest of the board are unhappy with me. Even though none of them have experienced anything like the SCAFFOLD procedure, they seem certain about how long it should take for a life-altering surgery to lead to profitability. I've endured months of nagging emails and voice messages. The latest missive, lobbed this afternoon, is filled with the usual accusations.

"You can't just coast forever. It's been almost a year since *Communion* and Mathilde's fan base is ravenous for more. The procedures and tests were expensive, and we can hold Mathilde liable for all of it."

Not the most effective threat since Monika and I share the same endless well of wealth, one I wouldn't hesitate to extend to Mathilde. But they are right. I've been neglecting my duties, instead savoring the discovery of Mathilde's mind. All my life, I've choked on the bitterness of having a mind that doesn't feel equipped to do what my soul wants. I was driven by the distance between what I could imagine and what I could put on paper. Eventually, I realized that what I lack isn't skill but imagination itself.

Now, in Mathilde's mind, my body depletes itself, drawing and painting and making. I could spend hours, days, entire lives looking at art through her eyes. The way she interprets the most quotidian objects and transforms them into things worthy of close attention is singular. The intuition with which she mixes paint colors to make shades never seen before is captivating. The brushes she chooses and how she grasps them, the occasional use of a soft press of the hand or the wood end of a brush to stipple or define— these are all revelatory things I adopt into my own art practice.

When I tell Mathilde how I feel, she shrugs it off. "Everyone does things in their own way. My intuition isn't necessarily good, it's just new to you. I'm sure I would feel the same way in your mind." I'm only grateful she will never know how untrue that is.

Now that I finally have the imagination, I realize that the appeal of being an artist has never been the prestige or fame, but the satisfaction of working toward a worthy goal. With this discovery, it's almost impossible to think about doing something as limited and limiting, as contrived, as an exhibit.

I give myself another few weeks to pass time in the screening room of Mathilde's brain. I read a book with her past self, or watch her thoughts collide in the present. I learn so much about her like this. How her losses caused her to resist relationships. How those losses also foster the fiercest attachments. On the screen, I especially love remembering our past together, realizing that every memory I have is only half remembered.

Eventually, I begin to mine Mathilde's consciousness for ideas. Each day, I drop into her mind, ambulating deeper amid the starry connections, the dense fleshy corridors, and the slow glug of traveling blood. One day, on one of these walks, the long pink passageway begins to darken until the landscape before me is completely gray. The tissue dries and the veined texture beneath my feet becomes more pronounced until I reach the edge of something I can't fathom. I walk in circles along the edge of the void, trying to understand the center. Not a wound like Beatrice; it's something mangled but alive and shuddering, not merely dead but necrotizing, threatening to engulf the tips of my feet when I get too close. I try to absorb as much of the trauma as I can by laying my hands on the affected places, but the surrounding darkness is unchanged. I've stumbled upon a place of such destructive and pervasive sadness, I worry my mind will be permanently altered by the experience.

For three days, I circle this memory and crawl back to the dripping pink flesh, climbing out of her mind defeated. Each day, the length of gray grows longer, the black void bleeding further. When I'm back safely in my own mind, I feel physical symptoms. A stickiness that lodges in my throat: I can't stop imagining the sick gray pustules from this mangled site infecting my own body.

On the fourth day, I allow my toes to tip over into the chaos, the rest of me slurped in before I have a chance to withdraw. I had expected an immediate plunge into darkness, a cold heavy sorrow that would be difficult to escape. Instead, as soon as I immerse myself, I'm drenched in a diffuse warmth.

A conduit opens between me and some other thing or person, comprised of an overwhelming love and directness. My ghost has never felt such peace. It's as if the body we share has been tranquilized. I put my hand through the golden strands of the conduit, watching how it makes my limbs glow. I pull on one and see it strengthen, the radiance obliterating my view for a moment. And now, in front of me, a small figure appears. A young Mathilde, gawky body and Buddha cheeks, flowing with a love that shines in her glistening black eyes. I have never seen anything so beautiful. I watch as she moves her lips and I listen closely to her intoning. From her childish voice a deeper resonance, an incantation. Out of her words, I hear only a few, including the name for the one she is speaking to. The gold around me, I realize, is her faith.

The strands start to flicker, and I pull my hand back, afraid I am causing the disruption. I sense something on the other end changing. The vastness has narrowed and solidified. It begins to speak. To make requests of Mathilde. My ghost watches as Mathilde fulfills those requests, horrific, diabolical requests, uttered by a robed proxy of her god. Slowly, the gold strands deaden, withering like straw. Heat radiates from our shared body and my consciousness understands this to be rage, even hatred. Eventually, the heat burns off, leaving agony and sorrow. Shame and self-hatred. I circle young Mathilde, wishing desperately to make her glow again, to bring back the joy I had seen. But there is nothing I can do. And while the narrowing had been a black time, responsible certainly for much of the trauma in Mathilde's life, it was the loss of her faith, that vast gold-edged love, that was ultimately most damaging and painful, impossible to come back from.

5

When I return to my own consciousness, I find blood on my arms from where my fingernails have dug into the flesh, my unconscious wanting nothing more than to hug Mathilde as tightly as I can.

She has never talked to me about the loss of her faith or the events that precipitated it. Now that I have experienced these horrors for myself, I understand her in a new way. Her entire oeuvre, especially the earliest works, are contextualized by these memories. The confessions in *He Is Risen* were a way to confront that deep betrayal by an authority figure, an attempt to suture the wound that ran through her life. But it didn't work, and she evades these memories, not knowing that avoidance keeps her stuck in a trauma loop. I had tried to absorb the trauma by putting a hand to the graying places—to no effect. Instead, the char transferred to my hands. Dimly, I remember the reason I had submerged myself in this memory—not only to heal Mathilde, but to discover something I can use artistically. I have to find something else . . . It would be too intrusive, exploitative even, to use this experience as material. But I have seen how the numbness is growing, needing to be cauterized, and I begin to dream of a work that could heal her.

To PUBLICIZE *ABSOLUTION*, a video is released a week before the exhibit opens, and it becomes one of the last things to go viral in the dying internet space. It's a short clip, showing me dressed in a white T-shirt, black jeans, and sneakers, walking up to a church and entering it. Inside, I happen upon a young man and ask for a name. He looks at the filming camera with apprehension, but leads me to an office behind the nave of the church.

"Father Patrick," I say when I reach an elderly man in his seventies.

"Yes?" he says, looking at me quizzically.

"You won't recognize me in this body, but my name is Mathilde Wojnot-Cho. I am a performance artist. For a duration of two years when I was a child, you molested me repeatedly during weekly confessions. I am not pressing charges, nor am I interested in retribution in any normal sense of that word. I would like to invite you to have a series of conversations with me over the span of a few months. I would like it to be something that is healing for both of us."

The video cuts to black with a last frame of the priest's face. What isn't shown in the video is his response. The way his face crumples. The quiet, strangled sobs. He puts a heavy hand on my shoulder, and in the lines of his lifted and sopping wet face, I read gratitude.

ABSOLUTION OPENS ON the first day of spring, and not since the Van Gogh show in 1936 have there been as many people queued outside of the MoMA for an opening. The overflow is content to stand outside: if they can't make it inside for the conversation, they can at least find out if the priest agreed to participate.

OVER THE COURSE of three months, Father Patrick sits on a platform in front of viewers for five hundred hours, in total silence. For the first week, I join him, describing in great detail how his actions affected Mathilde's life. Tears silently stream down his face—and this briefly brings back the popularity of the GIF.

Father Patrick continues to sit for the rest of the exhibition, showing up every day to large crowds jeering and protesting religious institutions, enduring death threats and physical intimidation. Every few days, I drop into Mathilde's mind to visit the site of her childhood trauma, and to watch it heal.

The seat I had occupied is opened to others and, slowly, people come to sit and speak to him. Other victims, his own and ones of other priests, come from all over the world to tell their stories. To be heard and held, to make peace and move on.

Reporters often wait for him before and after the exhibit hours. Most of them want to know why he agreed to do the exhibit and why he comes back daily. Only once does he break the vow of silence that followed him to the end of his life. He doesn't explain or justify his actions. He only gives thanks to Mathilde for giving him the opportunity to repent and atone.

6

On the last day of the exhibit, I sit across from him once more. At the end of our allotted time, I rise and ask the audience to bow in prayer.

"I absolve you of your sins in the name of my past, my present, and my future. I relinquish the power you have over my life. Amen." A chorus of amens follow.

A small reception for the highest tier of donors to the museum is scheduled for the evening, and I head to the room to wait, not wanting to run into any audience members or Father Patrick.

Mathilde appears in front of me when I enter, an apparition so sudden and unexpected, I freeze, unsure if she's real.

"Enka," Mathilde says.

"Hi," I say, trying to brush off the surprise.

The waiters around us run their fingers over the tablecloths and pour more ice into champagne buckets.

Awkwardly, Mathilde and I hug.

"Are you . . . yourself right now? Or are you me?"

A pause as I switch back to myself.

"I'm me," I say.

Relief on Mathilde's face. "Can we talk for a second?"

"Of course. I'm so happy to see you . . . I didn't think you'd be here. Monika said you might not be able to make it . . ."

"I know." She looks genuinely sorry. "I didn't know how to respond, I guess. When I got your message about *Absolution*."

"What do you mean?" I ask.

"I guess I was confused by it. The message informed me about the exhibit, instead of asking me about it . . . Why didn't you talk to me about it first?"

"Well, the message was meant to be the start of a dialogue."

"But . . . was it really? You were already so far along in the planning. I saw the promotional video before I heard from you." She takes a deep breath and lets it empty slowly. "You should have asked me about this before getting the foundation involved. Before working on it. If you had asked, I'm not sure I would have said yes."

"I *did* ask your blessing."

"You didn't, Enka."

Didn't I?

"I . . . get confused sometimes . . . I'm sorry. I thought for sure that I had asked."

"Enka, we've barely spoken since the procedure. It's impossible to get in touch with you . . . You never respond to my emails or messages, and you don't answer my calls. How can you possibly think that you asked me?"

"But that isn't true. Our weekly calls—"

"The ones that stopped more than a year ago?"

"I'm just so busy now . . . and you know that this is all for you, right? To produce something for your foundation. I could tell how challenging these memories were for you to face, and also how much you wanted to . . . Not only could I tell, I felt it *as* you. You're the one who said the public needs to be reminded of their own feelings, to keep from numbness. Don't you think that should apply to us, too? I saw it . . . *growing*, and I was afraid. I did it for you. That's what the SCAFFOLD is. You're not alone anymore. Every terrible thing that has happened to you is something that has happened to me, too. I thought it would be like Beatrice. That you'd just be so glad not to be alone in that pain anymore."

"Don't cry," Mathilde mumbles.

I wipe the tears from my face, feeling misunderstood and childishly sensitive. "Now I've made it all about myself."

"Enka, no. All I'm trying to say is, I didn't consent to being healed."

Her words come as a total shock to me. "But why would you want to hold on to this trauma? The whole point . . . is to heal you."

"When we were in school, what he did really defined me. I can see it in all of my past works, how reactive they were. I was frozen in this weird way in which my entire identity was just that of someone processing trauma. But I did it, and it was important to work through it in that way."

"I see."

"What happened to your promise, Enka? We were supposed to do everything together."

"We do! This is a collaboration with you!"

"You know what I mean. You promised to ask for permission before accessing parts of my mind. Should I have gotten that in writing? I mean, what's next? Are you going to magically heal the loss of my daughter, too? Am I going to wake up one day without the pain that has been the only reminder of the greatest thing that's ever happened to me?"

She takes another shaky breath. "I'm starting to wonder if this is really what I want. It's just so . . . unnatural."

"Well, I don't know if the person who escaped to the desert to kill herself while making an incense cone out of her dead daughter's body is the best judge of what 'natural' is."

Her dark eyes flicker between confusion and pain before landing on anger.

"I'm sorry, Mathilde, I didn't mean that. I don't know why I said it . . ."

"Leave Beatrice alone," she says in a hoarse, guttural tone I've never heard from her before.

I begin to cry again, this time out of an overwhelming sense of shame. "You're right. I should have asked. I mean, I did, but not the right you. I can see why that was an awful thing to do. I'm really sorry. I would never, with Beatrice. I'll ask, I—"

"I'm serious. You do not have my consent to go anywhere near Beatrice." She looks at me with distrust and something else. It takes all my strength not to dive into her mind, to see what she's thinking of me now.

"I won't. Please forgive me. This will never happen again."

"It shouldn't have happened in the first place."

"I know, and . . ."

"You know what the worst thing is about all of this?"

I can't help myself. "What?"

"There's no off switch. I can't just boot you out of my mind."

"Is that something you want?"

"It is." She softens. "Maybe not forever, but for now. I need a break, which means you need to take a break, too. Can you do that?"

"Of course." My words come out like a whisper.

7

But it isn't so easy to stop. I have responsibilities as Mathilde. Duties the foundation expects me to fulfill. Panicked, I call Monika to explain the situation. I'm worried that Mathilde has already called her . . . is somehow already in Gunter's chair, getting ready to undergo a removal of her pairing device.

"I don't see the problem. She won't know if you're inhabiting, right?" Monika asks.

"But if I continue to teach and work as her . . ."

"Leave it to me. Honestly, I'm a little surprised at the ingratitude. She's upset at you for healing her deepest, darkest traumas? Her identification with her pain is troubling. She's obviously not well enough to give or deny consent. You did the right thing, Enka. *Absolution* was a huge success. It was her most powerful work yet, and if she was a mentally healthy individual, she'd be able to see that, and to thank you for it."

Mathilde and I don't speak, but I know Monika has informed

her that the boundary she tried to put between us is in breach of her conservatorship. I'm sure my use of Monika as a go-between hurts her even more, but I keep myself busy so as not to think about it too much. This will blow over . . . and she'll understand someday.

Mathilde doesn't answer or return my calls, so I drop into her mind. I watch the moment Monika informed her of my continued visitation and feel the pain of that betrayal. All-encompassing. Immobilizing. It hurts to feel the anger she has toward the world, and especially toward me. It's painful enough that I begin to worry about her doing something we would both regret. What would happen if she were to take her own life? Would our connection sever? Would I experience it? Go with her? I think about helping her through this time without her knowledge, but I don't have the time or energy to hew the block of obsidian grief that envelops her. I need to focus on doing the best possible job as her representative. We can't both be depressed.

I stop dropping into her present. Focus on the past, where I'm able to control which thoughts and memories I see and hear. I only want to experience what is pertinent to me in the moment. Joy, instead of perpetual sadness.

Eventually, the guilt I have for continuing to work as her lessens and is replaced with frustration. She's making plenty of money from the work she does through me and, thus, has all the time in the world to devote to anything she wants. I've set her free in so many ways, and all she wants is a cage.

Although I miss her, I can't deny that this is the happiest time of my life. I am, in body, if not in name, established as a major artist. As Mathilde, I teach a few courses in addition to exhibiting once every year or two, after frenzied periods of thinking, creating, and producing. The rest of my time is spent being a dutiful wife, mother, and public figure. There are so many roles I'm expected to play, including hers, and they take all my energy. There are simultaneously a book, a movie, and a Broadway show in development about me and Mathilde, the best friends who became one artist. A "Day in the Life" article that chronicles how I split my time between motherly responsibilities and creative duties as Mathilde is so popular, they print and sell physical copies of it. The public can't seem to get enough of the talented yet haunted artist and her devoted best friend.

It's always been hard to stop inhabiting, but with each passing year, that difficulty only increases. I'll watch a movie with Logan and the boys and want to reexperience it from Mathilde's perspective. Something will happen with the twins, and I'll want to know how Mathilde would handle the situation. When the first few years after the SCAFFOLD integration transpire without incident, the monitoring is relaxed, and I'm more or less put in charge of overseeing my at-home equipment. Occasional surveillance by specialists is still necessary for their research, but as long as I'm productive, I'm trusted. As a result, it goes mostly unnoticed when I begin to inhabit Mathilde all the time.

8

Monika is easier to deal with when I have Mathilde's intelligence and artistic insights at my disposal, and though she sometimes looks as if she wants to ask who she's speaking to, she never does. The children can't seem to tell anymore, though I often imagine a slight preference for my company when I'm inhabiting Mathilde.

The only person who notices is Logan. I had been desperate to keep his interest when we first got together. After the twins were born, I wasn't so afraid of losing him. I allowed myself to be too tired, my body too sore from childbirth and nursing, for sex. And then he had been so busy for the next few years that when he was home, the passion we could ignite in each other was intense. That was before I knew the truth about him. Though I can see how confused and hurt he is when I rebuff his advances, I can't help but recoil from him. Sometimes I can forget that he wasn't born so much as made, but I always remember when he touches me. Sex with Logan has become something I stomach, not something I ever desire.

Besides, my assimilation with Mathilde's mind has dulled almost every other experience, especially sex, which is routinely touted as something that makes two or more people "one." The idea of physical union is so laughably superficial compared to what I have with Mathilde. So unnecessarily messy and emotionally ungratifying.

So one night, when Logan rolls over to my side of the bed and begins to trace lines on my arms with his fingertips, I slip into Mathilde's mind. And in the same way that I access her skills to think or to draw, I find the abilities she has in this craft. Dexterously, I flip myself over, angling my body in new ways. My back contorts as my stomach muscles twitch deeper and slower. I bring Logan's hands up to squeeze, marveling at the lack of self-consciousness in this body, the abundance of hunger, and the joy of its being fulfilled. Logan, not used to such assertiveness, loses control quickly, and for the first time since I learned of his true nature, my body responds. I tip my head back, hearing the pleasure erupt from my throat, my whole body a plucked instrument thrumming with rapture. I slither back into my own consciousness before he can notice anything, convulsing with aftershocks as I fall to the side of the bed. We catch our breath, a deep satisfaction and earned exhaustion spreading warmth throughout my body. That's when I notice Logan isn't his usual self, spread out on the bed with a look of quiet bliss.

"Everything OK?" I ask, registering his hunched compact form, his back to me.

"I'm not my dad," Logan says quietly.

I make a face, knowing he can't see me. *You literally are*, I think to myself.

"What do you mean by that?"

"I'm not a cheater, Enka. Did you think I wouldn't notice?"

When he turns to look at me, it's with an expression of betrayal.

"It was just something I was trying. For fun."

"Fun for who?"

"Isn't this every guy's dream? A threesome?" I chuckle, trying to lighten the mood.

"Do you even care that it wasn't consensual?" His face grimaces with pain.

"You know better than anyone that Mathilde didn't have any idea that was happening," I say.

"I don't just mean her. I mean me. Maybe I'm not every guy. Maybe I just want to have sex with my wife."

"I'm sorry," I say.

"I feel violated, Enka." The look of disgust and misery on his face makes me realize how serious he is.

"I wasn't thinking, Logan. But you're right, of course. It'll never happen again . . ."

"I wish . . ." Logan says before trailing off.

"What?"

He shakes his head.

"Say it."

"I wish you could just be yourself," he finally says.

"You don't even know how ironic that is, coming from you."

"What do you mean by that?"

"Nothing," I say, regretting going that far. "I'm just tired."

"I wish you could see yourself the way I see you," Logan says.

I tap the windows, enabling their screens to show a recent *Times* profile, issues of *Wired* and *Artforum*, their covers emblazoned with my face. "Logan, look at my life now. Look at these. What did being myself ever get me?"

Logan's expression becomes even more miserable and hopeless. "Me? Our beautiful sons?"

"That's not enough," I hear myself say.

Logan looks like I've slapped him.

"You don't mean that," he whispers.

"Logan, I just meant . . . I'm allowed to *want* a career. I'm allowed to be ambitious, to want success outside of a family."

"Of course, but you can be all of those things without being someone else. I've helped you so much with your career, Enka . . . I've given you everything. From the moment we met, I've given you everything."

Anger courses through my body, and something else I've never felt toward him. Resentment, for making things so easy for me. For erasing any difficulty or challenge that would have given me something to communicate. Once I let myself feel it, it overtakes everything.

"Given me everything? Maybe . . . but only as a way of holding on to me. Holding me back. Maybe I'd be happy being myself if I'd had more time to develop as an artist. Mathilde has never been emotionally entangled. If you hadn't made up some bullshit artist-in-residence role at Pathway to keep me invested in you and stuck in technology as a medium, who knows where I would be now?"

"What are you talking about? You were a technology artist before we met!" His voice lowers. "An unsuccessful one. You needed me to get anything shown."

My whole body feels like it's in flames. "Excuse me?"

"You heard me." His voice is rough and strangely hollow. "You needed me, just like you need Mathilde now. It's so fucked up. What you've done to her. You pretend it's all for her, but I see how much you like it. Tell me you can be honest with yourself, at least. You love having a little monkey in your mind that you can make dance whenever you want. I mean . . . there *has* to be a limit to how much you can take from a person. That's what I keep thinking to myself. I was sure that, eventually, you'd stop or create boundaries. But it's only gotten worse. You used to give me so much shit about my dad, but look at you now. You're more exploitative than he's ever been."

He couldn't have hurt me more if he'd physically hit me.

"Funny you should mention your dad. I wasn't going to say it earlier because I was being nice. But as long as we're being honest . . . you are the least yourself anyone has ever been. You're not even a real person, Logan. You're a prototype for Project Naiad. Yeah, Toru grew you in a petri dish."

The color has drained from Logan's face. "That isn't funny, Enka."

"Who's laughing? You think I like being married to my disgusting father-in-law's clone? Why else do you think I literally have to vacate my body to have sex with you?"

Big fat tears are falling from Logan's face now, and he looks just like the twins. He clenches his fists. "Take it back. Right now."

I open my mouth, suddenly wishing I could.

9

had tried to take it back. Laughter sputtered from my mouth as I tried to make him believe what should have been infinitely more believable: that I was joking, that I loved him, that I was just lashing out. But he grabbed the travel bag by the bedroom door and stopped unzipping to look at his hands. They were pale and shaking. He inspected his arms, as if searching for invisible ants, and began to claw at his wrists until he broke skin and drops of perfectly red blood came reluctantly. He crashed onto the bed. I tried to hold him, to comfort him. "Don't touch me," he choked. His eyes were wide with fear as he stood and backed away from me. He grabbed his things and ran.

Logan has always traveled incessantly for work, but this is different. He doesn't answer my calls. I leave messages pleading with him and his assistants, who haven't heard from him in days. "Your sons miss you," I tell him. *I miss you, too*, I want to add. And really, what's the difference? In the end, it's all semantics. Toru had said he was a real person. Each passing moment fills me with

more shame and remorse. The twins look so much like their father, I find myself apologizing to them late at night after they've
fallen asleep.

ABSOLUTION HAS BECOME a worldwide movement. Young men and
women everywhere are empowered to confront those who have
hurt them, often recording these exchanges and uploading them
to the internet, which becomes a community again, for just a moment, instead of a ghost town. I'm invited to speak at conferences
and important international gatherings, and to consult for well-
ness companies. I'm giving a talk about sexual harassment at a
local university when I collapse. Massive shocks threaten to rip my
head apart when I'm startled awake by a student moments later. I
drop back into my own consciousness and from there observe the
disturbances to the SCAFFOLD. I've never felt the actual device
before, but now my forehead grows hot from the inside out. The
hair at my temples begins to curl and I try not to panic. Just when
I think it'll burn through my skin, it begins to cool. When I lower
my hands, forty or so students are crowded around me. Watching
in silence.

I scramble to my feet and mumble excuses as I gather my
things. Outside, I take in deep breaths of the fresh campus air.
Part of me is still afraid that, at any moment, the device in my
head will become hostile again. *What the hell just happened?*

On the way home, I get a call from Monika. Her voice is so
frantic, I don't hear what she's telling me the first two times. Finally, I understand. The pairing device in Mathilde has been remotely tampered with and she's likely very ill. Have I heard from
her? *Not for months,* I think to myself. When I tell Monika what

happened in the classroom, she agrees that it was likely a reaction to the disturbance to Mathilde's pairing device. Has she finally decided to take back what's hers? I divert the car, finally heading toward the address she gave me long ago.

SMALL IS THE first thought I have upon seeing the space where Mathilde has been living for the last few years. I recognize it from the few glimpses I've seen during drop-ins. A small bed in the corner is topped with lumpy quilts and yellowed paperbacks. The sink is cluttered with mismatched dishes, and the kitchen counter is crusted with crumbs and food sediment. There's a bathtub in the kitchen, rusting through. While it's not without a certain charm, I can see at least a dozen health hazards. I'm just thinking that it doesn't look like a place Mathilde would live . . . doesn't look like the home of an artist—and then I see them: large, abstract black-and-white paintings. I recognize them as something "I" could have produced, but never thought to, which strikes me as strange. A brief glimpse of these works reminds me of that deeper intuition and organizational logic Mathilde has always had, that I hadn't been privy to. When I painted, I could arrange colors, but I never made them sing, never coaxed stories from them with oil, pigment, and goat hair. Her painting is so fine, it makes you question the canvas beneath. In certain places, it looks to be velvet, in others a crumbled powder, and still, in the corner, there is a bit of color you'd swear was painted on a swath of silk. And I can see how she painted with her hands, dipping, spreading, and etching paint onto the work, kissing the canvas with her fingertips.

I drag my eyes from the paintings to continue my search for

Mathilde and see her in the space between a dusty couch and a coffee table covered in abandoned mugs. Her face is the wrong color, and her limbs shouldn't be able to contort that way. I run to her, place a finger on her neck, and find an echo of life there. She's breathing, but she's hot, so terribly hot. I pull her out from the tight space and haul her to the car. I blast the air-conditioning as high as it will go, shivering as I drive us to the Dahlhouse. I drive recklessly, narrowly avoiding accident after accident. Almost daring something to happen. I don't know which I want more: for fate to spare me or to strike me down.

In the rearview mirror, I see sweat pouring from her body, leaving slick marks on the leather seats. *It's so fucked up. What you've done to her.*

Gunter will know what to do. I repeat that phrase to myself over and over until it stops being a statement, becomes a prayer.

10

When we finally get to the outer gate of the Dahl-house, something is wrong. The wrought iron hangs open, an unhinged jaw, and the guards are nowhere to be found. I'm going too fast, and the gravel beneath the car causes the tires to spin out, spewing thick clouds of dust. A dreadful bump and I stop the car. A terrible shrieking fills the air. When the sediment settles, I see the body of a massive boar, writhing. I drive on, trying to outpace the rasping groans and painful squealing, and park when the outline of the main house comes into view. Frances is stomping around the front porch in penny loafers and a crisp blue-striped shirt. Mathilde moans from inside the car.

"Help me, Frances!" I yell in her direction.

"We weren't expecting you, were we?" Frances asks, her voice preoccupied and a bit chilly.

"Something's happened to Mathilde. Monika said her device was tampered with . . . I thought Gunter or Dr. Hari—"

Frances starts walking toward the car, and when she moves, I see him behind her.

Logan.

On the ground behind her. I scramble out of the car and try to make my way toward him, but Frances grabs my arm, holding me in place.

My husband is filthy and barely moving. His shirt is torn, and through a gap in the fabric, I see blood.

"Enka," he says weakly. My heart stops at the pleading, pitiful sound of his voice.

I try to shake Frances off, but her grip tightens.

"Get off me!"

"Enka!" Logan's eyes widen with fear before his head hits the ground.

"What's happened to him?"

"Enka, you need to go home. Toru and I are handling it." Frances walks over to the car and opens the door, extracting Mathilde. "Did you hear me? You need to leave right now."

"I can't just leave him. Them. Logan—"

"I promise you. Logan is OK and he will be returned to you soon. Toru is handling it. I'll make sure Dr. Hari sees to Mathilde immediately. No one is better equipped to take care of this situation, but only if we can focus on the essentials."

"But . . . what happened?"

Frances, still holding Mathilde's limp body, trains her steely eyes on mine. Her fury is unmistakable.

"Enka. Every second you stay is a second you're taking away from their immediate care. We simply do not have time for you."

An enraged scream from behind. I look and see the mangled boar, tusks askew, heading toward me.

I get in the car and speed away, my heart breaking with every mile.

11

Sporadic updates from Dr. Hari. There isn't much he can do now, besides wait along with the rest of us.

An agonizing few days pass. I replay my argument with Logan in my mind. Each time, the hurt and confusion I caused him registers more fully, as does the realization of how much I love him.

"You're hurting me," Bastian cries. I had been stroking his hair, but in my worry, the pressure had become heavier and heavier until I was crushing his skull into the pillow.

"I'm so sorry, my love." I try to kiss it better, but he draws back from me.

"Where's Dad?" Roy asks meekly.

"Yeah, where's Dad?" Bastian repeats.

I force my lips into a smile, through the image of his body crumpling in my mind.

"He's working, sweetie."

FINALLY, ONE EVENING, Frances calls me.

"How is he? And Mathilde?"

"They are both recovering."

"Does that mean they'll be OK? What happened?"

"We've managed to contain everything for now, but some things have become clear during our ongoing internal investigation. That afternoon, when Logan came to the Dahlhouse, I was surprised. No one had been told to expect him. He was desperate for his father, but Dick was in Luxembourg. He refused to believe that his father was away. Accused me of lying. I became quite upset with him, and curtly told him to come back another time. That's when he struck me."

"He *hit* you? That's awful. I'm so sorry, Frances."

"I was shocked. In all my years of knowing that boy, I've never seen any proclivity toward violence. He wasn't himself. That's what I keep thinking . . . It's the only explanation. He was in such a state of profound agitation, it caused him not to be himself."

"What happened after that?"

"He continued to strike me until I became unconscious. Only for a moment or two, it turns out. But when I awakened, he was gone, as was his car. I assumed he'd left the compound. I was dazed. Went inside and looked at myself in the mirror. The bruises, the bleeding. All of it new to me. Gunter called the house line at that point, and that's when I found out that Logan hadn't left. He was driving around the compound, wreaking havoc. He unlocked the buildings that house Project Naiad. He scrambled the storerooms of genetic data for the Deszendant app, and broke into the art-storage facilities, smashing the protective glass and burning priceless artifacts and artworks. The damages there are somewhere in the millions, and when the public finds out about their data loss, I'm sure we'll face severe legal and regulatory consequences. When Toru caught up to him, he was in Gunter's lab, manually desynchronizing the SCAFFOLD link between you and Mathilde. He kept saying over and over that he was freeing her. The investigation is going to take some time. We have no idea what came over Logan, what possessed him to do all of this. But he's ready to go home."

"He is? Did he say that he wants to come home?"

"Yes. Someone will drive him tomorrow."

"No, please. Let me come get him."

THE GATE HAS been repaired and the guards calmly greet me. Everything looks undisturbed. Toru and Frances are waiting at the entrance to the main house. Frances nods at me and disappears through the front door. My stomach fills with dread at the prospect of being alone with Toru. He had entrusted me with information, and I had broken that trust. I only hope he doesn't know how I exploited it.

We walk together to the nearest greenhouse, where a healthy Logan is waiting. I'm relieved to see him, but he dips his head miserably when he sees me and barely accepts my embrace.

"Enka, I'm so sorry. You and the kids are my real priority. I should never have forgotten that, and if you'll give me another chance, I'll prove to you that I've changed." Logan's voice cracks with genuine regret.

I look at Toru, not understanding.

He puts a hand on Logan's shoulder. "Stay here. I'll talk to her."

Logan's arms hang in defeat as we walk to Toru's cabin.

"What's wrong? You don't like your new husband?" His mouth puckers, as if tasting something bitter.

"New husband?"

"We were able to heal the damage sustained by his body, but not his mind. Luckily, we had just started backing up his mind. But his memories end sometime last year."

"So he doesn't know?"

Toru shakes his head. "Thankfully, no. We'd obviously like to keep it that way. As you saw, things can be catastrophic when the clones become aware. Especially if it isn't done in the correct way."

In his cabin, one of the triplets sits in a chair, her eyes open and unblinking.

"Is she . . . ?"

Toru nods. "We're still collecting the many clones that escaped when Logan unlocked the Project Naiad buildings."

"There was a boar, when I was last here . . . Was that . . . ?"

"Yes, only the boars and a few Naiads managed to escape."

I study the alabaster hair and the limpid blue eyes, limbs as pale and sinewy as an aspen tree. Exactly how Frances must have looked as a teenager.

"Would you like some tea?"

His hands tremble as he fills the cups. I listen to the hiss of the leaves as they interact with the hot water, reading in the sound a gentle rebuke.

"What was he talking about? About giving him another chance?"

"A little lie I built in. He thinks he's been working nonstop with his father here and neglecting you and the kids. You ran away with them for a few days."

My eyes widen in confusion.

"It'll provide a buffer for you as you get used to him."

"Thank you, Toru. I suppose that will make things easier. And I'm glad he doesn't know. I regret it. All of it. I'm so sorry for hurting him. For hurting you."

"Enka, you still don't understand, do you? You didn't hurt him. You murdered him."

"Murder? No . . . he's right there," I say, sputtering over the bitterness of the green tea.

"He was a person, Enka. He was the first . . . original in his own way. Now there will only be copies made from other copies. Imagine every iteration of the *Mona Lisa* stemming from one fridge magnet. You're an artist, so you must have some idea. Have you ever worked on something you love? Something you pour everything of yourself into, only to have it be taken away and mass-produced?"

He rubs his head repeatedly, like he can erase it. Tears shake violently in his eyes as he looks up at me.

"I grew him, and then I raised him. Whether or not you could comprehend or respect his personhood, he was real. That was my son you killed."

12

ogan and I go home together that night. He holds my hand the entire way.

"I'm sorry," he keeps whispering. "Please don't cry, I'm so sorry. It will never happen again."

Each apology sickens me. I think back to this last year. The trips he took with the boys while I was busy being Mathilde. Trips to Chile and the Galápagos Islands. Teaching Bastian how to ski and Roy how to make s'mores. He will never have a chance to father his six-year-olds again. All the photos have been wiped from his devices. But the boys will remember, and this break in his consciousness will confuse them. No, not break. This end to his previous consciousness. Because the person who sits next to me and who caresses my hand isn't Logan. He's not the man I fell in love with, my faithful husband. This Logan is a facsimile, a shadow. Still, however diluted or impaired he is, I am just grateful to have him.

———————

LOGAN AND I are with Monika when she receives the call. Gunter explains that he was waiting for Mathilde's fever to break before trying to remove her pairing device, but after thirty-six hours, he had the epiphany that it wouldn't break while the device was still inserted. By then, it had overheated. In the end, he wasn't able to extract the burned and corroded object now permanently fixed in her head. Until she awakens, we won't know how she's doing, but Gunter suspects that her brain damage is extensive and irreparable. Logan's actions damaged the SCAFFOLD and severed us irrevocably. The shocks I felt when I collapsed during my lecture were a result of the sudden incompatibility of my consciousness in hers. Her mind stopped being hospitable to mine. It's hard to say what the sequence of events was like for her. For the first time since the SCAFFOLD procedure, I'm unable to access her experiences, memories, or thoughts. Gunter tells us it's a miracle she's still alive.

A FEW WEEKS after the incident, Gunter thinks Mathilde is finally stable. I'm afraid to return to the compound, but I want to be there when Mathilde is awakened. The drive is excruciating. In the cars that pass, I see friends on their way out of the city. Going to get lost in antique shops and oversized breweries. I've never felt more acutely that something is fundamentally wrong with me. Why have I never sought out their lives? Why does it take such extremes to fulfill me? I find myself missing my parents and wishing I had been able to accept the life they had offered me. Instead, I offered them mine, and lost them to it.

A few of the foundation members, including Monika and Otto, are already there when I arrive. Beneath the unforgiving lights in the operating room, Mathilde looks so much older. Her right temple is engorged, a hint of rusted metal showing through a mass of dried blood and burned skin. Beneath the thin layer of her medical gown, there is hardly a body. With a pang, I realize how malnourished she must be. Seeing her is overwhelming, as is the realization that I did this to her. And in the infinite moments that unraveled afterward, during the endless parade of chances I had to make things right, I did nothing. I chose this for her.

Only her hands are visible where they peek out from her giant sleeves. They are still beautiful and strong. Her fingers twitch as Gunter gives her the injection. I hold my breath for a second, exhaling when she stirs in the puddle of her gown and blinks her eyes open. Her face, when she recognizes me (*she recognizes me!*), breaks into a tired smile.

After a brief visit, Monika, Otto, and I leave so that Mathilde can rest. We didn't tell her the particulars of what had happened, only that she'd had an accident and that she needed to stay at the Dahlhouse for a few weeks, subject to surveillance and testing. After that, she'll be allowed to go home. Before we leave, Gunter asks if I want my SCAFFOLD removed. The connection is lost— what is the point of keeping it in? And yet I can't bring myself to part with it.

———————

WITH THE KNOWLEDGE that the connection between us is severed, the foundation goes into overdrive with the exhibits we have in production. It's only a matter of time before the public finds out that I no longer have Mathilde's magic touch, and the idea is to capitalize on their ignorance for as long as possible.

The foundation decides to exhibit the paintings they confiscated from Mathilde's home. A day before *Paintings, black and white* opens, an op-ed comes out in *The New York Times* lambasting Mathilde's evident need to differentiate herself from her other by sullying her oeuvre with permanent works. The article is unnecessarily harsh, especially the last line, which reads: "Why choose this version of Mathilde Wojnot-Cho over the unblemished one?"

The article brings some relief. I'd felt threatened by the release of artworks made by her alone. Swiftly, the relief turns to disgust. The article reeks of an all too familiar misogyny that has been leveled at Mathilde since the beginning of her career. Unless her art is one of visual vulnerability, positioning herself as a victim of men or the church, or something erring toward sensationalism, people are not interested. Whether this is because she boxed herself in from the beginning of her career or because she is a woman in art, I can't say.

A review of her exhibit comes out a few days after the opening, and I read it quickly, almost greedily.

It is with great trepidation that one goes to see their favorite impermanent structural artist in her first attempt at something permanent. *Paintings, black and white* was not a disappointment. The pieces have an emotive power that betrays what the artist may have been feeling at the time of painting. Careful, considered lines speak to a kind of cautious hopefulness while violent gestural strokes create a sense of desperation, a deep poverty of control. The intense pigmentation and the strength of the brushstrokes cohere in an experience that is revelatory. Compare this with the performance being shown across town.

The factory of Enka-Mathilde has created another piece of bait for those who would have the meaning of their art spelled out for them. *Habit*, which portrays the daily lives of practicing nuns, takes place over two months, and is available for view at all hours. The culmination, each day, of ten nuns pleasuring each other in a circle is said to be life-changingly cathartic, but I found it shockingly dull and a waste of the Tanztheater Wuppertal's great choreography skills. Enka-as-Mathilde's once-shocking art has become kitsch because it is produced by popular demand and based on tested formulas. A cheap formula with the aim to please, rather than to challenge. How else do E-M's pieces differ from the original performance pieces by Mathilde, you might ask? It's clear that Enka Yui-Dahl approaches the mind of her friend as something to be extracted, mining it for narrative and theme, whereas Mathilde is content to make works without prescribing their meaning. Where Enka constructs, Mathilde discovers, trusting an audience to complete her work with observation. Every recent exhibit by E-M has felt false or secondhand, too heavily engineered for a specific message or response. The constant churn of meaningful and defiant work that critiques basically the same thing every time betrays a lack of growth. This exhibit of Mathilde's paintings, spectacular webs of tar and white paint layered to look like heavy cloth, shows an artist grasping for something new. Something she doesn't know. It is a joy to reach into the unknown with her.

I sink to the ground after reading the review a few times. The familiar rush of shame and self-pity engulfs my body, but there's something else, too. A wayward smear of pride for the friend who is still the best, and who can still surprise us all.

13

nitially, Mathilde's regression was slow. She seemed more or less like herself for the first few years, a time when I could still convince myself that we had made the right decision. That I had done anything right during our friendship. Though he was busy with his Pathway work, Logan became my partner in Mathilde's care. He felt responsible for her condition, being the one who initially suggested the SCAFFOLD to her. I didn't have the courage to tell him differently. But no matter how much we nurtured her, Mathilde continued to deteriorate. When it became clear that she needed daily attention, we moved her back to our home, where she occupied the same room she had lived in after she lost Beatrice. It was the least I could do. Preparing meals, finding the best physical therapists and neurologists . . . ways to appease the guilt that weighed on me from every angle.

It was hard to see her slipping away. I could never have imagined she would look this way. I started taking photos of her every day, recording our conversations, tracking the erosion that took her from me, piece by piece. I am the only witness to her withering, her body the material for a final impermanent structural work.

Even her memory had been affected. She had forgotten about the last year of our friendship, when the SCAFFOLD was intact. Forgotten how angry she had been, how betrayed. She only remembers that I had helped her throughout our lives, during her greatest times of need. Our friendship was thus restored.

At first, I avoided speaking about art, for fear that it might be triggering, but when I realized she was forgetting her life as an artist, I began to talk freely about it, hoping to sustain her memory. She was no longer interested in creating art, but she wanted to support me and loved going to my exhibits. We removed all mention of her name from these shows so as not to cause unnecessary confusion for her.

During this time of attempted rehabilitation, I watched her closely, as did Monika, and we were both relieved to see that Mathilde seemed to have a newfound enjoyment of beauty in the world. She thrilled in the sun and seemed unable to keep herself from smelling any flower, caressing any leaf. She went on walks, eating simple meals three times a day, and spent most of her time with the boys, watching Roy paint or listening to Bastian practice piano. They were teenagers now, rebellious toward me and their father, but softened by pity or love for Mathilde. A few years passed in this way, with all of us together in our peaceful home.

"What is this?" Mathilde asks one day at lunch.

"It's the potato-leek soup from your birthday party last weekend," I reply. "I didn't want to waste it, so I just had Lionel put in new broth and vegetables."

"No, this," Mathilde says dreamily. She lifts her spoon to catch a sunbeam and turns it around in her fingers. "It's quite beautiful, isn't it?"

I laugh nervously in the moment, and then quickly try to forget about the incident. But Mathilde loses more objects and their names. Bastian walks into his piano room one day to find Mathilde naked from the waist up. She had forgotten to finish getting dressed. A full-time carer is hired for Mathilde. Then two, and eventually an entire team. The best cognitive researchers in the world are brought in for consultations, but make no progress. And though she continues to decline, though she has no sense of self or anything else, she seems to possess a deep happiness. She can often be heard laughing, something that disturbs the twins so much, she's moved to a different floor. A speech-language pathologist is brought in to help her relearn language, but despite our best efforts, she continues to degenerate. Six years after the bridge between us was severed, Mathilde is essentially nonverbal.

14

oday her hair is down. I drag a comb through the silver mass that crowds her shoulders. Without the general maintenance required of women in society, Mathilde has aged remarkably in the last few years. Although we are both nearing forty, I look much younger, thanks to daily genome scans and minor gene edits. Most of the time, though, she has a beatific expression on her face that makes me look dull in comparison.

It has been ten years since she came to live with us again. Ten harrowing years of memory and language loss. Ten years of daily photos and recorded conversations, which I will now turn into my next exhibit, *Born Again*. The board has hired an editor in these final stages of the exhibit preparations. They were correct to anticipate that the footage would be too difficult for me to watch.

Even without the need to gather footage, I still visit her every day. Comb her hair. Paint her nails. Massage her feet. As I braid, brush, and knead, I silently pray there's a part of her that can tell I'm here and that I care about her.

A sound brings me out of my thoughts: the comb clattering to the floor, my hand dropping it in shock at the sudden pain that bursts in my head. A lightning crack down the right side of my body. Followed by another, and another. I drop to my knees and hold my head. Mathilde's carers appear by my side and drag me from the room. The excruciating pain lessens, as does the noise. The shrieks and cries I now realize came from me. The shocks clear away, and what remains is the dull ache, the never-ending migraine, I've nursed for the last couple of years. The one no doctor or specialist has been able to cure.

FINOLA TAKES MY arm and accompanies me to my bedroom. I collapse into bed, pulling the covers tight around me, and feel sorry for myself. The persistent whine in my head is endlessly frustrating. In my sleep, I gnash my teeth, as evidenced by my dimpled molars and shaved incisors. I wake with a clenched jaw and am possessed by pain. People think me impatient and hostile as I grit my teeth through our interactions. In every photograph, a grimace of discomfort is plastered on my face. Worst of all, the headaches have been intensifying. The anticipation of pain as powerful as the pain itself.

I've asked Gunter if the SCAFFOLD might be the cause, but he assures me that would be impossible. "It's been nothing more than dead metal for more than ten years. Why would it start causing you pain eight years later? That doesn't make sense." I suppose he's right. Secretly, I worry that the headaches are a physicalization of my guilt. Maybe there exists in my subconscious a masochist hell-bent on punishing me. Another wave of pain and I grip my head with my hands.

If only there were a button I could press, or medication that would magically make any difference. When it's truly unbearable, I have to physically stop my fists from bashing my skull in. My fingertips graze a line of raised skin. What if Gunter is wrong?

I DON'T LIKE going to the Dahlhouse. Too many memories and too much history. The darkness and the dark acts it elicited from me are always at the edge of my mind: a blot I can't erase. The closer I get geographically, the more overwhelmed I am by feelings of remorse and shame. I feel especially uncomfortable knowing that Toru is nearby.

Frances opens the door, and I can see the deep gloom stretching behind her.

"Frances, I need to see Gunter urgently."

She looks behind me, as if to check that I'm alone. "Is he expecting you?"

"No," I say nervously.

A flicker of annoyance passes on her face before she smiles. "I'll come with you." She says this as if out of courtesy, but without her or someone else escorting me, I wouldn't get very far. The compound is rigged with various body-recognition devices. A face here, a thumb there, a calf muscle somewhere else . . . the randomness necessary now that people are swapping body parts and facial expressions regularly, according to which physical trends are currently favored. I can see that Frances herself has gotten a taut new neck and switched out her arched eyebrows for more linear ones.

"How's Logan?" Frances asks, the slightest hint of a threat in her voice.

"He's doing fine. On a camping trip with the boys now," I say.

"Good. Very glad to hear that," she says, softening. "And you?"

I hesitate, wondering if I should tell her the truth. "I've not been very well, to tell you the truth. I'm hoping Gunter can help."

Gunter opens the door, his blond hair shaved so close to his head, it's almost painful to see.

The surprise on his face becomes a spasm of frustration.

"I don't have time for extracurriculars today."

"She insisted," Frances says.

He relents, opening the door just wide enough for me to enter.

I sigh with relief as I step through, having successfully avoided Toru.

Gunter gestures for me to sit as he takes a seat across from me. He crosses his ankles and his hands before looking at me. "Is this about your SCAFFOLD again?"

"I'm sorry to ambush you like this, but I'm really suffering. I know you don't think the SCAFFOLD is responsible, but what's the harm in removing it? If there's even a chance it would help my headaches, I need to do it."

Gunter taps his long pale fingers on a metal tray in front of him. "The pain is that bad?"

"It is. I can barely fall asleep or . . . do anything. Every ounce of focus I have goes into bearing the pain at any given moment. I'm exhausted. I've tried everyone and everything . . . You're my last hope." I wipe furiously at the tears that have escaped my eyes.

"I'm sorry to hear how terrible it is. I suppose I thought it was just a nuisance. A headache."

"You're lucky you don't know how bad headaches can be." I can't keep the resentment out of my voice.

"If memory serves, we were never able to remove Mathilde's

device, is that right?" His long fingers spider across his face, as if they are thinking.

I nod. "It was too corroded. There was some worry that the removal would cause more damage."

"Hop in the chair, will you? Let's take a quick peek to see what's going on with your device. The connection has been severed, but your headaches could be from the device picking up feedback somehow. I don't know how much you see of her, but have you noticed the headaches worsening with proximity to Mathilde?"

"Yes," I say, surprised that I've never pinpointed the correlation.

We move to the other room, and I get onto the raised steel bed.

Gunter uses a long X-ray wand to take a photo of the SCAF-FOLD and get the serial number.

He turns on an ancient-looking computer terminal in the corner, and catches me looking while he waits for it to boot up. "We've found that these older terminals can be more difficult to hack. They've been retrofitted for our needs.

"And do you remember your password? It would have been something you and Mathilde agreed upon."

"'I breathe in, you breathe out,'" I say quietly. I haven't thought about those words for so long. They bring back memories, first joyful, then painful. Every important moment in our lives has been scored to these words . . . the scaffold of our relationship.

"That's odd . . ." Gunter says, bringing me back to the present. His fingers are flying rapidly on the keyboard.

"What is it?"

"Your device is a transmitter and a receiver. You receive Mathilde's skills, memories, and experiences. You also have limited capacity to transmit . . . the ability to heal her trauma, for example.

"Mathilde's device, however, is a receiver and a passive transmitter. It allows you access but isn't capable of transmitting anything that you haven't requested. Except that . . . it is."

"Excuse me?"

"She's actively transmitting. Right now, as we speak."

"What is she transmitting?"

"Just . . . pure feeling. Your headache."

"The pain I have . . . she's doing that? How?"

"There are two possible explanations. One: all those years ago, Logan didn't sever the connection, but actually reversed it. But that wouldn't necessarily explain why this is happening now." Gunter frowns and rubs his short hair frantically.

I'm almost afraid to ask. "The other possibility?"

"Mathilde has somehow managed to erode the device's limitations."

"But how could she have done that?"

"I'd have to examine her to be sure, but my best guess would be that we're witnessing the early stages of human-device chimerism. Her brain has accepted the device so fully, it has now become part of her."

ON THE WAY home, I crouch in the backseat, unable to enjoy the beautiful drive. Every fiber of my being is focused on mitigating pain. Gunter was more helpful than I had imagined he would be, but he didn't know why Mathilde would be transmitting this pain. I have an idea, one that breaks my heart to imagine. What if this is a cry for help? Trapped in her body and unable to communicate in any comprehensible way, is this all she can do? Is feeling the only thing she can send if words are as lost in her mind as they are in her throat?

HER BRAIN HAS accepted the device so fully, it has now become part of her. The words play over and over in my mind. *Does that mean . . . ?* The last time I was in her mind was that lecture long ago, when I collapsed. The shock of being thrown back into my own mind when Logan desynchronized us. From that moment on, I had assumed the inner recesses of Mathilde were closed to me forever. But if she and the device have somehow integrated . . . if Gunter is right . . . does that mean it might be possible to inhabit again?

15

The idea of inhabiting makes me nervous. What if something goes wrong? What if I get stuck in her mind? Or something happens during the moment of connection? What if it's painful? And the most terrifying fear: what if it works just like before, and I discover that the most beautiful mind is now barren?

At home, I lock the doors, barricade myself in bed, and tell Finola that no one is to disturb me. When the deep breaths have slowed my heartbeat to a reasonable speed, my mind jumps.

"I'VE BEEN WAITING for you for years."

I hear the voice before I become fully conscious.

"Mathilde, is that you?" I whisper, my words echoing.

"Let's give you a body, shall we?"

Hands and feet solidify in front of me, as does Mathilde. Around us, an intricate mesh of gold drips endlessly.

I begin to cry at the discovery that her mind is something I can still access—something that is whole and, shockingly, someone I can speak with.

"We've never . . . interacted before. How are we doing this?"

"I've been practicing," Mathilde says.

"And are you . . . oh, god, Mathilde. Are you OK? Are you in pain?"

"I'm not in pain."

More relief.

"But you are."

"I am. I thought because of you. Can you feel it?"

"I'm the one causing it. I was hoping it would lead you here, to me."

"I'm sorry it took me so long. I'm here now. If I had known earlier . . . Oh, Mathilde. You have no idea how much I've missed you. I visit you every—"

"I know about your daily visits documenting my decay for your next exhibit. I know everything now, Enka. You can't imagine my misery, withering away in here. Nothing to do, and no way to communicate, for years on end. I thought if I could find a way to you, we could figure a way out together. Slowly, I chipped away at the wall that allowed you, but denied me, passage. But when I finally got through, I almost wished I hadn't. Because what I found . . . At first, I felt so bad for you. Everyone is jealous, but they find a way through it. Not you. You nursed your envy. Used it to punish yourself. I saw how that toxicity bled into our relationship and made it one of comparison. And because you placed me so high, you could necessarily only be low and constantly wanting. Desperate enough to betray me again and again.

"You had every opportunity, Enka. So many chances to tell

the truth. To make a different decision . . . one that didn't end with me in a chair, unable to speak!"

"Mathilde, this isn't what was supposed to happen . . . All of this was meant to bring us closer. More collaborations . . . I wanted you to depend on me, not to leave me behind. It was a chance for us to be equals, a chance for me to catch up to you."

"But, Enka, we were equals."

"I . . . But if you can hear, you must know. I am so unbelievably sorry . . . I *hate* myself for what I've done to you." The hysterical edge in my voice makes everything sound performative and false.

"I don't need you to hate yourself, Enka. That helps neither of us." She looks at me with something close to pity.

"What can I do then? I feel so helpless."

"I assure you I'm more helpless than you. Logan, too. I know what you've done to him."

The full weight of my shame and guilt begins to collapse on me. "I don't know what I can do to make it right. Please. Tell me what to do. I'll do anything!"

"I don't think you can make any of it right. Your erasure of me has been too complete. Do you know what the saddest thing is? About all of this?"

I shake my head, even though she knows that I don't know.

"I loved you. So much, Enka. And I love you, still."

16

I sit up with a start, back in bed, in my own mind. The headache is gone. Both the low whine and the hammering shriek of it. But the pain that remains is infinitely worse. A pain of my own making. The realization that the person I've most truly loved in this world knows the full extent of my ugliness.

I SPEND A few days motionless, as if in paralysis. Because what do you do, what *can* you do, when you know someone is watching you? All the time? What can you think when you know someone is monitoring your thoughts? The headaches never come back, and I almost wish they would. I want her to punish me . . . I deserve to be punished, the SCAFFOLD a cilice for my repentance. Afraid of thinking anything else, I go through all the moments where I've hurt Logan or Mathilde. I, I, I, my self-flagellation a performance for her. But now that I know nothing is hidden from Mathilde, it becomes impossible to keep any self-deceptions in place. The performance becomes real. Being seen forces me to see myself, and I break under the weight of my gaze. The depravity of what I've done sinks in more, every day, until I have no choice but to accept myself as the monster I am.

The paranoia and processing eventually give way to something else: relief that someone knows the whole awful truth. Relief at finally owning every terrible thing I've done. And if she knows the worst of me, she must also know the best. She must know with certainty the love I've always had for her. But what good is a love like mine? I used my love again and again as an excuse, as absolution for the sins I committed against her. How much better would her life have been if I had hated her, or at least been indifferent? Whether or not she meant it to be, her presence becomes guidance, and shows me the only way forward.

17

will have to leave the bathroom eventually. I've been here too long, applying unnecessary layers of lipstick. Delaying the next chapter of my life. Five more breaths, in and out, before I show the world who I really am. The foundation, my friends, family, and followers. I'm terrified to face them all, but none are as formidable as the one I've already confronted.

The door opens, and Monika is silhouetted against the door, a hand on her hip. "There you are! Everyone is waiting," she says, a look of impatience and disapproval on her face. Careful not to step on her train of recycled prawn shells, I follow her out to the froth and churn of bodies assembled for the opening night of *Born Again*. My fingers leave a small wake on the backs of guests until we reach the small platform where Monika is about to introduce me.

"I've never seen you so nervous. I know there are a lot of people here, but that's to be expected. Surely you're used to it by now?

"Stop it," she says when she realizes I'm pulling my eyelashes out, one by one. "You're frightening me!"

I smile at that, knowing that I've never been less frightening in my life. I've made peace with what will happen next.

"THANK YOU ALL for being here tonight. It means so much to me, and I know it means everything to Mathilde Wojnot-Cho. She's the reason we are all here." I take a deep breath to try to steady myself. The lights are too bright, and for a second, I think that I can't do it.

"I'm sorry . . . I just . . ." A few more deep breaths. But my legs are trembling, the quaking threatening to throw me to the ground. And now the distinct feeling that something is tugging on my inhales and exhales, smoothing them out and stretching them longer. I look down at my chest, at the movements being made. I'm breathing in, and something or someone else is breathing out.

"I don't mean to cry. I, I need to come clean about something. Years ago, when Mathilde was being assessed, I sabotaged her test results. I made it look like she would never recover from her trauma . . . Worse . . . I made it look like she would degenerate." I don't let the gasps in the audience stop me for fear that if I do, I'll never continue.

"She was expected to make a full recovery, maybe more. I don't know. But it gets worse because I had so many chances to tell the truth. So many. That same night, and the next day and the next, but I didn't. Betrayal after betrayal. And I enjoyed it. Reaped the benefits. I loved being the medium by which her genius expressed herself. I loved being in her mind. As you can probably guess, it was a singular, addictive place. What I've done is unforgivable; we'll never know the artist Mathilde could have been. As of today, I am removing myself from Mathilde's exhibits, and leaving the art industry altogether."

ENOUGH, I THINK. *That's enough for now.* I can always confess more later, save the gory details for another day. I step offstage, holding on to what I can in the chaos that surrounds me. A riot of bulbs, flashing. Hands, grabbing. People are yelling unintelligible things and bodies are hurtling toward me. Vaguely, I see one of my bodyguards as I stumble off the platform in a daze. I stop walking. Begin to cry. Not because of the things people are screaming or because of the objects they're throwing, which pierce my arm, stomach, ear. But because of what I feel just now: a whisper of warmth that begins in my mind and spreads, reaching deeper and further, strengthening and solidifying until I fall, broken on the floor, sobbing, surrendering, to the unconditional embrace from Mathilde's mind, which envelops me completely.

18

Activists organize against me and the rest of Mathilde's foundation. The new #FreeMathilde movement calls on all museums to stop any and all exhibits by Enka-as-Mathilde. From the movement's official website: "What would Mathilde Wojnot-Cho actually think of all the merchandising? The posters of her past works where photography wasn't allowed? Postcards of silhouetted boners, stuffed nuns, and the cheap polyester habits that turn museum gift shops into a Party City during Halloween season—all of which are very permanent, by the way. The foundation is just trying to make money. There's no way they're honoring Mathilde's ethos or acting on her behalf."

I can't say I disagree. The timing is especially bad. On the heels of a successful launch between the military's Defense Innovation Unit and Project Naiad, Monika and Dick Dahl had just announced In Perpetuity, a conservation company that would use the SCAFFOLD technology to preserve artists, not just art. In the live statement, Monika had asked, "Can you imagine if we had been able to do this for Picasso? Van Gogh? Who knows what masterpieces we have been deprived of because we'll never know how these great masters would have evolved."

But the opposite is true. In continually giving established artists a platform, how many new artists and masterpieces will we never see? If we'd had an assembly line of Picassos, we might never have had a Mathilde Wojnot-Cho. The intensified scrutiny on the Dahl family and their involvement in Mathilde's captivity force them to shutter In Perpetuity before it even begins.

The SCAFFOLD has become available for commercial use, but further research has shed light on some of the incongruities, such as why I was never able to write Mathilde's name exactly as she did. Logan's team had underestimated the importance of a physical body to creativity and consciousness. Something of Mathilde's creativity was lost when Mathilde's mind and my body were connected; some unknown quantity of her creativity was stored in her body, out of reach to someone who could only access her mind. They also found definitive proof that Mathilde's creativity wasn't generated by trauma, but by experience. She would have outgrown thinking of everything as a middle finger to the church, and I wish so badly that I could have seen what she would have created next. The paintings, the permanent works, this new direction she had been going in. In an effort to preserve what we valued, everything of actual substance was irretrievably lost. The world will never see her ability to keep reinventing herself. Separate from the art that is absent, I deeply miss the person. The friend I could never know for certain, that dynamic and dangerous mind I have always admired, envied, even feared.

EVERYONE IS JEALOUS, but they find a way through it. In the coming days and months, I realize how right Mathilde had been. I *had* placed her high, making myself necessarily low. To me, she was the moon, and I, the tide, alternately lapping at her bright milky feet and receding toward the dark shore.

I HAD BELIEVED a lie I told myself, which was that I have always been my best, my most fulfilled, when I was envious. Really, it was love that has always made me my best. It has been my love for her that has most fulfilled, most fed me. The SCAFFOLD, like everything new, promised I would know her completely, but to know is to cease wondering. If jealousy was like a well, I'd never reached the bottom, hadn't realized the well was a tunnel to the mother of envy, which is awe. *I would like to do everything over again.* I have that thought a hundred times a day. *This time, Mathilde, I would choose to never learn you.*

ALMOST EVERY NIGHT, I dream the same dream. I am on a walk. Mathilde is with me, giving me directions. We pass the streetlamps and their yellow fever light, ignoring the mosquitoes and their frenzied dives against the glass, the music in the rhythm of their repeated hollow clinks. She nods at me and indicates the well. I climb down, the air becoming shallower and the walls rising from the damp moldering earth. She drops down next to me, and we crouch together, knuckles grazing the ground and nails etching the mud. When there is only brick in front of me, she insists I keep going. So I do, the skin on my forehead grating the lime-stone, my body a pestle to the earth's mortar. When I finally wear it down, my limbs are raw and broken by the slow rubbing, but we can see beyond the wall. Mathilde steps through the opening and runs ahead into a lacquered night, looking back to make sure I'm joining her. We have arrived under a silver orb in a sky of raw denim bejeweled by some teenage girl-gods in art school, and it only matters that we're here, looking out at the world together.

RETROSPECTIVE

As I get ready for the party, I touch the strands of white braiding themselves into my hair and look at the skin on my face, creased like paper that has been reused too many times. After the confession, the rest of my ego fell away. I let nature take its course. Lines run wild on my face, as do the children in my beginner art classes at the local community college.

It has been five years since I stepped out of the public eye. Beyond my weekly class, I no longer pursue art, even though I long to paint, to encounter myself on canvas, something I never did in my quest to become someone else. If only I hadn't assumed I had nothing to offer. In these two years, I haven't seen any of the foundation's board members. In many ways, today will be a reunion. I invited them to my forty-fifth birthday celebration, along with many of my old friends from art school. Polina, Mona, Yuki, and others. My parents are on their way from the airport. Bastian is back from their third year of university and their friends are at the party, as are many of Logan's colleagues. Roy still doesn't speak to me.

In the last few years, Logan has taken up carpentry, and his long beech tables have been moved outside to the backyard. His intricate carvings are covered with everyone's favorite dishes and a dozen or more bottles of wine. He catches my eye while fussing over one of the napkins, and I wonder for the hundredth time how I got so lucky. True, he's not the man I married, but I'm not the woman he married either. I turned out to be someone far worse than either of us had suspected, and yet, after the confession, and the initial shock of what I had done to Mathilde, he stood by me.

One of his colleagues has brought elaborate homemade kites, and the younger children are learning how to fly them. I look up at a vivid green grasshopper riding the waves in the sky and see a handprint pressed against a window. A smudge on an otherwise immaculate home, and day. I am so happy to see people from different times of my life in one place. I catch up with my old colleagues. Polina works as a consultant for production companies now, often running into Mona, who is an actress, most recently completing her seventh season playing the mother of a precocious vampire ballerina. Yuki has moved to a village in Japan, selling textiles dyed with persimmons and indigo plants she grows on her own little plot of land.

"Was it painful?" she asks.

"No," I say, touching my head lightly. After two years of waiting for contact from Mathilde, I'd had the SCAFFOLD removed, honoring her choice to be inaccessible to me. The scar on my right temple is one of the only things I have left of Mathilde, and I hope it never heals.

I can feel a palpable sadness to our interactions. Almost everyone in the world thinks that Mathilde Wojnot-Cho passed last year. Only the foundation knows that she continues to live under my care, at this very moment only four floors above the party. The lie is not far from the truth, as she hasn't been able to move of her own volition for years.

Bastian interrupts the conversation with my friends, brandishing a long knife. *Peace*, I think, as I'm surrounded by singing friends and family, about to blow out the candles. Their eyes shine with happiness, something unattainable to me now. A continuation of this peace is all I wish for. All my life I had chased after it, thinking it was something I needed to find or earn, instead of something to receive and accept.

I can accept now that I'm responsible for the annihilation of the two people I have loved most. Every day, I grieve the choices I made. I grieve my Logan and the family we might have had together. I grieve the life Mathilde might have had, the friendship that surely would have endured if I had only allowed it to continue. And I grieve myself—the art I might have made if I hadn't always seen it through the lens of someone else, framed by other standards. I would give it all up, anything and everything, for Mathilde to be by my side today.

Once everyone has their slice of cake, I speak with the people I have neglected for the first half of the party. Bastian's girlfriend is telling me about the kinds of policies she hopes to write one day when Jutta, one of the newer maids, interrupts our conversation.

"I'm sorry to interrupt, Ms. Enka, but Finola told me it was urgent." She fidgets with her hands, smoothing the front of her dress.

"What is it?" I ask. The kite drifts jerkily into view, plinking against a window.

"It's the woman upstairs. On the fifth floor. She asked for a pen and paper and has begun to draw."

ACKNOWLEDGMENTS

I am incredibly grateful for a second book and another opportunity to thank the many in my life who have sustained and nourished me.

Kirby Kim, you will always have my deepest gratitude for your constant support and wisdom. Thank you for all the ways you champion and challenge me.

Many thanks to Eloy Bleifuss Prados and Lansing Clark for generously providing your insightfulness and time to this work, and to everyone at Janklow & Nesbit who has been looking after me and working on my behalf.

Thank you, Jasmine Lake, for your continued advocacy in bringing my work to life in new forms.

Pilar Garcia-Brown, I still don't know what I may have done in a past life to have you as my editor in this one, but I remain incredibly grateful, if mystified, to work with you. I am also very thankful to work with my wonderful Dutton team again. Thank you, John Parsley, Lauren Morrow, Nicole Jarvis, Amanda Walker,

Stephanie Cooper, Alice Dalrymple, and Mary Beth Constant for everything you do to better my work and share it with the world. Thank you, Ella Kurki, for bringing your sharp-eyed sensitivity to the work, and Kaitlin Kall, for yet another stunning cover.

I am honored and humbled to play in the following orchestras: the Grand Teton Music Festival, the Oregon Symphony, the Experiential Orchestra, and the ProMusica Chamber Orchestra. Thank you for having me—the friendships I've found in each of these ensembles as well as the music we play together nurtures everything I do.

I am so thankful for my dear friends, especially: Adrianne Munden-Dixon, Audrey Belair, Brandie Albright, Carol Adams, Caroline Gilbert, Christy Fox, Dorothy Ro, Grace An, Isa Lussier, Jen Johnson, Jen Liu, Jenny Ross, Shanshan Zeng, and Susan Gulkis-Assadi. Thank you all for your unwavering support, love, and guidance.

I remain indebted to the many teachers in my life whose mentorship informs every facet of it. Susan McClary, for deepening my understanding of music. Larry Rachleff, for deepening my love for music and the work that goes into being a musician. May you rest in peace. Norman Fischer, for consistently feeding my imagination. Paul Kantor, for being the first to believe in me. Thank you for widening the definition of being a good musician into one that is synonymous with being a good human.

Immaculate Conception is largely a book about art. I owe my love of art to the many hours I spent wandering the Cleveland Museum of Art. What started as an easy practice-break pastime has become a deep and abiding love for art. And while I love art, I know very little about it . . . Thank you, Sharón Zoldan, for sharing your extensive art expertise with me.

Immaculate Conception is also a book about jealousy, which has been a source of much shame and growth in my life. I am thankful for the many lessons it has taught me.

My deepest gratitude to the doctors and nurses at Providence St. Vincent Medical Center who delivered my first child and cared for me in the aftermath. Dr. Elizabeth Reindl, Dr. Kelley E. Burkett, Macy, Trisha, Shelly, Olivia, Sarah, Emily, and Liesl: the kindness, instruction, and empathy shown toward me that week made the experience incredibly positive and joyful.

My wonderful readers. It has meant the world to see *Natural Beauty* in your hands. Thank you for taking a chance on me.

I am deeply thankful for my family.

Nainai, my grandmother, whom I miss every day.

Frank, Sarah, Amelia, Ellie, Brent, and Jackie, who fill my life with laughter and happiness.

Dalia, a source of consistent love and encouragement. Thank you for the invaluable ways you have supported me as a new mother.

Mama and Baba, the first storytellers of my life. I am so proud to be your daughter.

Boba, perpetual snuggler and bringer of gladness. Thank you for being the best writing companion.

Yochi, light, love, and joy of my life. Thank you for being the most wonderful partner and father to Boba and Indigo. You are the biggest blessing of my life and I never cease to be amazed by the life we share together.

ABOUT THE AUTHOR

Ling Ling Huang is a writer and violinist. She plays with several ensembles, including the Oregon Symphony, Grand Teton Music Festival Orchestra, ProMusica Chamber Orchestra, and the Experiential Orchestra, with whom she won a Grammy Award in 2021. Her debut novel, *Natural Beauty*, was a *Good Morning America* Buzz Pick, a *New York Times* Editors' Choice, and the winner of the Lambda Literary Award for Bisexual Fiction.